PERSON OR
PERSONS UNKNOWN

PERSON OR PERSONS UNKNOWN

Anthea Fraser

This first world edition published in Great Britain 2005 by
SEVERN HOUSE PUBLISHERS LTD of
9–15 High Street, Sutton, Surrey SM1 1DF.
This first world edition published in the USA 2005 by
SEVERN HOUSE PUBLISHERS INC of
595 Madison Avenue, New York, N.Y. 10022.

British Library Cataloguing in Publication Data

Fraser, Anthea
    Person or persons unknown
    1.   Genealogy - Research - Fiction
    2.   Murder - Investigation - Fiction
    3.   Detective and mystery stories
    I.   Title
    823.9'14 [F]

    ISBN 0-7278-6205-7 (cased)
    ISBN 0-7278-9135-9 (paper)

Typeset by Palimpsest Book Production Ltd.,
Polmont, Stirlingshire, Scotland.
Printed and bound in Great Britain by
MPG Books Ltd., Bodmin, Cornwall.

One

'I loathe drinks parties,' Max Allerdyce said irritably, as he slowed for a red light. 'All you do is stand around for hours in a crowded room, drinking inferior wine and making conversation with people you hope never to see again.'

Rona laughed. 'Come on, it won't be that bad. Not at Magda and Gavin's.'

'Oh, but it will; even good friends metamorphose into frenzied hosts and break up any promising conversation by introducing you to someone else.'

'Well, we could hardly turn it down, could we? It's Gavin's birthday, after all.'

'Then why couldn't they have a civilized lunch or dinner? Or a series of them, if numbers dictated? Drinks parties are a cop-out, a means of writing off outstanding invitations in one fell swoop. No one enjoys them, but duty is seen to be done.'

'I hope you're not going to be in this mood all evening,' Rona commented.

He made some reply, but she barely heard him. As they turned into Barrington Road, her thoughts had swung to the last occasion she'd visited the Ridgeways, when she'd seen her father walking along here with Catherine Bishop, a customer at the bank whom he'd professed to know only slightly. That had been a couple of months ago, and she still wasn't sure if he'd seen her drive past. The incident had never been referred to, but it had left a nebulous barrier between them. Lindsey, her twin sister, kept nagging at her to broach the subject, but she'd refused, feeling it an unwarranted intrusion.

Pushing the worry aside, she saw that a line of cars stretched

1

beyond the Ridgeways' gateway in both directions. Max, swearing under his breath, parked at the end of it.

'How long do we have to stay?' he demanded, as they walked up the path.

'You'll enjoy it once you're there,' Rona told him rallyingly, and was spared any further comment by Magda opening the door.

Half an hour later, she was prepared to concede he might have a point; most of the people in the room were unknown to her. Magda, though she and Rona had been close since childhood, did not make friends easily, and Rona suspected the guests were mostly Gavin's colleagues drawn from work and the various sports clubs to which he belonged.

Having extricated herself from a man whose breath smelt of garlic and who kept invading her space, she looked round, wondering whom to approach. Max, she noted with irritation, seemed to be enjoying himself more than she was; obviously in charm mode, his prematurely silver head was bent attentively to a short woman who was talking earnestly up at him.

'Excuse me,' said a voice behind her, 'are you Rona Parish?'

She turned to see a young woman regarding her with interest. 'I am, yes. And you're . . . ?'

'Zara Crane. This is my husband, Tony.'

The man beside her held out a damp hand. They seemed younger than the other guests, and Rona wondered at their connection with the Ridgeways. The girl was a few months pregnant and wore her hair, a pale red-gold, in a thick plait over one shoulder. Her husband, who just escaped being plump, had an incipient double chin, and his face was made the rounder by his curiously semicircular hairline, behind which his dark hair lay short and sleek as a seal's pelt.

'I work with Gavin,' he volunteered, confirming Rona's guess. 'And you're a friend of Magda's, I believe?'

'Of them both, I hope.' No need to add she'd nearly married Gavin.

'She was speaking about you last week,' Zara explained. 'At the office do.'

Rona smilingly raised an eyebrow. 'And what did she say?'

'That you don't live with your husband and haven't taken his name, and that you've been instrumental in catching two murderers.'

The words had come out pat and the girl, suddenly doubting the wisdom of them, flushed, her eyes falling to the glass of orange juice in her hand.

Rona's instant annoyance was tinged with a sense of betrayal. She would have words with Magda. The fact that the summing-up was more or less accurate was of little comfort.

Tony Crane hastily intervened. 'Please don't think we've been discussing you,' he said – though they clearly had. 'It's just that someone mentioned your articles in *Chiltern Life*; Magda told us she knew you, and that while writing them, you'd solved a murder and the killer proved to be someone she knew.'

Over the last months, Rona had been researching the history of Buckford, the county town, whose octocentenary was imminent. When she made no comment, Crane added, 'There's a souvenir binder for them with this month's edition. How many are you planning to do?'

'About half a dozen, I think.'

'Each on a different aspect?'

'That's right. I've done most of the research now, it's just a question of writing it up.'

'I enjoyed the one on the town's earliest beginnings. It must be absorbing, digging out all the facts and so on.'

'It is, yes.'

He hesitated. 'Will the murder feature in any of them?'

'No,' Rona said shortly. 'It isn't relevant.'

Zara moved impatiently, and they both turned to her. Her eyes were on Rona and there was sudden tension in them. 'Do you ever do research just for interest, with no thought of publication?'

Rona gave a short laugh. 'I'm not that high-minded! As any

journalist will tell you, everything's grist to the mill. It's how we make our living, after all.'

'But say you were paid for it?' Zara persisted. 'Then you wouldn't be out of pocket, but it would remain a – a private commission?'

Tony Crane said smoothly, 'There's something we'd like to find out, and we were wondering if, with all your contacts and so on, you might be able to help.'

Rona shook her head. 'That's not my brief, I'm afraid, but there are agencies you can approach.'

'So you wouldn't help unless you could publish the results?' Zara pressed.

'That's not quite—' Rona began, but Zara was pursuing her line of thought.

'I hadn't thought it through, but I suppose . . . Look, we can't discuss it here. Could we meet somewhere, so I can explain more fully?'

Rona hesitated, not wanting to become involved, and Zara, possibly misinterpreting her reluctance, added contritely, 'I'm sorry if I was tactless just now – about your lifestyle. You asked what Magda had said, but it came out wrong, not at all the way she put it.'

Rona smiled. 'It was fair comment,' she conceded.

'Then could we meet for coffee? I really think our project would interest you.'

'It sounds most mysterious.'

'What does?' Gavin had come up and slipped an arm round Rona's shoulders. In his other hand he held a bottle of wine, from which he topped up Tony and Rona's glasses.

Zara flushed again. 'Just something I want to discuss with her.'

'Well, any mystery you need solving, Rona's definitely your girl!' He squeezed her shoulder. 'Now, if these two will excuse us, I'd like you to meet someone who'd make an ideal subject for one of your biographies.'

Zara said quickly, 'Oh, but we . . .'

Rona extracted a card from her bag and handed it over.

'Give me a ring,' she invited, and allowed herself to be piloted across the room in the circle of Gavin's arm.

'So, who do you want me to meet?' she asked him.

He laughed. 'That was just an excuse – I thought you needed rescuing.'

'And there I was, thinking you'd found a new subject for me!'

'Are you considering another biography? Seriously? I thought your last experience might have put you off.'

Rona's recent venture in that field had resulted in murder.

'To be honest, I'm not sure what to do next,' she admitted. 'I'm coming to the end of the Buckford articles, and though Barnie has put forward a few ideas, nothing really grabs me. Immersing myself in a biography might be the answer, if I can find the right subject.'

A shrill of laughter reached them, emanating from the short woman with whom Max was still conversing. 'Max seems in good form,' Gavin commented. 'It's an age since we saw him; what's he doing with himself these days?'

'Actually, he's working on a portrait – his first for years. The local constituency has commissioned one of our MP.'

'James Latymer? Well, well, he is going up in the world! Where will they hang it? The Palace of Westminster?'

Rona smiled. 'More likely the Association office.'

The conversation was ended by Magda's announcing the food was ready, and Rona moved with everyone else into the dining room, where the table was spread with a delectable selection of savouries. It was half an hour later that, in search of a glass of water, she came across Magda alone in the kitchen, removing some minute pastries from the oven. At just under six foot, she was an imposing figure with her jet-black hair and large, heavy-lidded eyes, inherited from her Italian mother.

'Hi,' she greeted Rona. 'Everything OK?'

'Now that you mention it,' Rona answered lightly, taking a glass from the cupboard and filling it at the sink, 'I've a bone to pick with you.'

5

'Why, what have I done?' Magda asked with scant interest, sliding the pastries from the oven tray on to a plate.

'Divulged my marital arrangements, apparently, to total strangers.'

Magda turned to stare at her. 'What on earth are you talking about?'

'A young couple through there, who were at Gavin's office do.'

'Oh.' Her face cleared. 'We were discussing your articles and they seemed interested in you, for some reason, and asked a few questions. I didn't betray any secrets, though; everything I told them was common knowledge.'

'That Max and I don't live together?' Rona challenged her.

'I'm sure I didn't put it like that, but you don't, do you, *all* the time?'

Rona didn't argue the point. 'Anyway,' she said, leaning against the counter and sipping her water, 'do you know anything about them?'

'The Cranes? Nothing. I've only met them the once, at Palmer & Faraday's silver jubilee. Gavin says the man, whatever-his-name-is, is quite promising, and since he'd invited the rest of his team, he didn't want this guy to feel left out. What did they want with you, anyway?'

'From what I gathered, they'd like me to undertake some investigation or other. I declined, but the girl – Zara – still wants us to meet, to discuss whatever it is.'

Gavin put his head round the door. 'Sorry to break up the tête-à-tête, but I thought you were bringing the sausage rolls?'

Magda picked up the plate. 'Just coming,' she said.

'So, what's the verdict?' Rona asked Max as they drove home.

'Not bad as these things go; but give me a dinner party any day, where you can sit down in comfort instead of standing around all night like a spare part. Not to mention having to cope with a glass while balancing food on those flimsy plates.'

'Nevertheless, you seemed to be enjoying yourself,' she

said drily. 'Did you by any chance speak to that young couple?'

'No, I didn't come across them. Why?'

'They want me to look into something for them. I was pretty discouraging, though; with luck, I shan't hear from them again. Incidentally, Magda told them we don't live together.'

He gave a short laugh. 'There's friendship for you! Did you disabuse them?'

'No; I didn't see why I should explain myself to strangers. Anyway, as Magda pointed out when I tackled her, it's partially true. You *do* sleep at Farthings three nights a week, after your classes.'

'Because when I didn't, you'd either gone to bed by the time I came home or were burning the midnight oil meeting deadlines.'

'*I* know that, and *you* know that, and so does everyone else that matters.' And, Rona reflected privately, the space given by the arrangement made their marriage all the stronger.

Max grunted and drew in to the kerb, thankful to find a space almost opposite the gate. The tall Georgian houses in Lightbourne Avenue were not blessed with garages, and Rona's car was kept in one of a custom-built row in an adjacent street. Being so near the centre of town, she seldom used it anyway.

Although the day had been warm, the night air felt chill as they walked together up the short path to the door. Gus, their long-haired retriever, was awaiting them in the hall, and Max resignedly took down his lead.

'I won't be more than ten minutes,' he said, and went back down the steps, the dancing dog at his side.

Rona went down to the basement kitchen and laid the table for breakfast. The clock on the wall showed eleven thirty but she felt wide awake. Beyond the glass door the patio garden lay hidden beneath the reflection of the kitchen, its bright yellow walls giving the impression of sunlight.

She leaned her head on the glass, watching her doppel-ganger copy her. Discussion of the Buckford articles, together with a return to Barrington Road, had brought Catherine Bishop

7

sharply to mind, and instead of banishing the thought of her, as she usually did, she let her mind drift back.

It had been the vicar, Gordon Breen, who, on Rona and Max's first visit to Buckford, had mentioned Mrs Bishop as someone who might be of help, since she'd researched the history of several local schools. She'd been headmistress of one of them, but had since retired to Marsborough, Rona's home town, and was, it later transpired, a customer at her father's bank.

'What's she like?' she had asked him eagerly.

'I've hardly spoken to her,' her father replied, 'but she seemed quiet and unassuming.'

It was a sentence Rona had mentally replayed many times over the last couple of months.

Considering how large Mrs Bishop loomed in her mind, it was hard to realize that they'd met only once, when, at her invitation, Rona had called at her bungalow. And she'd liked her so much, Rona reflected bitterly. Though not conventionally attractive, the older woman had an air of stillness, of being at home in her skin, that was both charming and reassuring. Rona had felt relaxed with her, and looked forward to a continuing acquaintance. Seeing her with Pops had put paid to that.

I've hardly spoken to her, he had said. How could it be, then, that barely three weeks later, she had seen them strolling together near the bungalow, obviously enjoying each other's company?

Perhaps, she thought now, she should have brought up the matter the next time she saw him. If he realized she'd seen them, he would have been expecting her to comment. For that matter, even if he'd not noticed her car, surely the natural thing, in view of Rona's interest, would have been to mention having seen Mrs Bishop? The fact that neither of them had referred to it had lent the incident added – and probably unwarranted – importance.

It was for that reason that Rona'd made no move to see her again, even to return the scrapbooks containing the schools' histories that Mrs Bishop had so generously loaned her.

Admittedly, she had permission to keep them indefinitely, and she'd postponed writing the article on educational development partly for that reason and partly because of the memories it evoked of her own research on the subject. *Magda said you'd solved a murder, and the killer was someone she knew.*

An added problem, Rona thought, staring across the dark garden, was that she'd mentioned none of this to Max. At first, it had been out of loyalty to Pops – though why that phrase had come to mind she couldn't explain. Then, as time went by, it became increasingly difficult to broach the subject, especially since Max gave no sign of noticing any reserve between her father and herself. So it was only with Lindsey, from whom she had no secrets, that she was able to discuss the matter, and endless talk about it had profited them nothing.

On the floor above, she heard the front door close, and a minute later Gus's feet came skittering down the stairs, followed by Max's heavier tread.

'I thought you'd have gone up to bed,' he commented, coming up behind her and kissing the back of her neck.

'I've been thinking over the evening,' she said, only half truthfully.

'Wasn't it enough to go through it once?'

She laughed and turned to kiss him. 'You're right,' she said. 'Let's go to bed.'

Sunday morning, and the traditional lazy breakfast in their dressing gowns, with the newspapers divided between them.

Rona said, 'You've not forgotten we're due at the parents' for lunch?'

'Oh God!' said Max tonelessly, without looking up. 'Lindsey too?'

'Lindsey too; now Hugh's not on the scene, she's no excuse.' Even as she said it, Rona felt a twinge of guilt. But for months their mother's attitude had made visits home difficult, and now that there was tension, whether real or imagined, with her father, they'd become almost unbearable.

Hugh, from whom Lindsey was divorced, had briefly made

9

a comeback in her affections, on the strength of which he'd
transferred back to the Marsborough office: only to find that
his ex-wife, while enjoying his love-making – always the
strongest link between them – on weekend visits, had no intention of letting him move in on a permanent basis.

'Presumably he's still around, though?' Max asked,
smoothing out his paper.

'Still in Marsborough, yes. At first, Linz expected him to
be everywhere she went, but she hasn't seen hide nor hair of
him since that time in Sainsbury's. Actually,' she added slowly,
'I think there's a new man in her life. Someone from the
office.'

Max made an indeterminate sound, indicative of his opinion
of Lindsey's romantic liaisons. They'd landed her in trouble
in the past.

Rona said defensively, 'She really does seem to need a man
around. Someone to take her out to dinner or the theatre.'

'Or bed,' said Max baldly.

Rona flushed and did not reply.

Tom Parish stood at his dining-room window, staring unseeingly at the street. His daughters were coming to lunch, and
he couldn't believe that he was dreading it. The increasingly
infrequent times when they all gathered round the table had
always been a source of delight to him, a highlight in the
depressing life he led with Avril. Now, he knew sickly, he
must pretend not to notice Lindsey's accusing eyes or Rona's
averted ones.

She'd seen them, of course; she must have done. What's
more, she'd told Lindsey – and possibly Max, too, though
there'd been no appreciable difference in his manner. What
did they all make of it – of him? And – oh God! – what did
he make of it himself?

He wiped a hand over his face. It had been pure chance –
either good or bad, depending on how you looked at it – that
his meeting with Catherine should have occurred just when
he was finally accepting that his marriage was, to all intents,

over. For months he'd been dreading his retirement, urged on him by the bank following his heart attack that spring. True, he still tired easily, but that was infinitely preferable to being thrown more and more into his wife's company, without the escape route to the bank when she drove him to the point of distraction. That, he told himself grimly, was far more of a health hazard than the day-to-day routine at the bank.

Yet God knew he'd tried to keep his marriage alive, tried to rekindle what they'd undoubtedly once had. When had Avril become so irritable, so critical of the girls and himself, so constantly complaining? When, for that matter, had she last taken an interest in her appearance? Make-up was now a rarity, leaving her pale face with its colourless brows and lashes curiously undefined. As for clothes, she seemed simply to reach for what was nearest each morning, invariably an old jumper and skirt. Heaven help him, he was almost ashamed to be seen with her. Comparisons might be odious, but between Avril and Catherine, always so well groomed, they were startling.

On the day Rona had seen them together – if, indeed, she had – he'd had his first ever row with Avril. That's to say that instead of shrugging off her barbs, as he'd been doing for years, he had, to the astonishment of them both, lost his temper and lashed back at her. The row had simmered in his mind all day, and after work – knowing she'd be awaiting the apology he was incapable of making – he had driven almost without thought to Catherine's bungalow, where he sat miserably in the car, trying to work out the least damaging course of action.

There, Catherine had found him and, sensing his distress, suggested a walk to clear his head. And it was when she urged him to talk to Avril in an attempt to sort things out, that he'd realized, with a sense of shock, it was not that outcome for which he was hoping.

That had been over two months ago, and though he'd seen Catherine several times since, he'd still not so much as touched her hand. Nevertheless, there was no denying she filled his mind night and day, and he wasn't sure how long he could maintain the status quo. How, in God's name, could he attempt to explain this to his daughters?

'Are you going to lay that table, or stand gawping out of the window all day?' enquired an acid voice from the doorway, and, suppressing a sigh, Tom turned and belatedly applied himself to his task.

The Parishes lived on the western fringes of the town, in a residential district known as Belmont. It consisted chiefly of solid detached houses, 1930s in style, with gabled fronts and pebble-dash facades, though post-war development had extended its boundaries to incorporate, among other things, an estate of mock-Georgian town houses and an enlarged shopping parade. Rona and Lindsey had attended the neighbourhood primary school and been baptized and married in the local church.

Maple Drive was a twenty-minute car ride from Lightbourne Avenue, and Rona and Max passed most of it in silence. Since Avril didn't care for dogs, Gus had, as usual, been left at home.

As they drew up behind Lindsey's red sports car, Rona commented wryly, 'I hope you've got a series of topics lined up, in case of awkward silences.'

'Oh, your father will keep things going,' Max replied. 'He always does.'

Rona bit her lip and got out of the car.

Tom opened the door as they reached it, and she felt a rush of love for him. At first sight he looked the same as always – tall, tanned, iron-grey hair and slightly lined forehead. But the brown eyes that were so like her own had a guarded look, and when he spoke there was a false heartiness in his voice that tugged at her heart.

'Greetings, you two!' he exclaimed. 'Good to see you!'

She smiled, allowed him to kiss her cheek, and went ahead of him into the sitting room. Her mother was perched on an upright chair, an apron round her waist, and Rona dutifully kissed her before turning to her twin, reclining at her ease on the sofa.

'Hi, sis.'

'Hi yourself.'

Max, following his wife into the room, marvelled as he always did that the twins could be so alike and yet so different. They had the same dark hair – though Rona's flicked up on a level with her chin, while Lindsey's fell to beneath her shoulders – the same oval faces, the same straight noses and large brown eyes, albeit with differing expressions in them. Yet for all their similarity, while Rona was like a part of himself, his hackles invariably rose in Lindsey's presence. A state of armed neutrality existed between them, which all Rona's efforts had been unable to dispel.

As Tom began to pour the drinks, Avril came to her feet. 'Well, now you're all here, I'd better go and dish up.'

'Hang on a minute,' Tom protested mildly. 'Let them get their breath back and enjoy their drinks.'

'I did say twelve thirty,' Avril reminded them sharply, reluctantly sitting down again.

Rona glanced at the clock. It was twenty minutes to one. 'Sorry, but we're not pressed for time, are we?'

'Of course not!' Tom replied emphatically.

Avril threw him a venomous glance. 'Then don't blame me if the beef's overdone.'

There was a short silence. Oh God, God, God! Rona thought desperately. They'd not been here five minutes and already there was trouble brewing.

She addressed herself to Lindsey. 'What have you been doing since I last saw you?'

Lindsey sipped her drink with a self-satisfied air. 'Oh, wining, dining and so on.'

'New fella?'

'New fella.'

'You've met someone?' Tom asked eagerly.

'I told you, Pops. He's a colleague from work.'

'Married?' demanded Avril sharply.

Lindsey shrugged and did not reply. Rona avoided Max's eye.

13

'Well, at least it's not that Hugh,' Avril continued. 'Thank goodness you finally saw sense over him.'

Lindsey's hand tightened on her glass, and Rona's heart ached in sympathy. 'What's his name, your new man?' she asked brightly.

'Jonathan Hurst.'

'Are we going to meet him?'

'Probably, in due course.'

'Bring him to supper, if you like.'

'Thanks,' Lindsey said gratefully, adding with a grin, 'When Max is home, of course!'

'That goes without saying!'

Rona loathed cooking, and on his evenings at home, Max was in sole charge of the cuisine.

Avril stood up again. 'Right, you've got two minutes to finish your drinks, then lunch will be on the table.'

She left the room and Rona took a quick sip of her vodka.

'Don't rush it,' Tom said quietly. 'If necessary, you can take it through with you.'

'Thanks, Pops.' She glanced across at him, unprepared for the lurch her heart gave as their eyes met and held. God, she thought in confusion, he's really unhappy! Somehow, that aspect hadn't occurred to her. How long had he been feeling like this? And had Catherine Bishop anything to do with it? For the moment she didn't care. She simply wanted to jump up and put her arms round him.

'Ready for carving, Tom,' Avril called, and with a heavy heart Rona went through with the rest of them for Sunday lunch.

Two

Rona's thoughts continued to circle round her father and Catherine Bishop for the rest of the weekend.

Up in her study on Monday morning, she took out the scrapbooks detailing the schools' histories, telling herself it was time to stop procrastinating and complete the article on education. Weeks ago, she remembered, Mrs Bishop had left a message about something that might interest her, but, thrown off-balance by the unexpected sighting, Rona had never returned the call. Should she do so now? Would meeting her shed any light on the situation with her father?

Before her resolve could weaken, she checked the number and lifted the phone.

'Mrs Bishop,' she said quickly, when the quiet, remembered voice sounded in her ear. 'It's Rona Parish. I'm – sorry I've taken so long to get back to you. I believe you wanted to speak to me?'

There was a fractional pause, then: 'How nice to hear from you, Miss Parish. Yes, I did come across something. It mightn't be of interest, but I remembered your saying it was the offbeat rather than the factual that you were looking for.'

'That's right.' Rona moistened dry lips. Should she suggest—?

'If it's convenient, perhaps you could call round and have a look at it?'

How stilted they sounded! Rona thought despairingly, as she accepted the invitation.

'And do bring your delightful dog with you,' Catherine Bishop added, a smile in her voice.

Gus had broken the ice last time, Rona remembered. Perhaps he would again.

It was arranged that she should call at the bungalow the following morning, but the moment she rang off, misgivings swamped her. Suppose Mrs Bishop started talking about Pops? Should she admit to having seen them?

She pushed back her chair and went to switch on the cafetière. Then, a mug of coffee in her hand, she moved to the window and looked down on the small paved garden behind the house. In the plots on either side, a drift of leaves, brittle after the long, dry summer, had been dislodged by last night's wind and lay scattered on the grass. In their own, however, it was Rona rather than nature who set the pace, the only signs of the changing seasons the succession of flowers she planted in the tubs.

With a sigh she turned from the window and went back to her desk.

In the event, the article was not as onerous as she'd anticipated; she'd made copious notes while up in Buckford, and reading them brought back vivid memories of her visits to the schools, some of which dated from the sixteenth century. Material from Mrs Bishop's scrapbooks, which she had permission to use, helped to lighten the content, giving a human angle to the progression of education in the town.

By the time Max phoned that evening, the article was virtually finished. All that remained was to include, if she so wished, whatever Mrs Bishop had to show her.

'And that's the end of the exercise?' Max asked, when she reported on her day's work.

'Not quite; I'll have to go back with Andy for the last batch of photos. We've done the comparison bit – then and now. This time, I want original buildings that have remained virtually unchanged. And when all that's wrapped up,' she added, 'I'll have to decide what to do next.'

'Any ideas?'

'Not really, but Barnie has some thoughts. I'll have another chat with him.'

Barnie Trent was the features editor at *Chiltern Life*, a glossy monthly for which Rona occasionally wrote freelance. He and his wife were also personal friends.

'That reminds me,' Max said. 'I bumped into him in Guild Street at lunch time. They're expecting Mel and the children at the weekend.'

'Really? He didn't mention it last week.'

'It blew up suddenly; Mitch is being sent to the Gulf, and as he'll be away for a couple of months, it was decided Melissa and the kids should come over here. Also, the shorter distance will make it easier for him to fly back for the odd weekend.'

'Dinah will be ecstatic to have them for so long.'

'No doubt, but Barnie's anticipating some disturbed nights. The baby's still not sleeping through.'

Rona laughed. 'He'll survive,' she said.

Rona herself didn't sleep well that night – an unusual occurrence for her. Her mind circled continuously round Mrs Bishop and their coming meeting, dreading an awkwardness between them that hadn't been present at their first meeting. Any hint of embarrassment on her part would be a clear indication of her suspicions regarding her father, and, as she kept reminding herself, apart from that one glimpse of them together, she had nothing on which to base them. Nothing, that is, except the worsening atmosphere between her parents.

With an exclamation of impatience she sat up, punched her pillow into shape and, lying down again, firmly closed her eyes. *Che sera, sera*, she told herself philosophically, and finally went to sleep.

Whether or not Gus remembered his last visit three months earlier, he again went bounding down the path ahead of her, and, when Catherine Bishop opened the door, licked the hand she held out to him. As Rona had hoped, it helped to break the ice, and they were able to greet each other without the reserve she'd been dreading.

The morning was overcast and a cool wind ruled out sitting on the patio as they had before. Instead, Catherine invited her to take a seat in the room she'd only walked through on her last visit, and, alone for a minute, Rona looked about her. Like Catherine herself, it had an air of understated elegance: the wood of the spindly-legged chairs and bureau glowed warmly, the sofa and easy chairs were deep and comfortable. Two silver-framed photographs stood on the mantelpiece, one a man's head and shoulders, the other of a bride and groom, and the prints on the walls, cool and shimmering with light, were by some of the lesser-known Impressionists. Beyond the patio doors lay the remembered garden, still a blaze of colour. Rona drew a cautious breath of relief. So far, so good.

Gus settled himself at her feet as Catherine brought in a tray of coffee. In the intervening months, though she'd been constantly in Rona's thoughts, precise details of her appearance had become blurred, but seeing her again, Rona once more experienced that feeling of calm – which, she thought with a flash of unwelcome intuition, must be so restful for her father in contrast to her mother's spikiness.

Catherine poured the coffee and handed a cup to Rona.

'You've had a difficult time since we last met, haven't you?' she observed. 'I'm sorry your Buckford assignment proved so traumatic, but at least you put right a grave injustice.'

'Yes,' Rona murmured inadequately. Not wanting to pursue that line, she added quickly, 'I feel very guilty, keeping your scrapbooks for so long.' She bent to take them out of her brief-case and laid them beside her on the sofa. 'Thank you so much for lending them to me. They were fascinating.'

'I'm glad they proved useful. I'm really enjoying the articles, by the way; the complete set will be an invaluable collection.'

She offered Rona a plate of biscuits. 'The reason I wanted to see you,' she continued, reseating herself, 'was because I came across some papers at the back of my desk. They'd been lent to me when I was compiling the College history, and must have been overlooked when I returned the rest. I thought you might find them interesting.'

She smiled, savouring the moment. 'Forty-five years ago, Middle School held a mock election and pupils were required to write their own manifestos. One of them was by a certain James Latymer, aged thirteen.'

Rona put down her coffee cup. 'Really? Talk about coming events casting their shadows! I remember now, he was mentioned among famous old boys in the brochure. I should have interviewed him at the time, about education in his day.'

'Presumably you still could.'

Rona nodded. 'Oddly enough,' she went on, 'my husband has been commissioned to paint his portrait. He's working on it at the moment.'

'Now that *is* a coincidence. I'd forgotten he was an artist.'

Rona didn't recall ever having mentioned it. Had Pops? She said quickly, 'Yes, he has quite a broad range – landscapes, still life, portraits. He also gives evening classes, and teaches at the art school one day a week.'

'A busy schedule,' Catherine said smilingly. As soon as she'd spoken, she'd realized her gaffe, recalling too late that it had been Tom who'd mentioned his son-in-law's profession. 'I must look out for his work. What's his name again?'

'Max Allerdyce. He designed the latest set of postage stamps, but it's not been issued yet.'

'Versatile, as you said! Does he give exhibitions?'

'From time to time, yes.'

'I'm particularly interested,' Catherine went on diffidently, 'because I belong to an art appreciation society. Every so often we embark on a special project, selecting an artist, past or present, and studying his life and works in depth. We visit galleries, his birthplace if relevant, and any other places connected with his painting, accompanied by an expert on that artist. Is there any chance at all we might approach your husband?'

Rona smiled, shaking her head. 'I'm afraid not, it's just not

19

Max's thing. He's been asked several times in various connections, and always turned it down.'

'Ah well, it's our loss. Have you actually met James Latymer?'

'No. Max says he's pleasant enough, for a politician!'

'It might be amusing to show him the manifesto, and ask if his priorities have changed.'

'A leading question, certainly, but I can't see him answering it!'

Catherine went to the bureau and took out several dog-eared sheets of lined paper, which she handed to Rona. The writing was a forward-sloping scrawl, and there were some succinct comments in red ink in the margin.

'I suppose you'd need his permission to quote from it?'

'No question.' Rona was scanning the top sheet. 'Apart from common courtesy, it's his copyright.' She flicked a glance at the sheet beneath. 'May I take it home with me?'

'Of course, but I'll need it back eventually; I shall have to return it to the College with suitable apologies.'

Which, Rona thought, would involve her in another visit – unless she opted out and posted it back.

As she was leaving a few minutes later, Catherine remarked, 'I met your sister in town. Did she tell you?'

'She mentioned it, yes.'

'I'd no idea you had a twin, and naturally I mistook her for you. I felt very foolish.'

'No need to, lots of people do.'

'Actually, as soon as I spoke to her, I began to have doubts. You're not quite identical, are you?'

'Not to people who know us, though if we try, we can create quite a bit of confusion!'

'I can well believe it!' Catherine said.

She stood at the door as Rona and the dog went down the path and got into the car, returning her wave as she drove away. Then she closed the door and returned to the sitting room, staring down at the tray of coffee cups as she thought over the visit. She'd hoped to learn, by some process of osmosis, whether or not Rona had seen her with Tom that evening, but she still couldn't be sure. Either she hadn't, or she was playing Catherine at her own game. And Catherine realized, despairingly, that she'd been hoping the outcome of this meeting would help her decide what to do.

There was no longer any point in denying she was deeply attracted to Tom – she still balked at the phrase 'in love'. It had all been so totally unexpected, overwhelming her before she was even aware it was happening. In the fourteen years since Neil's death, she'd had no interest whatever in men, gently rebuffing any venturing too close. She was financially independent, thank God – even comfortably off since her mother's recent death – and despite having to give up teaching, the other love of her life, to nurse her during her last illness, her life was still full and interesting. She saw quite a bit of Daniel and Jenny, and despite her basic reserve, had made several friends since she'd come to Marsborough, mainly through the societies she'd joined. She did not, she told herself, need a man in her life, let alone one who was already married and whose daughters she had met.

She put her hands to her head. God, what a mess! Several times she'd decided not to see Tom again, had gone so far as to turn down one or two of his proposed meetings. What always undermined her, though, was the knowledge that he was profoundly unhappy. Was that her fault? He'd intimated that his marriage hadn't been right for years, but she suspected it was only when the two of them so obviously enjoyed each other's company that he'd appreciated quite how much it had deteriorated. In which case, she was at least partially responsible.

She knew, too, how much he was dreading his retirement at the end of the year, when he would be forced into his wife's company. Catherine had a consuming, if ambivalent, desire to meet Avril Parish; she couldn't conceive of a woman not appreciating Tom as a husband.

Tom! He filled her mind with disconcerting suddenness, bringing a sharp, painful stab of desire that literally took her breath away. She sat down abruptly, her heart hammering. That hadn't happened before. It was over fourteen years since that particular urgency had assailed her. Holding her mind in abeyance, she forced herself to breath slowly and deeply until, gradually, the heat left her body.

No longer nearly so sure of herself, she gathered together the coffee cups and carried them through to the kitchen.

Rona, too, had found the visit vaguely unsatisfactory. It had reinforced her liking for Catherine, but left her with no inkling of the current position between her and her father. The manifesto was a find, though, she told herself more positively; surely Latymer would have no objection to her quoting from it? What politician was averse to a little extra publicity? He could even make capital out of it: 'All my life, I've had political ambitions!' No need to explain it had been a school exercise.

She garaged the car and walked back to Lightbourne Avenue, Gus trotting happily at her side. In the hall, she at once lifted the phone and dialled Max.

'You haven't by any chance got James Latymer there with you?' she asked, when he answered.

'No, I haven't. Why?'

'I'd like to meet him.'

'You've not shown any interest before. Why now? Thinking of becoming a parliamentary candidate?'

'Hardly. No, I've been to see Catherine Bishop – you know, the scrapbook woman I mentioned last night – and she produced a manifesto that he'd written for a mock election when he was thirteen.'

'What was his platform? Save the Whales?'

'I've not had time to read it, but at a guess it's more altruistic than he'd go in for now.'

'Such cynicism!'

'She also wondered if her arts appreciation society could approach you.'

'No way.'

'That's what I told her. But to come back to Latymer, what's the position, exactly? Is he still sitting for you?'

'He's done a stint and at the moment I'm working from preliminary sketches and photographs. He's due for another session in a week or two.'

'But I need to speak to him now, if I'm to incorporate any of it in the article. Barnie's restive about its non-delivery as it is.'

'Can't help you, I'm afraid. Write to him at the House of Commons – or call in at the local offices. They might be able to help.'

'OK, thanks. Speak to you tonight, then.'

She'd no sooner put down the phone than it started to ring, and she lifted it to hear Lindsey's voice enquire, 'All right if I pop round for lunch?'

'As long as you take pot luck.'

'Larder luck, you mean.'

'Very funny.'

'I could pick up something on the way if you like? Pizza? Fish and chips?'

'There's an offer I can't refuse. Fish and chips would go down a treat.'

'Put the plates in the oven, then. See you.'

The cool breeze had dropped, and they ate companionably at the kitchen table beside the open patio doors. A scent of herbs from the trough outside drifted tantalizingly in, overlaying the smell of chips.

'I saw Catherine Bishop this morning,' Rona said, shaking on more vinegar.

Lindsey's eyes narrowed. 'And?'

'And nothing, really. If I'd hoped to glean anything, I was unsuccessful.'

'Heaven knows what Pops sees in her. She's no oil painting.'

'I've told you before, she grows on you. And her face has character.'

'It's what that character is that worries me.'

23

'I honestly can't think there's any malice there. She seems so pleasant and self-assured.'

'Probably comes from always getting her own way. She was a headmistress, don't forget.'

'Mum looked ghastly on Sunday,' Rona said gloomily.

'Mum *always* looks ghastly nowadays. She just doesn't seem to care.' Lindsey speared a piece of fish angrily. 'I'd like to take her by the shoulders and shake her, ask if she can't see that she's driving Pops away. Because that's what'll happen, whether to this Catherine woman or someone else. Damn it, he's an attractive man, Ro; there'd be plenty of women only too ready to snap him up if he became available.'

'Can't you talk to her? You've always been closer than I have.'

'And say what? "Take a look in the mirror"?'

'Exactly that.'

'And then duck! But I never get the chance to see her alone. I'm at work all week, and Pops is there at weekends.'

'Suggest a girls' day out one Saturday. Say you want to buy a new suit or something and would she like to go with you.'

Lindsey eyed her doubtfully. 'Do you think it would work?'

'It just might. Perhaps, in the glamorous surroundings of Netherby's, it'll strike her that what she's wearing isn't exactly *le dernier cri.*'

'Talking of Netherby's, guess who I met the other evening? Some people in the road had us all in for drinks, and our friend the "battered wife" was there, complete with spouse.'

'Lord, I'd forgotten all about her,' Rona said.

The Yarboroughs had moved into Lindsey's cul-de-sac during the summer. Adele joined Max's watercolour class, and on her first attendance he'd glimpsed bruising on her arms, which caused him concern. Rona and Lindsey, called upon to meet her and assess the situation, had concluded that, with the house move so recent, she'd simply banged herself while moving furniture.

'Her husband works at Netherby's, doesn't he?'

'Sales director, no less,' Lindsey confirmed.

'What's he like?'

'Seemed OK. Quite a charmer, in fact.'

'And the fair Adele?'

'Still fluttery and still wearing long sleeves.'

'Could be she just prefers them,' Rona commented, pushing her empty plate aside. 'Max hasn't mentioned her lately; perhaps she didn't rejoin this term. How were they as a couple?'

'Same as any other. Far from seeming afraid of him, she was on the clingy side.'

'That figures.'

The sisters had not taken to Adele.

'Anyway, they seem to be settling in, though there are still workmen's vans there every day. God knows what they're doing to the place.' Lindsey glanced at her watch. 'I must go; I promised to meet Jonathan for a coffee before going back to the office.'

'*Is* he married, Linz?'

'In the process of divorcing, actually.'

'Are you sure?'

'Yes, I'm sure. All right?'

'It's not just that "his wife doesn't understand him"?'

'God, Rona!' Lindsey stood up angrily. 'If I'd known I was going to face the third degree, I'd never have come! You're worse than the parents!'

'I just don't want you to get hurt.'

'That's their line.'

'OK, OK, sorry.' She gave her sister a contrite hug. 'When are we going to meet him, anyway?'

'I don't know – I'll play it by ear.'

They went together up the basement stairs and Rona opened the front door. 'Don't forget what we said about Mum.'

'Girls' day out? It'll be a barrel of laughs, all right.'

'Please, Linz.'

'All right, I'll give it a try and report back.'

'You're a star,' Rona said.

After she'd gone, Rona went up to the study and read through James Latymer's manifesto. Without seeing those of the rest of his class, there was no way of making a comparison, but as far as she could judge, it made some sound points and was well put together. It would be interesting to know if it had earned him election.

Determined not to hold on to it indefinitely, as she had the scrapbooks, she made two photocopies, marking on one the passages she might, with his permission, quote in her article. Obtaining that permission was her next priority. Or one of them. Another thing she'd been putting off had been a final visit to Buckford to complete the photographic record. Better to arrange that now, while she was on a roll. She rang *Chiltern Life* and asked to be put through to Barnie.

'I hear you're expecting a US invasion,' she greeted him.

'We surely are,' he returned in a drawl.

'It'll be lovely to have Mel and the children, won't it?'

'Of course, though I don't doubt the entire house will be turned upside down, and anything approaching normal routine thrown to the winds.'

'Worth it, though.'

'You've been talking to Dinah!'

'Come on, you old grump, you'll love playing grandpa!'

He laughed. 'You rumbled me! Right, what can I do for you?'

'You'll be glad to hear I've all but finished the education article, and I wondered when Andy would be available for the final fling?'

'Hang on a minute while I check with him.'

There was a brief silence, broken by Barnie's voice on the other line.

'You're in luck,' he announced, when he came back to her. 'He has a window free tomorrow, if that's all right with you?'

'Perfect. I'll ring him direct, shall I, and make the arrangements?'

'You do that. And once the family's arrived, you must come round and see them.'

'That'd be great. Love to Dinah in the meantime.'

*   *   *

26

Andy Hume was waiting outside the pub where she'd arranged to pick him up. At a little under average height he was shorter than Rona, a fact she'd always felt he resented. He stood huddled into his raincoat, its collar turned up against the thin, persistent drizzle and his precious camera well protected from the weather.

A man of few words, he simply nodded a greeting as he climbed in beside her. Photography was his overriding obsession, and as far as Rona knew, he'd no other interests or hobbies. Which, she felt, must be daunting for his wife.

'Thanks for this, Andy,' she said. 'After all this time, it'll be good to put the Buckford project to bed.'

'Aye, it has dragged on a bit. What are you wanting this time?'

They'd already made one photographic foray together.

'Well, last time we concentrated on how the town had changed over the centuries, taking shots, if you remember, from the same points as in the archive photos, to reveal a totally different view – shopping mall, police station and so on. But what struck me when I was there was how many buildings were actually *un*changed, still standing where they'd always stood, and still in use. The churches are obvious examples, but some of the schools too – St Stephen's in particular – and Market Square with its stone cross, and the Counting House, and Clement Lane, where the houses lean together and almost touch across the alley. And there are little flights of stone steps that lead from one level to another, and cobbled squares and ancient wells—'

'Am I right in thinking we're only here for the day?' Andy interrupted drily, and Rona laughed.

'The old bit's confined into quite a small area. It won't involve much moving around.'

'You say you're meeting someone for lunch?'

'Yes, if you don't mind – the family I stayed with when I was up there. There's a good pub nearby, which I'm sure will do you proud, and my friends know I'm on a tight schedule.'

'OK by me,' Andy said. 'Let's hope the rain lifts. These fine buildings of yours won't look so good swathed in mist.'

'The sky seems to be brightening,' Rona said hopefully, but he merely grunted.

Her optimism was, however, justified, and by the time they reached Buckford, a watery sun had broken through the clouds and the wet pavements steamed gently in its heat. They parked in the multi-storey, and for the next couple of hours moved purposefully about the old town. Parts of it held strong memories for Rona, particularly the thatched almshouses and Witch's Pond with its sinister stocks.

'They actually ducked witches here,' she told Andy as he angled his shot. 'I'm glad the sun's out; last time I came it was almost dark, and too atmospheric for comfort.'

At twelve thirty she left him at the King's Head and walked up the cobbled path to Parsonage Place and the house where, for a month, she had stayed two nights a week while she gathered her material. And eventful nights they had been.

Will was at school, but it was good to see Nuala and her father again and hear their news.

'We're keeping the articles, of course,' Nuala told her eagerly. 'Every now and then, I come across bits that I told you about myself – the Goose Fair, for instance, and celebrations for the Royal wedding. It's quite exciting!'

'You were an invaluable source!' Rona assured her.

When it was time to go, she was touched with sadness. They'd become good friends during her stay, and although Buckford was only a two-and-a-half-hour drive from Marsborough, in the normal course of things they were unlikely to meet again.

'If you marry the bank manager, send me an invitation!' she called from the gate, and both Jack's laugh and Nuala's heightened colour told her she'd hit the mark.

'You can count on it!' Nuala promised.

They'd covered most of what Rona wanted during the morning, and by four o'clock were ready to leave.

'You've whetted my appetite with this place,' Andy admitted. 'I might well come back under my own steam. Plenty of scope if I need something to enter for a competition.'

'It's picturesque, certainly,' Rona agreed as they left the old town behind them, 'but a bit too claustrophobic for me. I much prefer Marsborough, with its wide, tree-lined streets and elegant buildings.'

Andy shot her a sideways glance. Small wonder she had reservations about the place, he thought, considering the traumas that had accompanied the writing of the articles. Still, she'd never mentioned them to him, and he wasn't going to bring them up now.

'Probably because it's home,' he said.

Three

Rona spent the next day in front of a screen at *Chiltern Life*, sorting through photographs to accompany the four as yet unpublished articles, and periodically checking her preferences with Barnie. The first two had been well received, and, whether fortuitously or not, a rise in circulation had coincided with publication of the second. Complimentary letters had also been received, and Barnie congratulated her on her suggestion of printing them as a pull-out, complete with binder in which to keep them.

'You're getting 'em hooked, girl!' he said enthusiastically. 'We should do more of this.'

It was on the Friday evening, as Max was preparing their meal, that the phone rang. Rona lifted it, but before she could speak, a high, staccato voice broke in. 'Rona Parish?'

Rona frowned. 'Yes?' she said cautiously, lifting her shoulders in reply to Max's inquiring eyebrows.

'This is Zara Crane. We met at Gavin and Magda's.'

'I remember.' A picture came to mind of a pointed little face and a thick braid of red-gold hair.

'You were kind enough to agree to discuss a – project I have in mind.'

That didn't correspond with Rona's memory. 'I don't think I—' she began, but Zara again cut in quickly.

'It's taken me all week to pluck up the courage to phone you,' she said. 'Would it be at all possible to meet tomorrow morning?'

'I'm sorry,' Rona said firmly, 'I prefer to keep my weekends free.'

'Oh.' She sounded quite downcast. 'The trouble is, I'm at work all week.' A pause. 'I could meet you about four thirty, though?'

Anyone would think she was doing me a favour, Rona thought irritably. 'You'll have finished work by then?'

'I'm a schoolteacher, at Belmont Primary. Do you—?'

'I went there myself,' Rona told her.

Zara gave a relieved laugh. 'Well, that makes things easier! We live just round the corner from the school, in one of the town houses. Could you possibly come over, so we can discuss things?'

'Zara, I'm not at all sure—'

'Don't worry about the publishing angle,' Zara hurried on. 'I've thought it over since we met, and I can't see it would do any harm. It might even help. Shall we say Monday? The address is fourteen Grosvenor Terrace.'

It seemed she wouldn't take a refusal. 'I'll come,' Rona said, 'provided you realize I'm not committing myself to anything other than a discussion.'

'All right, but as I said, I think you'll be interested. Four thirty on Monday, then?'

'Four thirty on Monday,' Rona confirmed resignedly, and rang off.

'What was that all about?' Max asked curiously, sprinkling salt into the casserole.

'Remember that young couple at the Ridgeways'?'

'Whom you thought you'd discouraged from contacting you?'

'The same. It seems I wasn't discouraging enough.'

'Well,' Max remarked, 'you're always saying ideas come from the most unlikely sources, and you're in need of one at the moment, aren't you?'

'I suppose that's true. She's a forceful young woman, that. Used to getting her own way, I shouldn't wonder.'

'Takes one to know one!' Max commented, and ducked as she threw a tea towel at him.

*   *   *

Number fourteen was halfway along the terrace of mock-Georgian town houses, and since there was a vacant parking bay close by, Rona slid into it. Perhaps not surprisingly, the house bore more than a passing resemblance to her own, genuine, Georgian home, though it was considerably smaller.

Zara, wearing a blue tunic and grey flannel skirt, opened the door before the bell had stopped ringing.

'Thanks so much for coming!' she exclaimed breathlessly.

Inside, any similarity to home disappeared. There was no basement in this modern house, and the ground floor consisted of a kitchen-diner, glimpsed through a half-open door, and an integral garage. Zara showed her upstairs to the sitting room, which took up the whole of the first floor. Another flight led presumably to the bedrooms and bathroom.

The room in which she found herself owed its light, open aspect to three sash windows overlooking the front of the house. The roof of the school was just visible between the houses opposite.

'You certainly haven't far to commute,' Rona commented, taking the seat indicated.

'No, it's very convenient. Excuse me a moment, while I bring up the teapot.'

Rona looked about her, at the magnolia walls, the pale blue upholstery and the collection of china dogs on the mantel-piece. Her quick glance detected no photographs and the walls were devoid of pictures. The adjective that came to mind was 'antiseptic', though she couldn't have said why.

Zara returned with the teapot and seated herself opposite, beside a small table already bearing a tray with mugs, plates, and what looked like a shop-bought sponge cake.

'I know I bulldozed you into coming,' she began disarmingly, with an apologetic little smile, 'but I really am desperate for your help.'

Rona raised an eyebrow and accepted the mug and plate handed to her, shaking her head at the proffered sugar bowl. Zara cut the cake into alarmingly large slices, and she perforce took one with a murmur of thanks.

Zara sat back in her chair and stared down into her lap, twisting her wedding ring round her finger. The silence lengthened, and Rona, increasingly impatient to learn the object of the visit, was about to speak when she looked up, squared her shoulders and said without preamble: 'I was adopted as a baby. My parents didn't tell me till I was ten, but to be honest it didn't make much difference. Even when I was eighteen, and could have done something about it, I didn't try to trace my birth parents.' She paused. 'I think my attitude was, *If they didn't want me, I don't want them, either.* It's only in the last few months, since I became pregnant, that it seemed important to find out about myself.'

'That's understandable,' Rona murmured, but Zara was already continuing.

'My parents were against the idea from the start, and did all they could to dissuade me. But when they realized I was set on it, they finally told me what they'd known all along, that my mother was dead and my father's identity unknown. "So you see," they said, "there's really no point in bothering."'

'That *is* bad luck!' Rona sympathized. 'A double blow.'

'Yes.' Zara bit her lip. 'I could have been the result of a one-night stand.'

She looked up, meeting Rona's compassionate gaze. 'Still, I was determined to go ahead, and as my adoption papers were no help, I sent off for my original birth certificate, to find out my mother's name and where she'd been living. The weirdest part was that *my* name was given as Amanda Jane. Amanda Jane Grant, and my mother was Gemma Grant.' She shook her head wonderingly. 'I don't feel at all like an Amanda. It's as though we're two different people.'

After a moment's reflection, she went on. 'So then I sent off for her death certificate. I was adopted at six months, so I sort of assumed she'd died having me.'

This time she was silent for so long that Rona prompted, 'But she hadn't?'

Zara shook her head, and, reaching down beside her chair, retrieved a piece of paper which she handed across.

33

As Rona had anticipated, it was a death certificate. Skipping over names and dates, her eyes flicked immediately to the portion headed *Cause of Death*, totally unprepared for the stark words that leapt up at her: *Asphyxiation by ligature.*

'Oh God!' she said softly. 'Zara, I'm so sorry. What a shock for you.'

Zara said rapidly, 'The address given – in Stokely – is the same as that on my birth certificate, two months earlier. Well, Tony and I scoured all the press archives we could find. The papers had been full of the story: police interviews, house to house enquiries, Lord knows what. They were anxious to trace the baby's father – *my* father – but a friend told them he'd moved to Australia with his family months before. He'd not even known Gemma was pregnant.' She flashed Rona a glance. 'I think of her as Gemma – it's easier, somehow.'

'So if it wasn't him, who did kill her?'

'As far as we know, they never found out. The verdict at the inquest was "murder by person or persons unknown". Does that mean there might have been two of them?'

'I think it's just a legal phrase,' Rona said.

'Well, we checked through the rest of the year, hoping they caught someone later, but the story just died away.'

'What exactly happened to her?' Rona asked tentatively.

'The friend she was sharing with – Selina someone – found her in the bath, with her tights knotted round her throat. I was screaming in my cot in the next room. They thought it might have been a burglar, but nothing was taken. She'd left the door on the latch for Selina.'

After a minute, Rona leaned forward and passed back the death certificate. 'It's a terrible story and I'm very, very sorry, but I don't see where I come into it.'

Zara smiled wanly. 'When I heard you'd unearthed two murderers, it seemed like the answer to a prayer. I – hoped you might unearth me a third.' And as Rona stared at her, aghast, she added with a terrible little laugh, 'And when you've done that, perhaps you could find my father.'

'I take it you're not serious?' Rona's voice was hoarse.

'But I am, Rona! This has made all the difference, don't you see? My birth parents didn't abandon me as I'd thought; my father never even knew I existed, and my mother kept me, even though she was only twenty and on her own. I owe it to her to find out who killed her.'

'But after – what – twenty-five years? If you're really determined to go ahead, you should get in touch with a private investigator. He'd—'

'No,' Zara broke in determinedly. 'I'd much rather you did it – you'd go at it from a different angle. Magda said you write biographies; you must know how to dig out buried facts.'

When Rona, her head spinning, remained silent, she leaned forward, her hands clasped between her knees. 'Will you help me? Please?'

'Zara, how can I?'

'You've done it before,' Zara said stubbornly.

'But that was just luck. And as for your father, there are agencies whose job it is to trace birth parents. I'm sure—'

'They'd need a name first.'

'For that matter, so would I.'

Zara's eyes dropped. 'If you're wondering about the fee,' she said awkwardly, 'I have a savings account; it won't be a problem.'

Rona flushed and shook her head. 'That doesn't come into it. *If* I decide to go ahead – and it's a big "if", because there are all kinds of considerations to take into account – it'll be *Chiltern Life* who signs my cheque.'

She met Zara's wide, uncomprehending gaze. 'You did say I'd be free to publish my findings?'

'Well, yes – yes, I suppose so.'

'Then the first thing I'd have to do is discuss the ins and outs with my editor. I'd need to be sure he'd take it. He might agree if, for instance, we ran a series on people searching for their birth parents. There are plenty of them, though I hope for their sakes they don't come up with situations like yours.'

35

'How soon could you let me know?'

'The end of the week?'

Zara gave a small sigh. 'I'd hoped to have an answer today, one way or the other.'

Rona shook her head. 'And even if I go for it, there are no guarantees. For a start, this is quite different from the other cases I stumbled into. In the first one, the death had been written off as suicide, and in the second, someone else had been charged with the murder, so the police weren't interested in either of them. But from what you say, this case remains open, and even if they're not still actively working on it, they wouldn't thank me for butting in.'

Briefly, she thought of her confrontation with DI Barrett in Buckford. Thank God Stokely would be in a different division.

'It's my bet they've forgotten all about it,' Zara said bitterly.

'Well, as I said, I'll have to weigh up the pros and cons before coming to a decision. I still think you'd do better to employ someone whose job it is to do this sort of thing.'

A sudden thought struck her. 'Have you told your parents you're approaching me?'

Zara shook her head. 'First, I wanted to see what you'd say.'

'I'd probably need their cooperation.'

'But they don't *know* anything! That's the trouble!'

Privately, Rona thought they might know more than they realized – or, at any rate, admitted. Her mind elsewhere, she ate the last of the cake on her plate. There was no denying she was intrigued by the story, but Barnie's reaction could be iffy – he erred on the side of caution – and she was only too aware what Max's would be.

She refused Zara's offer of more tea and rose to her feet. As Zara also stood, Rona was momentarily aware of the rounded shape beneath her tunic. Whether that baby would know anything of its maternal grandparents might depend on her. It was a responsibility she wasn't sure she wanted.

* * *

It would have been natural, being in the neighbourhood, to have dropped in on her mother in the adjacent street, but Rona, though torn by guilt, had no wish to see her. Instead she drove quickly back into town, along Guild Street and up Dean's Crescent North to Farthings, the little house where Max had his studio and where, before going to see Zara, she had left Gus.

Between Farthings and the house next door was an alley leading to Max's garage, and she turned the car into it. A gate in the wall to her right gave access to the tiny piece of ground that served as a garden, and as she got out she could hear Gus barking a welcome. She tried the latch but the gate was bolted.

'Sorry, boy,' she told him. 'I'll have to go round the front.'

The solid wooden door opened directly off the pavement, opening on to a small passage with doors to left and right and another, standing open, straight ahead. Through this Gus now came skittering, paws sliding on the polished boards, tail wagging as though he'd endured a week's absence rather than a couple of hours'. Rona bent to fondle his ears.

'Hi!' she called up the steep, open staircase.

'Hi!' Max responded. 'Come for the hound?'

'Yep, but I'd like a word, if you can spare the time.'

It was an unwritten rule that she didn't disturb him during working hours, nor he her, unless it was urgent.

'Yes, I'm knocking off now. Come on up while I finish off.'

Leaving Gus in the hall, she went up to the studio that spread across the entire upper level. It had originally been a loft, but the carpenter next door, who had done a lot of work for Max when he first bought the cottage, had transformed it, putting in skylights and opening up dark corners.

As her head and shoulders emerged above the stairwell, she saw him drape a cloth over the easel, and knew better than to ask to see his work. He'd show it to her when he was ready.

'I need to get things ready for the class,' he said, 'but fire away; I can listen while I'm doing it.'

She walked to the window and looked down at the street, not many feet below. It was homecoming time; men and women with briefcases, and old ladies with shopping baskets, were making their way along the narrow pavements, and Guild Street, running along the end of the road, was now clogged with traffic. Behind her, she could hear Max setting up the stools and easels for his students.

'I have a problem,' she said, her eyes following two boys cycling, to the peril of pedestrians, on the opposite pavement. 'You know I went to see Zara?'

'Don't tell me,' Max replied. 'She wants you to investigate a murder!'

Rona spun round. His back was towards her, but when she didn't respond, she saw his shoulders stiffen before he turned slowly to face her.

'Joke!' he said heavily. 'Rona, that was a *joke*. Right?'

For a minute longer they stared at each other. Then he let go of the stool he was holding and it fell with a clatter to the floor. 'God Almighty!' he said explosively. Then, turning towards the stairs, 'We'd better go down and you can tell me about it. I have to get supper, anyway.'

Class evenings necessitated an early meal.

He clattered down the stairs ahead of her. Gus, seeing their set faces, waved his tail uncertainly and trotted after them into the kitchen.

'Going back outside?' Max asked him, and the dog hastily sat down and looked up at him, tongue lolling. 'Apparently not.' He closed the back door. 'There's a bottle of wine in the fridge,' he added. 'Help yourself, and pour one for me. Are you staying for supper?'

'I'm not hungry,' Rona replied. 'I've just had the most enormous piece of cake.'

'Then you'll have to sit and watch me, and while I eat, you can recount your problem. Though I might as well tell you, if murder really is involved, I wash my hands of it. You've put the fear of God into me twice already this year.'

She watched as he took a dish of lasagne out of the oven, crisply brown on top, sauce bubbling round the edges. He spooned a generous portion on to a plate, set it on a tray together with knife, fork and his wine glass and, motioning to her to follow, went through to the living room and placed the tray on the small table at one end. Beyond it, the little walled garden lay bathed in mellow sunshine. Gus settled himself in his usual position under the table.

'Right,' Max said, 'you'd better fill me in.'

Slowly, sorting it out in her mind as she went, she did so.

'So, you have a mother who got herself murdered,' he summarized, 'and a father who scarpered. Connected, obviously.'

'It seems not. He emigrated before he even knew she was pregnant.'

'If they know that much about him, they must know his name,' Max argued.

'You'd think so, but Zara swears not.'

'What about her grandparents? Surely they must have known him?'

Rona sipped her wine thoughtfully. 'I didn't think to ask, but Gemma wasn't living at home. She was sharing a flat with another girl – the one who found her.'

Max shook his head despairingly. 'God, love, you attract them like a magnet, don't you? The Harvey business was bad enough, but once it was cleared up, I thought that was that. I never dreamed it was the start of your becoming a pseudo-detective. I tell you, my nerves won't stand it. How many more times are you going to put yourself in danger?'

'It needn't be dangerous,' Rona protested unconvincingly. 'People are searching for their birth parents every day.'

'Well, she's already found her mother, hasn't she? Or rather, she knows who she was. The fact that she's dead should be the end of it. As to her father, are you proposing to fly to Australia and search the outback for him?'

'Don't be facetious, Max,' Rona said crisply. 'I came to you for advice.'

'Well, that's easy enough: don't touch it with a bargepole.' He eyed her over a laden forkful of lasagne. 'Not that I flatter myself you'll take it. You're using me as a sounding board, aren't you?'

She smiled wryly. 'I hoped you wouldn't notice!'

'What's your gut feeling about it?'

'I don't know. It smacks of banging my head against a brick wall, but I admit I'm intrigued. If Barnie's agreeable and I *do* take it, I'll set myself a time limit. If I don't get anywhere in, say, six weeks, I'll give up.'

'I thought these things could take years.'

'I can't spare years. I need to earn a living.'

The clock on the mantelpiece chimed seven.

Max put his empty plate on the tray. 'I'll have to make a move, love. I didn't finish preparing upstairs, and they start to arrive at quarter past.'

'OK. Thanks for listening.'

'Let me know what you decide.'

Rona garaged the car in Charlton Road, snapped on Gus's lead, and turned towards home. The dog, ever hopeful, tugged in the direction of the footpath leading up to the park, but she shook her head. It would be dark soon.

'Tomorrow,' she promised.

As she walked slowly back to the house, her mind replayed the conversations she'd had, first with Zara Crane and then with Max. He had a point, she thought; Gemma's parents must surely have known who the father was. She wondered if Zara had obtained her mother's birth certificate, which would give their names.

Back in the house she fed the dog, but still wasn't hungry herself. She went up to the study, switched on the computer, and typed out everything she could remember that Zara had told her. Then she sat staring at the screen, trying to decide what to do. Would Barnie be interested in articles on the search for birth parents? Surely it would be fascinating to learn of the different reactions – parent to child, child to parent, and how often parents refused even to meet their offspring? She would have to sell it to him if she were to proceed with Zara's request; though she was freelance, she tended to confine herself to *Chiltern Life*, and couldn't offhand think of anyone else to whom to send the article. And the more she thought about it, the more she felt she'd like to do it.

Finally, hunger at last beginning to stir, she turned off the computer and went downstairs, deciding to go along to Dino's for a meal. She hadn't booked, but a Monday evening shouldn't be too busy, and she was confident he would squeeze her in. She and Max were regular customers and, hating cooking as she did, she often went alone when he was working.

Ten minutes later, with Gus at her side, she set off down the avenue and turned into Fullers Walk, at the top of which lay Guild Street, the main shopping area. Dean's Crescent, however, branched off about two thirds of the way along, winding its way past the restaurant and the offices of *Chiltern Life* to the upper end of Guild Street, and, having crossed it, became Dean's Crescent North, where she'd left Max an hour or so earlier.

Dino greeted her with his usual exuberance. 'Ah signora! *Benvenuto*! You are alone this evening? We will find you a nice table.'

She was following him across the room when a voice hailed her, and she turned to see Gavin Ridgeway rising to his feet at a table nearby. 'Rona! Max not with you? Come and join me.'

'Hello, Gavin. Are you on your own, too?'

'Magda's off on a buying trip. Let's be lonely together!'

She hesitated, not sure she wanted an evening in Gavin's exclusive company; it unsettled her that he should look so exactly the same as when they'd been together – attractively irregular features, thick, ash-blond hair. However, she could scarcely decline. With an apologetic glance at Dino, she went to join him, and he pulled out a chair as Dino signalled a waiter to lay another place. She was being foolish, she told herself; their romance was five years in the past and both were now happily married. All the same, an underlying guilt remained that, while considering his proposal, she had met and fallen for Max.

41

He handed her the menu and, recalling the appetizing smell of Max's supper, she ordered *lasagne al forno*.

'It was a good party the other week,' she began, as he poured her some wine.

'Glad you enjoyed it. The trouble with that sort of do is there's never time for a proper conversation, especially if you happen to be the host.'

Rona toyed with the roll on her plate. 'That couple I was talking to when you "rescued" me,' she began diffidently.

'The Cranes?'

'Yes. You were right; I *was* in need of rescuing.'

He smiled. 'To be honest, I wasn't sure they'd fit in, but I like young Crane and he's been a bit down in the mouth lately.'

Rona looked up quickly. 'Oh?'

'Turns out his wife was adopted, and, now they're expecting a family, she's set her heart on tracing her parents.' He hesitated. 'And strictly *entre nous*, they had rather a shock when they looked into it.'

'Oh?' Rona said again, conscious of her quickened heartbeat.

'Her mother had been *murdered*, would you believe?'

She took a quick decision; Zara had not requested secrecy, and if she undertook the task, her involvement would soon become common knowledge. 'Actually, Gavin, I know about it,' she admitted. 'That's what I meant about needing to be rescued. She wants me to find her killer.'

He put down his glass and stared at her. Then he gave a shout of laughter. 'God, Rona, you're not serious? How the hell did she . . . ? Ah, I remember now: Magda was proclaiming your successes in that field last time we saw them. I thought at the time young Zara seemed unduly interested. Did she ask you at the party?'

'Only to discuss something; I went round this afternoon.'

'Are you going to do it?'

'I don't know.'

Their plates were set before them and they began to eat in silence. Then Rona said tentatively, 'You say her husband seems depressed?'

42

Gavin shrugged. 'He wants her to drop it, obviously. Thinks it might harm the baby if she has any more upsets. Whether that's feasible or not, I wouldn't know.'

'It's odd they never found out who did it. The absent father seems to have been the only suspect, and he had the best of alibis.'

'How so?'

'By emigrating to Australia months earlier, blissfully unaware of impending parenthood.'

'Ah! That, I didn't know.' Gavin glanced at her. 'How does Max feel about this? Your taking it on, I mean?'

Rona pulled a face. 'As you'd expect.'

'Can't say I blame him. You've had some narrow escapes this last year.'

'His point exactly.' The corners of her mouth lifted. 'I have to say, though, that hunting murderers adds a certain piquancy to life!'

'Well, for God's sake be careful.'

'Oh, I shall. Now, that's enough about me. Where's Magda swanned off to?'

'Paris,' he replied, refilling her glass. 'Some people have all the luck.'

'Is she still planning on putting cafés into her boutiques?'

'In principle, yes; there are a few where it wouldn't be practicable, but she's doing some market research.'

'The one in Buckford was great.'

Gavin smiled. 'That's her flagship.'

The waiter approached to enquire if they'd like a dessert, but they settled for coffee and the accompanying amaretti.

'And separate bills, please,' Rona added as he moved away.

'Oh, now look—' Gavin began, but Rona cut in.

'No, Gavin, I mean it. The last time we met here, with Magda, you insisted on paying, which was very generous, but I can't let you make a habit of it. This is one of my favourite haunts, and I can't run the risk, every time I come, of someone I know trying to treat me. It was great having your company, but I pay my own way. OK?'

'Far be it for me to argue, *Ms* Parish.'

'Good,' she said, and purposefully took out her credit card.

Minutes later they were on the pavement outside. Gavin's car was parked in the small yard behind the restaurant. 'Can I run you home?' he offered, but she shook her head.

'As you know, it's just round the corner, and Gus will protect me from any bogeymen.'

'As long as you're sure. It was good to see you, Rona. Mind how you go.'

'I will. Love to Magda. Goodnight, Gavin.'

With Gus's lead tightly in her hand, she walked swiftly down the pavement and rounded the corner without looking back. Where Gavin was concerned, she thought, it was a policy she'd be well advised to follow.

Four

The next morning, Rona was still wondering how best to put the proposal to Barnie when Dinah phoned.

'Rona – ages since I saw you! How about you and Max coming over and meeting the family? Melissa would love to see you again, and I don't think you've ever met Sam, have you, let alone little Martha?'

'That would be great, Dinah.'

'Lunch time would be better than evening, from the children's point of view. How about Sunday? Are you free?'

Fleetingly, Rona thought of her parents, but no invitation had been forthcoming. 'Yes, that'd be fine, thanks.'

'Come over about twelve, then – and pray for a fine, warm day! Indoors, the noise level can be excruciating if they let rip together. The cats flee to the top of my wardrobe!'

The Trents had three Siamese, who had long ago formed a non-aggression pact with Gus.

As soon as Dinah rang off, Rona pressed the button for *Chiltern Life* and asked to be put through to Barnie.

'Telepathy!' he greeted her. 'We were talking about you at breakfast; you'll be getting a call from Dinah later.'

'I already have,' Rona told him. 'Lunch on Sunday.'

'Well, she doesn't waste time, I'll say that for her! What can I do for you?'

Quickly and as succinctly as possible, Rona outlined her proposal. When she finished, there was a lengthy silence.

'What do you think?' she asked, when the suspense became unbearable.

'Not too keen, to be honest. Principally because I don't

want to be responsible for you getting into deep water, and it seems to me that's the way you're heading.'

'But surely it would be interesting to follow someone's search for her birth parents?'

'Don't be naïve, Rona; you know as well as I do it's the murder angle that interests you. Oh, I know you've been there before, but at least on those occasions you stumbled into it unknowingly.'

'Surely being aware of it would give me an advantage? Quite apart from that, though, I'd like to have a go at running the father to earth. OK, so he went to Oz twenty-five years ago, but he might have come back since. If I could find *one* parent for her, it would be something.'

There was another pause. 'If I said no, would you still go ahead?'

Rona considered the question. 'Possibly. I was saying to Max that, either way, I'd set myself a time limit to come up with something. If there was absolutely nothing after six weeks, I'd give up. And I reckon, if I have to, I can afford to waste six weeks.'

'And if something *did* come up?'

'Well—'

'I take that as a "yes". Tell you what: I'm not going to commission this article, and if you write it, I might not publish it. We may need the lawyers to look at it, for one thing. But if you produce something interesting and I feel it's appropriate to the magazine, then I'll certainly consider it. Will that do?'

Rona sighed. 'I suppose it'll have to,' she said.

That evening, she phoned Zara.

'Rona! I wasn't expecting – you said the end of the week.'

'I know, but I've reached my decision.' No need to tell her of Barnie's reservations. 'I'm prepared to spend six weeks looking into your family, on the understanding that if I can't find anything in that time, I'll give up. Are you agreeable to that?'

'Oh.' Pause. 'I suppose so.'

Take it or leave it, Rona thought. 'If you want me to go ahead on those terms, I'll need quite a lot more information.'

'Of course – such as what?'

'For a start, photocopies of your birth and your mother's death certificates. And I could do with *her* birth certificate, too; that would give your grandparents' full names and address.'

'Oh, yes! I never—'

'Did you check for a marriage certificate, by the way?'

'I checked, but I never expected to find one.'

'And you didn't?'

'No.'

'The next thing is, did you by any chance take copies of the write-ups in the papers?'

'Yes – every mention we could find.'

'That's great – could I borrow them? There's no point in duplicating the work.'

Selina Someone's proper name might appear in the reports, Rona reckoned; failing that, she'd turn up the electoral register. The girl was sharing with Gemma, dammit; it was inconceivable that she hadn't known more than she'd said.

Now for the tricky bit. 'There's one thing more, Zara. If I find what we're looking for, or any part of it, I must have complete freedom in writing it up. You can read it before I submit it, but on the understanding that the only changes I'll agree to are errors of fact. In other words, even if there are parts you'd rather I left out, they'd have to stand.'

'You mean, once you've started, I can't change my mind?'

'Not without very good reason.'

'OK, I suppose that's fair enough.'

'Fine. Well, once you have Gemma's birth certificate, we can arrange a meeting to hand over all the relevant papers.' She hesitated, then added gently, 'It's still not too late to withdraw, if you're having second thoughts.'

Zara gave a little laugh. 'It just seems so – official, all of a sudden. But no, I've set my heart on finding out as much as I can, and you're my best bet. I'd like you to go ahead.'

'Fine. We'll be in touch, then.'

The phone rang immediately she put it down, and as she lifted it again, her mother's voice said, 'Lunch on Sunday all right?'

'Oh Mum, I'm sorry! You're about twelve hours too late!' Thank goodness! Rona thought involuntarily, hating herself.

'I didn't realize you required so much notice,' Avril said stiffly.

'Mel and the children are over from the States – the Trents' daughter, you know – and Dinah's invited us to meet them.'

'But Sunday's a family day; surely she knows that? Why can't you go on Saturday?'

'We weren't invited for Saturday,' Rona said, an edge creeping into her voice. Then, against her better judgement, 'Could we come to you then?'

'No, that won't do; I've already got something on.'

I, not *we*?

'Sounds interesting; what are you doing?'

'Playing in a bridge tournament, as it happens.'

'At the weekend?' A pause. 'What about Pops?'

'What about him?'

'What's he doing while you're out playing bridge?'

'I've no idea,' Avril said coldly, 'but don't concern yourself on his account; he spends more time out than in these days – I'm sure he'll think of something.'

Rona drew in her breath, but Avril was continuing: 'Since you won't even *try* to alter your arrangements, I suppose there's no more to be said. Visits home seem to be a low priority these days.'

'Oh, for God's sake, Mum!'

'Perhaps you'll consult your diary and let me know when you're free.' And she rang off.

Rona sat for several minutes before, with deliberation, she put the phone back on its rest. Her irritation with her mother – a more or less permanent state at the moment – was overlaid by acute anxiety about her father. *He spends more time out than in these days.* With Catherine Bishop?

And the thought of Catherine reminded her she still hadn't returned James Latymer's manifesto. Added to which, if she wanted a clear slate by the time she started on her next project, the sooner she obtained his permission to quote from it, the better. There remained, however, the problem of the best way to approach him; she didn't want to butt in on one of his sittings with Max, yet on the other hand, it hardly seemed worth attending one of his surgeries.

The solution was presented to her half an hour later, when Max made his nightly call.

'Dust off your tiara,' he told her. 'The Conservatives are having a fundraising cheese and wine party next week, and we've received a personal invitation, courtesy of James Latymer. When I say "invitation", I am, of course, using the word loosely; we have to pay for the privilege, but you were wanting to meet him, weren't you?'

'I was indeed; in fact, I'd just been wondering how to wangle it. The invitation went to Farthings?'

'It's the only address he has for me.'

'So when is it?'

'Next Wednesday, six to eight p.m., at the Clarendon.'

'Lucky it's one of your free evenings. I've had two invitations myself today, both for Sunday lunch.'

'Uh-oh!'

'You can relax – Dinah got in first!'

'The other was presumably your parents?'

'Yes, and Mamma was not best pleased at being pre-empted.'

'Another black mark, then. We're building up quite a stockpile.'

Rona said heatedly, 'And we've done nothing to deserve any of them!'

'OK, sweetie, don't let it get to you.'

She drew a steadying breath. 'Sorry.'

'Any more thoughts on this parent search?'

'I spoke to Barnie and he wasn't too keen. He's hedging his bets.'

'I'm not too keen either, in case it escaped your notice.'

'It'll be all right, Max, honestly.'

'From which I deduce you're going ahead?'

'I phoned Zara this evening and said I'll give it six weeks. We'll see how it goes.'

'Well, if you're going to publicize it, for God's sake only admit to searching for the father. I don't want yet another hitherto undetected murderer coming after you.'

She smiled bleakly. 'I can't say I do, either. Don't worry, I'll be discreet.'

His sigh reached her down the phone. 'I thought I was married to a biographer, not a private detective.'

'You are. And I promise, after this, I really will embark on another. My publishers are getting restive, for one thing, and I have some possibilities in mind.'

The fact that murder had put paid to her last attempt at biography was not mentioned by either of them.

The following morning, before she could find an excuse to delay, she phoned Catherine Bishop.

'I was wondering when it would be convenient to return the manifesto,' she began brightly.

'Oh – there's really no hurry. Keep it as long as you need it.'

'Actually, I don't need it any more; I've made photocopies.'

'I see. Well, don't make a special journey out here; I'm coming into town this morning to do some shopping. Could we meet for a coffee, say at the Gallery?'

'That would be fine, thanks.'

'Eleven o'clock?'

'I'll be there.'

Rona was thoughtful as she made her way up Fullers Walk towards Guild Street, Gus trotting at her side. She'd been wondering if there was any casual way she could introduce her father into the conversation, in order to gauge Catherine's reactions. On reflection, though, it was an undertaking fraught with peril; if there was any sounding out to do, much better to pick on Pops; at least she knew where she was with him.

The Gallery Café was approached up a wrought-iron staircase between two shopfronts on Guild Street, and led to a walkway above the pavement containing a few boutiques, an art shop, and the café itself, which straddled the corner of Guild Street and Fullers Walk, offering a choice of viewpoint from its window tables.

Catherine was already seated at one of them as Rona and Gus walked in. Gus went straight to her, tail wagging, and accepted a pat before settling himself under the table, careful to avoid the stack of carrier bags propped against the wall.

'What a pleasure it is to see a well-trained dog!' Catherine remarked, as she picked up the menu. 'Now, I've decided to be wicked and indulge in a Danish pastry. Can I tempt you?'

Rona smiled. 'I don't need much tempting.'

'Fine.' She signalled the waitress and gave the order, checking Rona's preference from the dozen or so types of coffee listed.

'I come up here for lunch sometimes,' she confided as the waitress moved away, 'and sit here unashamedly people watching. It's fascinating.'

'Do you ever see anyone you know?' Rona asked, remembering a shock sighting she'd once had from this very table.

'Not so far, but then I don't know that many people here.'

Rona took out the envelope containing the manifesto and passed it across the table. 'Before I forget,' she said. 'Thanks so much for showing it to me.'

'Have you asked permission to quote from it?'

'Not yet, but I'm hoping to meet Mr Latymer next week, at a fundraising event.'

'I wonder if he remembers writing it,' Catherine mused.

'How's the portrait coming along?'

'All right, I believe.'

'You haven't seen it?'

'Oh no; work in progress is kept strictly under wraps. Quite literally, in fact: last time I went into the studio, Max draped a cloth over the easel.'

Catherine laughed. 'I'm sure if I were having my portrait done, I'd want to look at it after every session.' She hesitated. 'Did you ask him about speaking to our group?'

'Yes, but I'm afraid the response was as I expected.'

Their coffee and pastries arrived, and Rona embarked on her Viennese slice.

'You seem to have had a successful shop,' she commented, glancing at the packages on the floor.

'So-so. I still haven't found a present for my son; it's his birthday next week.'

Rona looked up in surprise. 'You have a son?'

'I have indeed, and a daughter-in-law. They live in Cricklehurst.'

'I don't know why, but I never—' Rona broke off in confusion, belatedly remembering the young couple in the photograph who, for some reason, she'd assumed to be a niece or nephew.

'Don't I look maternal?' Catherine asked, with an amused smile. 'Let me try to redeem myself: Daniel works for a computer firm in Stokely and his wife, Jenny, manages a flower shop. They've been married three years now, and one reason I didn't leave Marsborough when my mother died was because it was within easy reach of them without being on their doorstep.'

Rona's face was flushed. 'I'm sorry – I didn't mean to—'

'My dear, there's nothing to apologize for; I'm just surprised I've never happened to mention them. Your—' She broke off, flushing in her turn.

There was a brief, taut silence, then Catherine said quietly, 'This is ridiculous; what I was going to say is that your father has met them – or, at least, Daniel.'

Rona gazed at her, mouth suddenly dry, and she went on quickly, 'He very gallantly came to our rescue – twice, in fact. I was waiting for a bus one day when my car was in dock, and he kindly stopped and ran me home. And as if that weren't imposition enough, while we were having a cup of tea, Daniel phoned to say Jenny was having a miscarriage.' Her brows drew together, remembering. 'It would have meant a taxi all the way to Stokely, but your father insisted on driving me there. It was so kind of him.'

Some comment seemed called for, and Rona forced herself to say, 'I see.' And she did – partly. It explained how the friendship – if that's what it was – had begun, but she'd seen them together on a totally different occasion.

Catherine was watching her a little warily, perhaps anticipating further questioning, but loyalty to her father prevented it. Instead, Rona added simply, 'That sounds like Pops.'

Embarrassed and uncertain, she'd suddenly had enough of the discussion, and, hurriedly finishing her coffee, she retrieved her handbag and took out her purse.

Catherine shook her head. 'This is on me,' she said firmly, as she signalled for the bill. 'I was glad of the chance to see you again. I do hope, now our professional contact is over, we can still meet occasionally?'

'I'd like that,' Rona said awkwardly, wondering, even as she spoke, if it was the truth. Certainly when she'd first met Catherine, she'd hoped a friendship would develop between them; she had found the older woman's sense of calm relaxing and somehow comforting. But that was before she'd seen her strolling with Pops on a summer evening.

She stood up and clicked her fingers at Gus. 'Thanks for the coffee, and for all your help over Buckford.'

'It was a pleasure,' Catherine replied formally, knowing it would be unwise to press further. Though she couldn't resist adding, 'Give my regards to your father.'

Rona shot her a quick look, nodded, and, with a final smile, walked quickly from the room, the golden retriever at her heels. Catherine watched her go with mixed feelings.

She saw us that evening, she thought, *I'm sure of it. I hope to God I haven't put my foot in it for Tom.* And she turned with a slightly strained smile to take the bill from the waitress.

Rona walked along Guild Street until she was out of sight of the Gallery windows before stepping into a doorway, where she took out her mobile and dialled her sister's number. Lindsey answered almost at once.

'Any chance of your slipping out for a couple of minutes?' Rona asked. 'I've something to tell you. Two things, actually.'

'I suppose I could take an early lunch. Where are you?'

'A couple of hundred yards down the road.'

'You don't give much notice, do you?'

'Please, sis?'

'OK. We can go to the wine bar in Market Street. I'll meet you outside the offices in five minutes.'

'So,' Lindsey said, when they were seated with glasses of wine in front of them. 'What is it that's so urgent?'

'I've just had coffee with Catherine Bishop, and she admitted knowing Pops. Apart from the bank, I mean.'

'She didn't!'

Rona recounted what Catherine had told her. 'But it still doesn't explain what they were doing in Barrington Road,' she finished.

'If it was all so innocent, how come neither of them mentioned it?' Lindsey asked suspiciously.

'That was what I was wondering. And she nearly didn't tell me. She stopped herself at first, then she said, "This is ridiculous," and came out with it.'

'What was ridiculous? Skirting round the subject?'

'That's how it struck me.'

'So what do we do now?'

Rona said slowly, 'I wonder if she'll tell Pops the cat's at least partially out of the bag.'

'If she does, do you think he'll say anything?'

'Time will tell,' Rona replied philosophically.

Lindsey sipped at her wine, thinking over what she'd heard. 'And the other thing?' she asked after a minute.

'What?'

'You said you'd two things to tell me.'

'Oh – my latest assignment, that's all.'

'Which is?'

'A parent search.' And she went on to tell Lindsey about her meetings with Zara, and Barnie and Max's reservations.

'I see their point. It sounds a bit dodgy to me.'

'Quite interesting, I'd say, trying to track down the errant father.'

'Oh, come on, Ro! This is me you're talking to! It's the murder that attracts you, and you know it. *That's* why Barnie and Max don't like the sound of it.'

Rona shook her head impatiently. 'It's old hat, Linz. Twenty-five years old, to be exact. Even if I wanted to, I wouldn't have a hope in hell of nailing him.'

'You underestimate yourself,' Lindsey said darkly.

The second phone call resulting from the café meeting was put through to Tom's office at the bank.

'I think I should warn you that I had coffee with Rona this morning.'

He frowned. 'Warn me?'

'I told her about the Stokely trip.'

He drew in his breath sharply. 'However did that come up?'

'We were talking about Daniel and Jenny, and it more or less slipped out. I tried to retrieve it, saw how futile that was, and decided to – make a clean breast of it.' She added anxiously, 'I hope I didn't do wrong?'

'Of course not.' He paused. 'Did you mention that we've met since?'

'No, but I'm almost certain she saw us that evening.'

'What makes you think so?'

'Just – her manner, somehow.'

'But nothing was actually said?'

55

'No. She left soon afterwards.'

'All right, Catherine. Thanks for letting me know.' He glanced at the closed door of his office and lowered his voice. 'I was wondering – that is, I'll have the day to myself on Saturday. Will you be free, by any chance?'

'I think so, yes.'

'Perhaps we could spend it together?'

'That would be lovely, Tom.'

'I'll be in touch, then. In the meantime, thanks for phoning.'

'Goodbye,' she said.

Tom put down the phone, leaned back in his chair and surveyed the ceiling, his lips pursed. There'd been another contretemps with Avril the previous evening: Lindsey was coming to lunch on Sunday, he'd been told, but Rona was 'too busy'. Tom had wondered, with a sinking heart, whether she was trying to avoid him, but then Avril had added, 'She wanted to know what you'd be doing with yourself while I was out on Saturday. As if I wasn't the last person to ask.'

He'd made the mistake of remarking that he hadn't in fact known she was going out, whereupon she'd insisted that she'd told him, adding that he should try listening to her occasionally and he might learn what was going on. The situation was becoming farcical, he thought despairingly, but, more seriously, the stress of it was getting to him. He'd been alarmed last night to feel a warning twinge in his chest.

Now, added to everything else, Rona knew about the Stokely trip. She'd be expecting him to say something, but what the hell *could* he say? *My marriage is a sham and I've fallen for Catherine?*

A wave of heat washed over him. He'd never put it so baldly before, even to himself. Furthermore, he hadn't the slightest idea how Catherine felt. Oh, she valued his friendship, he knew that, but she'd given no indication that she wanted to take it further. After all, she was an intelligent, cultured woman with wide and varied interests; what would she want with an almost retired bank manager with a dicky heart?

At least, he thought, cheering up slightly, she'd agreed to spend the day with him on Saturday. That was something to look forward to.

After a week of cloud and early-morning mist, Saturday dawned warm and sunny. A coach was taking the bridge team to Chilswood, and Avril left the house soon after nine. An hour later, Tom drove to Willow Crescent to collect Catherine.

It had been agreed they would drive out to Penbury Court, a stately home fifteen miles south of Marsborough, which was famous, among other things, for its gardens. It was the last weekend in September, and the roads were busy with families intent on making the most of the good weather. But they were in no hurry; the drive itself was part of the day out, and Tom relaxed, responding to Catherine's light-hearted mood, and suffering the numerous hold-ups with good-humoured resignation. How different, had Avril been beside him.

When they eventually reached the property, they had to queue for several minutes while those in front of them either presented their National Trust cards or paid the entrance fee. Then, having parked and armed themselves with an up-to-date leaflet of attractions, they set off in the direction of the lily pond. Catherine was wearing a coffee-coloured dress and leather sandals, and, on leaving the car, had put on a sunhat. 'To stop me getting freckles!' she'd smiled. Informally dressed, she appeared somehow younger and more carefree, and it seemed entirely natural when she slipped her arm through his.

They walked slowly round the pond, looking at the brightly coloured fish that swam there and the plants that grew along the edge, about which Catherine proved quite knowledgeable. And as they walked, they talked easily about a variety of topics that, while interesting them both, didn't touch on the personal. Tom always enjoyed their conversations, the gentle thrust and parry, the exchange of opinions and ideas as each of them stimulated the other to an increasingly wide range of hypotheses.

For an hour or more they admired borders and gazebos, statues and sunken gardens, fortuitously coming across the Courtyard Restaurant just as a table was being vacated. The midday sun was now directly overhead, and they seated themselves under the umbrella with a sigh of relief. Catherine removed her sunhat and tossed it on a chair.

'I don't know about you, but I'm ready for a long, cold drink,' she announced, and smiled as a pleasant-faced young waitress appeared as if by magic and set a jug of iced water on the table, together with two glasses.

After studying the menu, Catherine selected prawn mayonnaise and Tom a Caesar salad. He ordered a bottle of wine, and sat back to look about him. Dotted round the courtyard were some two dozen tables, where couples or families laughed and talked over their meal, while inside the restaurant itself, he could see others who had opted to avoid the sun. The complex was an old mews, and the buildings surrounding the yard would originally have been stables. The tiled roof of the restaurant was surmounted by a small clock tower that, he noted, corroborated the time showing on his watch. Halfway through the day already.

And suddenly his happiness evaporated into misery. He didn't want this day to end – ever. He didn't want to go back to his wife's unsmiling face, her barbed comments, her perpetual discontent. He wanted – and he knew this with a blinding flash of certainty – to spend the rest of his life with Catherine.

'Tom? *Tom!*'

He looked up, meeting her concerned eyes.

'What's the matter?' she asked anxiously. 'You've been staring into your glass as though you'd like to drown yourself in it!'

'I've decided to leave Avril,' he said.

She drew in her breath, staring at him with an expression he couldn't decipher. A waiter materialized beside them. He opened a bottle, invited Tom to taste the wine, poured two glasses, and placed the bottle in an ice bucket alongside the table. Throughout this performance, the two of them sat in silence, avoiding each other's eyes. As he finally left them, Catherine asked quietly, 'When did you reach this decision?'

He smiled wryly. 'Just now. As you know, life has become increasingly difficult lately, but last night . . . '

'Last night?' she prompted, when he didn't continue.

'Last night, after yet another row, I – didn't feel too good, and it rather scared me.'

She said sharply, 'Your heart, you mean?'

He nodded, not meeting her eyes.

'Oh, Tom,' she said softly. Then, 'What will you do?'

'I've no idea. I've not had time to work it out.' He glanced at her, then down at the fork he was turning over in his fingers. 'I don't want you to think our seeing each other has had any bearing on this; the marriage has been going downhill for years and I've refused to acknowledge it. But I wouldn't be honest if I didn't say that since I met you . . .'

He broke off and she sat unmoving.

'Since I met you,' he continued after a moment, 'I've discovered that I'm not after all fit only for the scrap heap, that I can still feel. . .' Again he stumbled to a halt.

'Feel what, Tom?' Her voice was low.

He forced himself to come out with it. 'Like making love,' he said in a rush. Not daring to look at her, he added ruefully, 'You now have permission to slap my face!'

'Suppose I don't want to?' A smile came into her voice. 'Slap your face, that is!'

His head jerked up and, meeting her eyes, he felt such an intensity of joy that he was momentarily winded. She put a hand over his.

'Tom, the last thing I wanted was to contribute to the breakdown of your marriage. I kept telling myself we shouldn't keep seeing each other – if you remember, I made several excuses. But I could tell how miserable you were, and I could hardly bear it. I kept wanting to hold you and tell you everything would be all right.'

Their salads arrived and Catherine hastily released his hand.

Tom's mind was reeling, unable to take in the momentous possibilities suddenly opening up before him. 'God, Catherine, I can't believe this. I – don't know what to say.'

'I don't think either of us does, so let's just eat this delicious lunch and try to absorb it.'

'But – am I right in thinking that you – that we . . . ?' He drew a deep breath. 'What I'm trying to say is – if – when – I'm free, will you – marry me?'

'I don't see why not!' she said.

'God!' he exclaimed in frustration. 'I can't believe that we're sitting here over prawn salad discussing things that will change our lives, and I can't so much as take your hand because we're surrounded by all these bloody people!'

She laughed. 'Never mind; going down on one knee has gone out of fashion. Seriously, though, I don't think we should rush things. You came out with your decision as soon as you made it; possibly if you'd given yourself time to think about it—'

'It would have been exactly the same.'

'Nevertheless,' she went on, 'there are a lot of things to consider – principally, of course, your family, but also how the bank might react if you suddenly flee the nest. I suggest we take a step back until you've had a chance to think it through. We've waited a long time to find each other; it won't hurt to wait a little longer.'

She met his eye and laughed softly. 'All right, it may hurt just a little, but it'll be worth it in the long run. We've agreed that we have what the Victorians called "an understanding"; let's leave it at that for the moment, and just enjoy our lovely day as we were doing this morning.' She paused. 'All right?' she asked softly.

He didn't want to step back, he thought protestingly. On the contrary, he wanted to shout his joy from the rooftops, to give exuberant expression to this intoxicating feeling of release.

'All right?' she said again, and, seeing the sense of it, he reluctantly nodded.

'All right,' he said.

Five

First impressions indicated that Sunday would be as warm and sunny as the day before. Dinah's prayers had been answered, Rona thought, as she drew back the curtains.

'What do you bet Barnie'll do a barbecue?' said Max lazily from the bed behind her.

'Well, I can't see Sam sitting through a meal in the dining room.'

'How old will he be now?'

'Two and a half, I think, and Martha's three months.'

'I hope to God we're not going to be subjected to baby talk all day!'

Rona laughed. 'You and Barnie can go and grump in a corner.'

He got out of bed, shrugged on his towelling robe, and stretched hugely. 'Breakfast in ten minutes,' he said, and pattered barefoot down the stairs.

Melissa had changed since Rona had last seen her, on her wedding day. Although still slim, after two children she was more curved than Rona remembered, and had acquired a slight American accent.

'It's great to see you again!' she cried, enveloping her in a hug. 'From what I hear, you're leading quite an adventurous life these days!'

'That's one way of putting it,' Max murmured, adding, as he was hugged in turn, 'Marriage and motherhood certainly seem to suit you.'

'Oh, they do!'

Admittedly there was no sign of the difficult pregnancy she had undergone, that had caused her mother to fly out to be with her for the last weeks, and resulted in Martha's premature birth. Nor was this visible in the baby herself, lying in a Moses basket under the trees, and kicking lazily as she watched the moving leaves above her head. Rona stood with Mel and Dinah looking down on her.

'She's gorgeous, Mel!'

'She's gaining weight steadily now,' Mel said contentedly.

Barnie came out of the house, his grandson on his shoulders. Sam was familiar to Rona from the photograph in the sitting room, his blond hair and blue eyes inherited from his father. He gave Rona a shy smile but refused to say 'Hi!' as instructed by his mother.

'He doesn't say a great deal anyway,' Melissa admitted.

'Just be thankful!' Dinah told her darkly. 'Once he starts, there'll be no way of stopping him!'

As Max had predicted, the barbecue was already lit, and he was keeping a wary eye on Gus, who had stationed himself near the meat laid ready. Barnie handed the child over to his mother and went to join him.

Melissa said, 'If you'll excuse us, I'll take Sam to the bathroom before we start eating. He's not totally reliable yet.'

'You're in your element, aren't you?' Rona teased Dinah, who was looking fondly after them.

'Of course I am! I don't see nearly enough of my grandchildren. But – Sam and Martha – I ask you! Did you ever hear such oldie-worldie names?'

A natural enough reaction, Rona supposed, from one who'd called her own daughter Melissa. 'The old names are coming back,' she said diplomatically.

Dinah shrugged resignedly. 'Anyway, what have you been up to? I haven't seen you for a while.'

'Mainly finishing off the articles on Buckford. I had to go back again last week.'

'I gather Barnie's not too happy about your new project.'

Rona pulled a face. 'He's keeping a diplomatic distance till he's sure I'm not going to be murdered in my bed.'

Dinah shuddered. 'Don't joke about it. It's true, then, that you're going after another killer?'

'That could be a by-product, I suppose, but my main objective is to research the birth parents of someone I met. She was adopted as a baby and knows less than nothing about them.'

'But the mother's murderer was never caught?' Dinah persisted.

'No, but that was twenty-five years ago. He's probably long dead by now.'

'I sincerely hope so,' Dinah said quietly. 'Take care, that's all I ask, and if you find you're getting out of your depth, drop everything and get out.'

'Yes, ma'am!' Rona saluted.

Dinah smiled briefly and patted her arm. 'Let's go and join the men,' she said.

Oddly, her warning left Rona with a vague unease that neither Max's nor Barnie's had engendered, and as they settled themselves round the large wooden table, she wondered why. There was no denying Dinah was a forceful character: though under five foot, she made up for her lack of inches by strength of personality, displaying a passionate interest in everyone and everything, and once formed, her opinions were not easily swayed. Watching her as she darted about distributing plates of meat and bowls of salad, Rona thought she resembled a small dynamo, her deep voice and rich laugh ringing out over the hum of general conversation.

As for Melissa, she seemed the unifying factor that melded them into a family. The wide divergence in her parents' heights – Barnie was over six foot – had evened out to make her average, as her mother's wiry black hair and Barnie's softer, rapidly thinning thatch had merged into the cascade of brown curls that fell to her shoulders. As to temperament, Rona couldn't say: Barnie was renowned at *Chiltern Life* for the shortness of his temper, and she had before now seen Dinah fly into a fury when thwarted. Perhaps, she thought with amusement, it would be as well to remain in Melissa's good books.

Gus, who had been provided with his own piece of steak, slept contentedly in the shade alongside Martha's Moses basket, and Sam had left the table to play in the sandpit hastily provided by his grandparents.

'I wonder how many more weekends we'll have like this,' Dinah remarked, as the adults sat drinking coffee after the meal. 'I always hate it when the time comes to put covers on the barbecue and lock the chairs in the shed for the winter.'

'Oh, I don't know,' Max said lazily. 'Autumn's my favourite time of year: crisp frosts, bonfires, and cosy evenings with the curtains drawn. Will you still be here at Christmas?' he asked Melissa.

'Yes, Mitch is coming to spend it with us.'

'We'll see him long before that, though,' Dinah put in quickly, noting her daughter's downcast face. 'He's flying back for the weekend in three weeks' time.'

'Sam keeps asking for him,' Melissa said.

Poor little boy, Rona thought, missing his father. But at least he knows who his father is. And her thoughts again turned, as they so frequently did at the moment, to Zara Crane. The rest of them could utter their dire warnings, but she was determined to do all she could to solve the mystery of Zara's birth.

They had not long been home when the phone rang, and Lindsey's indignant voice demanded, 'Why the hell didn't you tell me you weren't going to the parents'?'

'Sorry, it never occurred to me. Why, did you go?'

'Of course I bloody went! Sundays are a dead loss anyway, since Jonathan has to spend them with his family, but Mum never let on it would be only the three of us.'

'Perhaps she rang you before me.' Rona paused, glancing through the sitting-room doorway at Max, ensconced with the Sunday papers. 'How was it?' she asked quietly.

'Much as usual; Mum narking away and Pops letting it wash over him. Come to think of it, though, he seemed more relaxed than usual, as though he really didn't care what she said, instead of just pretending not to.'

With another glance at Max, still impervious behind his paper, Rona moved further down the hall. 'I suppose you heard about the bridge tournament?' she asked in a low voice.

'Indeed I did. I was given a blow-by-blow account of every hand, as though it meant anything to me!'

'Did Pops say what he did while Mum was out?'

'No, and I didn't ask. Why? He probably spent the day gardening, as usual.' There was a pause, then Lindsey said, 'Oh God! You think he was with that woman, and that's what accounted for his good spirits?'

'It's a possibility, that's all. Linz, this is getting serious. We can't just sit back and let Mum destroy their marriage.' Rona paused, mentally reviewing courses of action. 'How about that girlie day out? If she'd agree to make an effort, meet him halfway, it might still not be too late.'

'OK, I'll see if I can fix it for next weekend. Where were you today, anyway? Mum said you were too busy to come.'

Rona's temper flared at the injustice, but she answered steadily. 'A prior engagement, perfectly genuine. Dinah asked us over to meet Mel and the children; they're here for a fairly lengthy stay while her husband's working in the Gulf. He's with some American oil company.'

'I don't think I've met the daughter. What's she like?'

'Very pleasant, and the children are sweet.'

'Getting broody, sister dear?'

'Not a chance. Not yet, anyway.'

Lindsey laughed. 'Well, I'll try to get Mum organized, and let you know how it goes.'

'You're a brick,' Rona said gratefully.

The Clarendon was Marsborough's premier hotel, situated on the corner of Guild Street and Alban Road.

Rona and Max were directed to the Albany Room at the rear of the building, from where a babble of conversation was spilling out into the foyer. As they went in, Rona at once spotted James

Latymer standing in a group, and in the moments before he caught sight of them, subjected him to a rapid inspection, interested to compare the television image with the living man.

Even in the flesh, he seemed larger than life, with his dark hair, florid face, and, it had to be said, expanding girth – due, no doubt, to House of Commons lunches. The woman beside him, presumably his wife, was striking in her own right – tall and slim, her hair very short but with strands curling on to her face in a style reminiscent of Audrey Hepburn. She was wearing a hyacinth-blue tunic in raw silk over wide-legged palazzo pants – so wide-legged, in fact, that Rona at first thought it was a skirt.

Possibly conscious of her gaze, Latymer glanced towards the door, and, on seeing them, excused himself to the group and led his wife over to meet them.

'Max! Good to see you!' he exclaimed, holding out his hand. 'And Mrs Allerdyce – this is a pleasure! Darling –' he turned to his wife – 'this is the brave man who's painting my portrait! My wife, Hester.'

She smiled and took their hands in turn. 'Mr Allerdyce – Mrs Allerdyce.'

'Let me get you a drink,' Latymer said, signalling to a waiter who moved swiftly forward with a tray of glasses.

'Actually,' Max said, taking one, 'Rona prefers to use her professional name. She's known to all and sundry as Rona Parish.'

'The biographer?' Hester Latymer exclaimed, her eyes widening.

'Guilty as charged,' Rona admitted.

'What a talented family!' murmured James.

'But that's wonderful!' Hester was continuing. 'I've read all your books, and thoroughly enjoyed them. And aren't you also doing that series in *Chiltern Life*?'

'I am, yes. In fact,' she turned to James, 'I was hoping for a word with you, Mr Latymer.' She opened her handbag and took out the photocopy. 'I wonder if you remember writing this?'

'Oh dear!' he said with a humorous grimace. 'Is my past catching up with me?'

He unfolded it, watched with interest by the three of them, and ran his eyes down the page. 'Good God! Wherever did you unearth this?'

'In the Buckford College archives,' Rona said. 'I was wondering if you'd give me permission to quote from it in my article on education?'

'Not until I've read it!' he replied, with a politician's caution. 'May I borrow it?'

'Oh, that copy's for you; I thought you'd like to have it.'

'Thank you. I promise to come back to you on it.' He folded the sheets, slipped them into an inside pocket, and looked about him, conscious of his duties to his other guests. 'Now, I'm sure you know a lot of the people here, but is there anyone I can introduce you to?'

'Please don't bother,' Rona said quickly. 'We've already taken up your time, and we're very adept at mingling.'

'Excellent. Well, a pleasure to have met you, and I'll be in touch.'

Hester Latymer turned to Rona. 'I'd enjoy discussing your books with you sometime, if that would be possible?'

'I'd be delighted.'

She smiled, nodded, and moved away to join her husband, who was already greeting another couple.

There were indeed quite a few people they knew and, the main object of the evening having been achieved, Rona relaxed and enjoyed herself, chatting to friends, buying the requisite raffle tickets and helping herself to the delicious canapés. It was approaching eight o'clock and she was beginning to wonder if they should make a move when she heard Max say, 'Hello, Adele! I didn't realize you were here!'

She turned quickly, and found herself face to face with the pretty, timid, and possibly abused Adele Yarborough. The man at her side was, to Rona's surprise, smiling at her and holding out his hand.

'Lindsey, isn't it? Nice to see you again.'

Adele flushed a deep rose on his behalf. 'No, Philip, this is her sister Rona, Mr Allerdyce's wife.'

Philip Yarborough looked confused and embarrassed. 'I do beg your pardon; I'd no idea—'

'It happens all the time,' Rona assured him quickly. 'Please don't worry about it. You're Adele's husband, I presume?'

'Philip Yarborough, yes.' He took her hand.

'Rona Parish.'

If the difference in surnames threw him, he hid the fact, simply turning to Max as Adele introduced them. While the two men shook hands, she murmured to Rona, 'We met your sister at a neighbour's party.'

'Yes, she told me.'

The pink silk blouse, Rona saw, had the usual long sleeves, and she found herself wondering if they really did hide bruises. To her untutored eye, Philip Yarborough didn't look violent: in his mid forties, he was of average height, with a broad nose and thick brown hair that sprang up from either side of his off-centre parting. He also, she noted, had the practised, easy manner of the salesman. Quite a charmer, as Lindsey had said.

Since the men were still talking, Rona asked, 'Have the children settled in at school?'

As usual, Adele wasn't meeting her eye. 'They've only just started, so it's a little soon to say.'

Of course; they'd stayed with their grandparents till the end of last term. 'How about you, then? Are you getting to know more people?'

'Yes, everyone seems friendly, but with workmen still in the house, I can't get out much. It takes me all my time to fit in Max's class.'

So she was still going, Rona noted. Max hadn't mentioned her.

'You enjoy it?'

'Oh, very much. It's the highlight of my week!' Adele flicked a glance at her husband and, catching his eye, murmured apologetically, 'We really should be going, Philip.'

'But I haven't spoken to Rona yet!' he protested, raising his eyebrows in mock dismay.

'We told the babysitter eight thirty.'

'Oh, very well. The burdens of parenthood!' He turned to Rona with an unexpectedly attractive smile. 'Perhaps we'll have a chance to speak next time we meet.'

She smiled back. 'I hope so.'

As they moved away, Max commented, 'We'd better go, too. I booked the table for quarter past.'

By the time they'd said their goodbyes and collected their coats from the cloakroom, it was already eight fifteen.

'I enjoyed it more than I expected,' Max remarked as they set off briskly along Guild Street. 'What did you think of our esteemed MP?'

'I agree with your assessment: pleasant enough, for a politician.'

'He's in the shadow cabinet, you know,' Max commented. 'I'd say he has an illustrious future ahead of him.'

At Dino's, they were ushered to their usual table and their order taken. It wasn't until their main course had arrived that Rona said casually, 'I didn't know Adele had signed on again this year. You never speak of her.'

Max shot her a glance from under his eyebrows. 'Do you wonder? Every time I mentioned her name, we had a row.'

Rona flushed. 'That's a slight exaggeration.'

'Not as I remember it.'

'It was just that you set yourself up as guardian angel on the flimsiest of evidence.'

'You didn't see those bruises,' he returned, stabbing an artichoke heart.

'So what did you make of her husband?'

'Plausible.'

'*Plausible?* What kind of judgement is that?'

'The words "snow" and "Eskimo" come to mind.'

'Well, he *is* in sales,' she pointed out, mildly surprised to find herself defending Philip Yarborough.

'Exactly. And the first thing a salesman learns to sell is himself.'

'Oh, come on! He's a director of a highly reputable store, not a second-hand car dealer!'

'The basics are the same.'

'So you still think he knocks her about?'

'For God's sake!' Max looked quickly about him, but no one appeared to have heard.

'Have there been any more signs of it?' she pursued.

He hesitated. 'Not physical signs, no.'

Rona leant back in her chair. 'Oh, so we're back on the psychological kick? I was forgetting you were a trained therapist.'

Max threw down his fork. 'What did I tell you? Every time! Do you wonder I never mention her? It's obvious you've taken a dislike to her.'

'I think she's manipulating you, that's all, and you're falling for it.'

'Exactly how is she manipulating me, when she keeps herself covered up all the time?'

'By doing just that; she knows you saw the original bruises and were suspicious of them, even if they were only a result of heaving furniture around during the move. She's playing on your sympathy by making you wonder what she's hiding.'

He raised a hand wearily. 'Can we just drop it, please, and enjoy our meal? This is giving me indigestion.'

Rona did not reply.

It took a while for the conversation to teeter back on to an even keel, and they were still being careful with each other as they prepared for bed. She stood listening to the running water as Max brushed his teeth in the en suite, and when he came back into the bedroom she went to him and put her arms round his neck. After a minute he responded, and they stood in silence, holding each other.

'I'm sorry,' she whispered contritely. 'I didn't mean to spoil the evening.'

'I just don't understand what you have against her,' he said, kissing her hair.

'Nor do I, really, but now that I've met him, I honestly can't see Philip Yarborough as a wife beater.'

'They don't wear badges, you know.' He sighed, gently putting her aside. 'All right, I might have overreacted to the bruises. I hope to God I did, because either way there's nothing I can do about it. Now,' he added, his voice lightening as he climbed into bed, 'we've wasted enough time arguing, so let's start making up for it.'

And, harmony restored, Rona thankfully complied.

Zara phoned at lunch time the next day. 'The certificates came in this morning's post,' she said. 'I'll be in town after school; would you like me to drop them in?'

'It would be a help, if it's not out of your way.' Rona gave her directions to the house, adding, 'It looks rather like the big brother of yours!'

'I'll find it. I want to go to the supermarket first, so will it be OK if I get there about six?'

'Fine; I'll be here.'

When she rang off, Rona took out a clean folder, labelled it *Zara Crane* and set it aside. Tomorrow, she thought with a twinge of excitement, it would be bulging with the photo-copies Zara was bringing with her. Then she could really get to work.

'I see what you mean!' Zara commented, staring up at the frontage of the house. 'The difference is, yours is the real thing.'

Rona stood to one side and she came in, looking about her with interest. 'Oh, you have a basement! Lucky you! How many bedrooms are there?'

'Would you believe only one?'

At her look of surprise, Rona added, 'We made a lot of changes when we moved in. For instance –' walking into the sitting room – 'this was originally two rooms and we knocked down the dividing wall.'

Zara looked admiringly at the marble fireplace, the antique

tables, comfortable armchairs, and the duck-egg walls displaying Max's collection of modern paintings, harmoniously blending the new with the old. 'It has such character!' she exclaimed, and Rona remembered the bare magnolia walls in Grosvenor Terrace.

'Would you like a quick tour?' she offered.

'Oh, yes please! I love looking at other people's houses.'

She dumped the heavy carrier bag at the foot of the stairs and Rona led the way up, showing her into the large bedroom with its en suite. 'This is the only floor that we didn't knock into one room,' she said. 'Principally because I needed somewhere to work.'

Zara walked to the window and looked out at the leafy avenue. 'It's like being in a tree house!' she said. 'You see everything through a screen of leaves.'

'In summer, yes.'

They moved on to the study and it, too, met with approval, in particular the miniature fridge and electric ring. 'The kitchen's in the basement,' Rona explained, 'so this saves me going down two flights in search of refreshment. When I'm busy, I have lunch up here – to the frustration of my dog, who's not allowed above the ground floor.'

'It's a brilliant idea!' Zara enthused. 'I spend half my time running up and down stairs.'

Back on the landing, she glanced at the flight of stairs leading upwards. 'What's on the top floor?'

'Nothing of interest. It was Max's studio for a while, but we disturbed each other, so, as you know, he now works at our other house.'

Zara flushed. 'Me and my big mouth!' she said.

Her most fervent enthusiasm was, however, elicited by the sunshine-yellow kitchen, the patio garden seen through its glass door, and Gus, who, waking from his nap, came to greet her.

'I've always wanted a dog,' she said, scratching his ears with both hands, 'but with our lifestyle it wasn't practical, and now with the baby coming, goodness knows when we'll get round to it.'

Rona handed over the carrier bag she'd collected on the way down. 'Take a seat. Would you like a glass of wine while we look at these?'

'No, I'm off booze, thanks, but don't let me stop you having one.'

'Fruit juice, then?'

'That'd be lovely.'

They sat at the table and Zara took out the bundle of papers.

'These are what we copied from the newspapers,' she said, extracting a thick pile of sheets from a manila envelope. 'And here are the copies of the birth and death certificates. They weren't as easy to get as mine; I hadn't got all the dates and addresses, and had to go through the General Register Office. Still, I got there in the end.'

She smiled ruefully. 'You know that phrase from the inquest verdict, about persons unknown? It could just as easily be a description of my parents, couldn't it? My father's a total mystery, and I can't really picture Gemma, either. All I've got is that grainy photo they kept reprinting when she was killed. I'd give anything to see a proper one.'

'If we can trace your grandparents, they're sure to have one.'

Her face lit up. 'That's true. But what about my father? Is there any hope at all of finding him? I might have a complete family of half-brothers and sisters in Australia.'

'We'll advertise on the web,' Rona said, 'but unfortunately, since he's not even aware of your existence, he's not likely to log on to those sites.'

She reached across for the certificates, picking up the one that lay on top. It was Zara's birth certificate – or rather, that of Amanda Grant.

'That's interesting!' she commented. 'Gemma's occupation is given as radio reporter. With luck, we'll be able to trace people who knew her.'

'Where will you start?' Zara enquired, sipping her fruit juice.

'First, I'd like to meet your adoptive parents. They do know now that you've approached me?'

'Yes, but they won't be much help. They've told me all they know.'

'Something might emerge. Could I have their name and address?'

'Margot and Dennis Fairchild,' Zara said reluctantly. 'The Gables, Swing Gate Lane, Cricklehurst.'

Rona's heart jerked. The last time she'd been in Cricklehurst, she'd come face to face with murder. 'Phone number?' she asked, and Zara gave it, adding, 'Let me know how you get on.'

'Actually, Zara, that's something I need to explain: I know you instigated this search, but as I told you at the beginning, I'll be working as a journalist, not a professional people-finder. Which means, to put it bluntly, that I won't be under an obligation to keep reporting back to you. That might sound harsh, but it's in your interests too; suppose I had a lead, told you about it, and then it faded away, having raised your hopes for nothing?'

Zara looked mutinous. 'You mean you're not going to tell me *anything*?'

'Not unless it's definite. And, as I explained, I'm limiting the search to six weeks. If something arises in that time – which I very much hope – fine, I'll carry on working on it. But if, despite all the feelers I put out, we don't get anywhere, then that's it. OK?'

'I've already said so,' she answered sulkily.

'You do see my point, don't you? It could take years, and obviously I can't afford to spend an indefinite time on it. As I said at the beginning, you'd be much better advised—'

'I want you to do it,' Zara broke in. 'All right, I won't keep pestering you. I've waited this long, I can wait a little longer.' She glanced at her watch, then pushed her chair back. 'I must be going; Tony'll be home by now.'

She stood up a little clumsily, one hand going to the small of her back.

'OK?' Rona asked quickly.

Zara nodded. 'It's just that I get tired by the end of the day, and my back starts to ache.'

Rona led the way up the stairs. 'I'll do my very best to come up with something,' she promised as she opened the front door.

'I know you will. Thanks for taking it on.'

Rona closed the door behind her, and wondered belatedly what to do about supper. Not Dino's, two nights running; in any case, she was impatient to read through the papers Zara had brought and make some initial notes. She'd ring for a take-away, she decided, and eat it at the kitchen table with the papers spread about her. Not for the first time, she reflected that there were advantages in spending some of her evenings alone. However, before phoning her order through, she'd ring the Fairchilds and try to make an appointment for the next day. Nothing like striking while the iron was hot.

With the tingle of anticipation any new project engendered, she ran back down the stairs to check their number.

Six

Swing Gate Lane led off the main road through the village, its detached houses standing in good-sized gardens. The Gables, about halfway down, was a long, low house approached by a curving drive. Since the gates stood open and the lane was fairly narrow, Rona drove inside.

The appointment was for eleven o'clock, and having assumed Mr Fairchild would be at work, she was surprised when he opened the door to her. Perhaps, she thought, he was needed for moral support. He was a tall, sandy-haired man with light-blue eyes, who shook her hand with a grave smile and shepherded her through the palely panelled hall to a conservatory built on the back of the house. His wife was standing nervously by a table bearing a silver coffee pot and cups and saucers. Like her husband, she appeared to be in her mid to late fifties. She was a small, plump woman, smartly dressed in a silk blouse and tailored skirt, and was regarding Rona with apprehension.

'It's good of you to see me,' Rona said, taking her hand. 'I know this must be hard for you.'

'It's come as a shock,' Margot Fairchild admitted. 'We didn't think Zara was interested in her birth parents.'

Dennis Fairchild said gruffly, 'We took our time telling her she was adopted. She was a happy, secure child and there seemed no point in unsettling her, especially when her mother was dead and her father unknown; it wasn't as though they might try to contact her at some stage. Whether we did right, I don't know; nowadays, received wisdom says they should be told from the word go.'

'In any case, it didn't seem to make much impression.' Mrs

Fairchild waved Rona towards the wickerwork sofa, and, when she'd seated herself, handed her a cup of coffee. 'She never referred to it again. In fact, we congratulated ourselves on how smoothly it had gone.'

'Would you have any objection to my recording this?' Rona asked tentatively. 'It's hard to remember, later, exactly what was said, and it would save me having to take notes.'

'Go ahead,' Fairchild said, and Margot, after a quick glance at him, nodded.

Rona extracted the recorder from her handbag and switched it on. 'So what was the first indication you had that she *did* want to find her father?'

Margot passed round a plate of shortbread – home-made, by the look of it. 'When she and Tony came to tell us she was pregnant. She was obviously delighted, but there was an under-lying tension that I picked up at once. And then she came out with it: now she was having her own baby, she needed to know where she had come from. That's how she put it. It – was like a physical blow.'

Dennis put his hand briefly over hers. 'We'd assumed we were all the family she needed. Wrongly, as it turned out.'

'How old was she when you adopted her?'

'Well, she had to live with us for three months before we could start proceedings,' Margot replied, surreptitiously wiping her eyes, 'so she'd have been about six months when it became official; but we've had her since she was ten weeks old.'

'I don't know much about the procedure,' Rona confessed. 'You'd been on a waiting list, had you?'

'Yes, for some time. But to give these people their due, they do try to match you up if possible. In those days, Dennis's hair was more auburn than it is now, and so, of course, is Zara's. It's surprising how often people say she looks like him.'

Personally, Rona couldn't see it, but she smiled and nodded. 'And you knew about her parents?'

'Yes. Naturally, we'd heard about the case at the time, that poor girl found dead in the bath and the baby crying in the next room.' Her eyes filled again. 'It made us want her all the more, so we could make up for what had happened. We changed her name too, partly to give her a fresh start, and partly because it made her more ours.'

'Did you ever meet her grandparents?'

It was Dennis Fairchild who answered. 'No; initially, we were afraid they might want the child, but we learned from the newspapers that Gemma's father had died when she was sixteen, and her mother later moved to South Africa.' This would be in the photocopies, Rona reflected; she'd only had time to flick through them.

'She flew back for the funeral,' Fairchild added, 'but that was it.' He met Rona's eyes. 'Forgive me, but I don't see what you can possibly hope to achieve. Even if Zara's father didn't know of the pregnancy, it could never have been serious. Not if he was prepared to up stakes and emigrate, leaving his girl-friend behind. Furthermore,' he went on before Rona could speak, 'you haven't even got a name for him, have you? How can you even *start* looking, without that?'

'It's a challenge, I grant you, but I can't believe absolutely *no one* knew his identity. So my first step is to advertise – on the Web and in local papers – for anyone who knew Gemma. She worked in radio, apparently, so plenty of people must have done.'

'But she wouldn't have been anyone *important*!' Dennis protested. 'Not at twenty years old! She was probably the gofer or tea girl, and put "radio reporter" on the birth certificate because she thought it would look better.'

'Well,' Rona said stubbornly, 'it's my best lead, so that's what I'll start with. I particularly want to trace her flatmate, which will mean a trawl through the electoral registers. *She* must have known more than she admitted.'

There was a brief silence. Then Margot said in a low voice, 'Zara's also got a bee in her bonnet about her mother's murder. Did she tell you?'

'Yes, but that's hardly my remit. If the police couldn't solve it at the time, how can I, twenty-five years later? He's probably dead himself by now.'

I sincerely hope so, Dinah had said. Again the unsettling frisson.

Dennis Fairchild pursed his lips. 'I can't help feeling it would be better to let sleeping dogs lie,' he said. 'Still, once Zara's set her mind on something, it would take more than us to dissuade her. That's something we learned very early on.'

'There's nothing else you can remember that might help in the search?'

They both shook their heads.

'And you never heard any more of the grandmother?'

'No reason why we should. We certainly didn't try to contact her; we were just relieved she wasn't making a claim.'

Rona reflected on the conversation as she ate a solitary pub lunch on the outskirts of Cricklehurst. Gemma's birth certificate had named her parents as Joyce and Harold Grant. She'd now learned that Harold had died some thirty years ago – had his widow remarried? It would be worth checking for a marriage certificate in the name of Joyce Grant, though if she was still in South Africa, it might not be recorded here.

Back home at the computer, she discovered to her frustration that Stokely Town Hall held only the current electoral registers. Out-of-date ones could be viewed at the Family History and Archive Centre in Buckford, and a phone number was given to enable would-be searchers to book a reading machine.

Damn! Rona thought. She'd hoped to follow her search at Stokely with visits to both the local paper and radio station. Now, a return journey to Buckford would also be necessary. Still, the registers were her first priority, so there was nothing for it but to phone through and book a machine for eleven a.m. on Monday.

'How's the project going?' Max asked later that evening, as they were sitting over dinner.

'Early days,' Rona replied. 'As I expected, the adoptive parents weren't much help. What I need now is publicity, so I'm going to contact Tess Chadwick at the *Stokely Gazette* and arrange to see her on Tuesday. I'm sure she'll give me a plug. With luck, she might even be able to put me on to someone at County Radio.'

'With what end in view?'

'Tracking down people who knew Gemma, of course. Stokely is where she lived and worked – and died, for that matter.'

'But surely it's the father you're after?'

'I've already put a message on a contact site. The trouble is, as I told Zara, if he doesn't know she exists, he won't be looking for her. What I need is a name, which is why I'm concentrating on her friends here. I can't believe a pregnant twenty-year-old, with no parents to hand, wouldn't confide in *someone*. And the most likely someone is her flatmate, which is why I have to trail up to Buckford yet again, to check the electoral register.'

Max topped up their glasses. 'You've not forgotten there's a murderer lurking in the background?'

'No, I haven't.'

'Suppose all this attracts his attention?'

'I doubt if it'd worry him; he must think he's safe after all this time.'

'But God, Rona, the girl probably knew him! He might *be* one of these friends you're happily looking for! There's no evidence she was killed by a burglar, is there? Nothing was stolen?'

'No, but if he'd just strangled her in the bath, he'd hardly waste time opening drawers on the off-chance of something to hock, especially if the baby was screaming blue murder. Anyway,' she added a little sulkily, 'all known friends and acquaintances were interviewed at the time.'

Max looked at her thoughtfully. 'Obviously, you won't be mentioning Zara?'

'Obviously not by name. She assures me only her family

and the adoption agency know her history, so it would be impossible for anyone to identify her.'

'But not so hard to identify you, if someone put his mind to it. So no names, OK? Leave a contact number, nothing else. Your mobile, or even your email address, since it doesn't include your name.'

Rona gave an exasperated sigh. Then, seeing the concern in his eyes, her expression softened and she reached for his hand. 'Don't worry, Guardian Angel; I'll be careful, I promise.'

He raised her hand to his lips and kissed it. 'Just mind that you are,' he said.

As Lindsey turned into Maple Drive, her father's car was just approaching the corner. They both wound down their windows.

'An unscheduled visit, love? I wasn't expecting you.'

'Mum should be; I'm taking her shopping.'

Tom looked surprised. 'Oh? She didn't mention it.'

'Lunch included,' Lindsey added. 'Hope that's OK?'

'Of course – no problem. I'm off to the garden centre to look for a new shed. Enjoy yourselves.'

As she drove the few yards to the house, Lindsey wondered if she'd unwittingly given him carte blanche to visit Catherine Bishop, but there was little she could do about it. She tried the front door, found it unlocked, and let herself in.

'Mum?' she called. 'Ready for our shopping spree?'

Avril appeared in the kitchen doorway, drying her hands on her apron. 'I think I'll give it a miss, dear,' she said listlessly. 'You don't need my opinion on what you're buying.'

'Oh no,' Lindsey told her firmly, 'you're not getting out of it now! I've booked a table for lunch at Netherby's, so we can revive ourselves halfway through.'

'Lunch?' Avril echoed. 'I didn't realize—'

'You'll need your coat – there's quite a sharp wind this morning.' Lindsey eyed her mother's drab skirt and blouse. 'Or would you like to change first?'

'Why should I change?' Avril asked in surprise. 'Not meeting the Queen, are we?'

'I – just thought you'd like to wear something smarter, for going into town,' Lindsey said lamely.

Avril's eyes traversed her daughter, taking in the knee-length skirt, the boxy jacket, the bright scarf at her throat. 'Well, I'm sorry if what I've got on doesn't suit you, but it's that or nothing.'

Lindsey suppressed a sigh. 'Some lipstick, then?'

Avril snorted. 'At my age? What's the point?'

Lindsey's temper snapped. 'If you were a *hundred*, you could still make the best of yourself!' She seized her mother's shoulders and spun her to face the hall mirror. 'Look at you!' she commanded. '*Really* look! When did you last have your hair done? Or buy any new clothes? When did you stop *caring*, Mum?'

Avril's startled eyes met hers in the mirror and she gave an uncertain laugh. 'All this, because I'm not wearing lipstick?'

'I just don't understand – you used to be so smart. Ro and I were always so proud of the pair of you.' She paused, then added deliberately, 'And Pops still looks great.'

'Well, he has to. The bank—'

'Mum, he's an attractive man, and he meets attractive women every day in the course of his work. And then—'

'And then he comes home to me,' Avril finished for her. 'You don't need to worry on that score; it's a long time since your father afforded me a second glance.'

'Do you blame him?'

Avril turned quickly. 'Now look, if you've come here to insult me—'

'Mum, I'm here because I *love* you, and I don't like what you've turned yourself into. Nothing seems to please you any more. Today was supposed to be a treat, just the two of us together, but I'm having to beg you to come out with me, and you're not prepared to make the slightest effort to—'

To her annoyance, her eyes filled with tears of frustration. 'Sorry,' she said in a low voice, feeling for a handkerchief. Her mother was regarding her with a frown.

'If it means so much to you, of course I'll come. But don't

83

imagine that a shopping trip will turn an ugly old duck into a swan.'

'You could be a swan again any time you wanted,' Lindsey retorted, dabbing at her eyes, but Avril, reaching for an old duffle coat, simply shook her head, and, having run out of arguments, Lindsey silently opened the front door.

The feeling of constraint lasted throughout the drive to town and the parking of the car, but as they emerged on to the main thoroughfare, both of them began to relax. The sun was shining and a brisk wind blew the first autumn leaves down the pavement ahead of them. Guild Street was thronged with shoppers, the windows were full of tempting displays, and Lindsey's heart rose again. Come hell or high water, she'd see her mother bought at least one outfit today.

Tom did indeed try to phone Catherine from the garden centre, but there was no reply and he didn't care to leave a message. Only as he rang off did he remember that she was expecting visitors this weekend; no doubt they'd gone out for the day. With a metaphorical shrug of his shoulders, he went to look at the sheds.

It was almost four o'clock when Lindsey drew up at the gate, but she declined the offer of a cup of tea. Avril gave her a quick hug before getting out of the car.

'Thanks, love,' she said gruffly.

'We must do it again.'

Avril nodded, hurried up the path with her parcels, and, after turning at the door to wave, disappeared inside. Lindsey started the car and slowly moved off. The hug had taken her by surprise – her mother wasn't demonstrative – but she was gratified by it. Perhaps it and the day they'd spent together heralded the beginning of a thaw that would bring her parents closer. She could only hope so.

Still clutching her parcels, Avril went into the kitchen. Through the window, she could see Tom at the bottom of the garden with Bob from next door, both of them bent over wooden panels laid out on the grass. The new shed, no doubt. She watched them for a minute or two, while a host of thoughts blundered around in her head. Then she went upstairs, took her purchases one by one out of their carrier bags, and laid them on the bed: a dress in soft rose-pink wool, an oatmeal jacket, a heather tweed skirt, and – a wild extravagance – a cashmere sweater in pale mauve. She stared down at them with something approaching panic. She must have been mad to allow Lindsey to talk her into this! She'd spent more money on clothes in one day than she had over the last five years. The final two bags, smaller than the rest, disgorged mascara, an eyebrow pencil, and a lipstick the same shade as the dress.

Lindsey had been all for whisking her into the beauty salon to have her hair styled, but at that Avril had drawn the line. Nevertheless, she conceded, it could do with a wash. Still hardly believing what she'd done that day, she went to the bathroom and turned on the shower.

She was still upstairs when, an hour later, Tom called, 'Bob and I are off to the pub. I'll be back by seven.'

'All right,' she called back from a dry throat. She was seated on the dressing-stool, staring at her image in the mirror. Her wispy hair was twisted into large blue rollers, and her face was an unaccustomed shade of beige. It was a wonder the liquid hadn't dried up in the bottle, she reflected; she'd not used it since the Harris wedding more than two years ago. Several times over the last hour she'd been on the point of running to the bathroom to wash it all off. And yet – a flicker of long-dead vanity stirred inside her. It *did* make a difference, having a little colour in her face. Almost fearfully, she reached for the blusher.

'Something's happened, hasn't it?'

Catherine shot a quick look at her cousin, who, seated at the kitchen table, was neatly slicing beans into a colander.

'How do you mean?'

'You seem – different, somehow. As though you're hugging a secret to yourself.'

'You're imagining it,' Catherine said with a smile.

'Talking of which,' Elizabeth mused, as though she hadn't spoken, 'did you ever realize that when we were young I was always pretending to have secrets, in the hope of inveigling one out of you in return? It never worked; you were always infuriatingly self-contained.'

Catherine glanced at her fondly. Both only children, they had early on formed a deep friendship that had stood them in good stead over the years, sustaining them through life's ups and downs. Though, Catherine reflected ruefully, when real tragedy had struck and Neil so unexpectedly died, she had not allowed even Elizabeth to penetrate her wall of grief.

'So, since I've rumbled you,' her cousin was continuing, 'you might as well come out with it. Is Jenny pregnant again? Or is it Daniel?' Her voice sharpened. 'He's not being transferred to another office, is he? One that'll involve them moving away? I do hope not, when you're so nicely settled.'

'Relax, Lizzie! Jenny is not pregnant and there's no prospect of their moving, at least for the present. Daniel's promotion hasn't come through, but when it does, he'll still be based in Stokely.'

'Well, whatever you say, *something's* happened; I've been aware of it all day – over lunch at the pub, during the walk afterwards . . . If Colin hadn't been there, I'd have tackled you earlier.'

'Talking of Colin, it's too bad to leave him alone while we chat in here. You go through and let me finish those.'

'Sorry, that's not good enough. He's watching the match, and wouldn't thank me for joining him.' Elizabeth peered at her over the top of her glasses, which, as usual, had slid down her nose.

'Good Lord!' she exclaimed suddenly. 'You haven't met someone, have you? Yes!' Her voice rose in triumph. 'You have! You're blushing like a sixteen-year-old.'

Catherine turned hastily back to the sink. 'Can we drop this? It's not getting us anywhere.'

'Only because you won't let it! Oh Catherine, come on! Surely you can tell me? You know I wouldn't breathe a word, and it would be so wonderful if—'

'Look,' Catherine broke in, still busying herself at the sink, 'if and when there *is* anything to impart, I promise you'll be the first to know. Will that do?'

Elizabeth stared at her back for a moment, then, seeing it was hopeless, capitulated and, with a sigh, returned to the beans. 'Seems I've no choice,' she said.

On his return just after seven, Tom was surprised to see through the dining room door that the table was laid. He frowned. Was someone expected to dinner? With a flicker of hope, he wondered if Lindsey had come back with Avril and been persuaded to stay. Certainly they'd long since stopped using the dining room for just the two of them; supper was usually eaten in front of the television, a convenient device, since it spared both of them from having to make conversation.

He paused in the doorway to look more closely and saw, to his further surprise, that though only two places were laid, the best silver was set out and there were candles in the holders. What the hell was going on? It wasn't his birthday, or their anniversary.

'Avril?' He glanced into the kitchen, but it was empty. 'Where are you?'

'In the sitting room.'

He pushed open the door and stopped abruptly. She was standing by the fireplace, tension in every muscle and a look of nervous defiance on her face. His breath knotted in his throat and his heart set up a thick, uneven beat. For this was his wife as he hadn't seen her in many a long day – hair softly curled, lips tinted, and a dress he didn't recognize flattering a figure long hidden under shapeless jumpers and skirts.

A dozen bewildered thoughts struggled for supremacy. This was Lindsey's doing – because she knew of his perfidy. But

87

he didn't *want* Avril to change! Part of his rationalization for loving Catherine had been the contrasting frumpish image of his wife. Now, by transforming herself, she'd thrown the blame squarely back on him. And overriding all this reasoning came the numbing awareness that she'd made this effort for him, and that with every second he hesitated, the uncertain hope beneath her defiance was fading a little more. God help him, he couldn't throw it back in her face. Though he longed to turn and rush from the house, he forced himself to say, 'My goodness, Avril! Your fairy godmother's been busy!'

'Well, I haven't made much effort lately,' she acknowledged awkwardly. 'Seeing all the glamour pusses in Guild Street brought it home to me.'

'And – dinner in the dining room?'

'Same thing applies – I've let things slip. We have the room, we shouldn't keep it just for company.' She paused, still watching him anxiously. 'You – approve, then?'

'You look – lovely,' he said. And wanted to weep.

Tony Crane looked up from his newspaper for the third time in as many minutes to glance at his wife. She'd been standing at the window for some time, arms crossed over her chest and each hand cupping the opposite shoulder. It was as if she were either hugging or protecting herself, and she shouldn't feel the need to do either.

Finally he laid his paper aside and went over to her, slipping his arms round her from behind and letting his hands rest lightly on her swelling stomach. It was dark outside; their reflections were mirrored in the cold glass, and beneath them the street lamps glowed hazily through the evening mist. 'What is it, sweetheart?' he asked softly.

She gave a little shrug, and her hands came down to cover his. 'Nothing, really. I'm just being silly.'

'In what way?'

'Cold feet, I suppose.'

'About the parent search?'

'Yes.' She turned in the circle of his arms, and he saw that her eyes were wide and frightened. 'Oh, Tony, why did I do it? Why did I ask her? I wish things could just go on as they are.'

'Darling, they will. Nothing'll change, whatever she finds out. We're still us, looking forward to having our baby. Nothing can alter that.'

'I wish we'd never gone to the Ridgeways' party!' she exclaimed passionately. 'That I'd never even *heard* of Rona Parish!'

'If you feel like that, phone her and cancel it.'

'I can't; she made that clear. She gave me one last chance to withdraw, and I didn't take it. After that, she said she'd continue with it like any other job, whatever she found out.'

'That seems a bit high-handed.'

'No, just businesslike. I don't blame her; she can't spend hours on a project, only to have someone change their mind and make her scrap it.'

'What exactly is worrying you?' Tony asked after a minute.

'Oh, all kinds of things. Getting my hopes up, and nothing happening. Or, even worse, Rona tracking down my father and him not wanting to know. It would be a second rejection.'

Tony laid a finger on her lips. 'Now that's enough, Zara. You know perfectly well you've never been rejected in your life. Your father didn't know about you, so there was nothing he could do, and your mother hardly got herself murdered on purpose. She'd kept you, remember, though it wasn't nearly as easy for single mothers in those days.'

Zara's eyes filled with tears. 'I know, I'm being thoroughly unreasonable.' She gave him a watery smile. 'Put it down to my condition!'

He laughed. 'I've a feeling I'll be hearing a lot more of that excuse over the next few months. Seriously, though, even if Rona does track him down, you've no need to take it any further. It'll be entirely up to you whether or not you want to arrange a meeting.'

'That's true.' She looked a little happier. 'It might be enough, just to know who and where he is, without actually meeting him.'

89

'So there's nothing to worry about, is there?' He patted her stomach. 'Little One already has four perfectly good grandparents waiting to welcome him or her. Anything else is an optional extra.'

She gave a gurgle of laughter. 'That's a novel way to describe my father!'

'Best to keep him in his place! Now, come and sit down, like a good girl. There's quite a chill coming off that glass. Would you like me to get you a hot drink?'

She allowed him to lead her back to the gas fire and help her into a chair. 'That'd be lovely,' she said.

Tom lay wide awake, his eyes staring into the darkness. Beside him, Avril had started to emit the rhythmic little puffs that preceded her soft snores and, knowing she slept, he allowed himself to relax slightly.

The evening had been like none other he could remember. He had duly lit the candles on the table, and poured out the wine she had ready at room temperature. The casserole, prepared, he suspected, before all thoughts of her metamorphosis, was not as sophisticated as she might have liked, but she'd creamed the potatoes – an unusual refinement – and added slivers of almonds to the carrots. In all, it was a very good meal, and he was careful to tell her so.

'Remember you mentioned going on a world trip when you retire?' she had startled him by asking, over the baked custard.

God, yes, so he had, in a previous existence. BC, he thought with mild blasphemy. Before Catherine.

'Well, I've been thinking it over, and you're right – it's an excellent idea. We'd be able to take our time over it, wouldn't we, staying as long as we wanted in places we particularly liked?'

He murmured something noncommittal, aware of a rising tide of panic. Next thing, she'd be sending off for travel brochures, and then what would he do? He couldn't stall her indefinitely. One way and another, this evening, with his disconcertingly pretty wife at the elegant dining table, had been the most stressful of his life, and he'd give anything if she'd only revert to her previous incarnation.

When bedtime came, another terror materialized. Would she expect him to make love to her? To his untold relief, however, she had merely bent over and kissed his cheek – another innovation – before turning on her side and settling to sleep. Perhaps, he thought thankfully, she had decided to take one step at a time.

Down in the hall he heard the clock strike midnight. And quite suddenly, he needed to hear Catherine's voice – needed, somehow, to speak to her, to reassure himself that she actually existed, and he'd not been whisked back a decade to when he and Avril had lived a more harmonious life.

Carefully, so as not to disturb her, he slid out of bed and silently padded downstairs, lifted the phone off its charger and carried it into the kitchen, shutting the door quietly behind him. She had visitors, he told himself; perhaps they wouldn't yet have gone to bed. Though in his urgent selfishness, he knew it made no difference. Had it been three o'clock rather than twelve, he would still have had to phone.

'Hello?' Her anxious voice in his ear, doubtless alarmed by the lateness of the call.

'Catherine, it's me,' he said quickly. 'Can you talk?'

'Tom! Yes – yes, they've just gone to their room, and I'm laying the breakfast table. Whatever is it? Has something happened?'

He hesitated, longing to pour out his fears about Avril's sudden change and the difficulties it might entail, but restrained by an illogical loyalty to his wife. Loyalty! he mocked himself, as the thought registered. How did he rate phoning another woman at midnight?

'Tom? Are you all right?'

'Yes, yes, I'm all right. I just suddenly needed to know if – if you loved me?'

Her low laugh, which set his pulses racing. 'You phoned to ask me that?'

'Please, Catherine – I need to hear you say it.'

91

'I love you, Tom Parish. Now and forever. Is that good enough for you?'

He let his breath out in a long sigh. 'We need to talk soon,' he said, 'but bless you for that. Goodnight, my darling.'

And before she could make any other comment, he rang off, replaced the phone, and made his way silently back to bed.

Seven

Lindsey phoned on the Sunday morning.

'I thought you'd like to hear how I got on with Mum.'

'Oh, of course – it was yesterday, wasn't it? How did it go?'

'A bit like swimming in treacle, but progress was made. I coerced her into buying a couple of outfits.'

'Well done!'

'And some make-up. God knows if she'll use it, but I did labour the point about Pops still being virile—'

'Linz!'

'Relax – "attractive" is the way I put it – and I think it went home. So now we cross our fingers.'

'And hope she changes her attitude as well as her looks. Did you witness the transformation?'

'Not fully fledged, but she looked surprisingly good when she tried things on. The assistant produced what she called the "petite" range, and the clothes really suited her – it was quite an eye-opener. She protested every step of the way, but at least she bought them, and I made her promise to wear the dress last night. I'd give anything to have seen Pops's face . . . Ro – are you still there?'

'Sorry, yes. I was just wondering if it isn't all too late; shutting the stable door, etc.'

'Well, I've done all I can. Now it's up to her.'

After they'd rung off, Rona remained thoughtful. Lindsey wished she could have seen their father's reaction, but she was concerned with what he wouldn't have revealed. If he were indeed attracted to Catherine Bishop, this could be the catalyst. He was a kind man; faced with his wife's olive branch, would he give up his private dreams and stay with her? And if so, was that really what Rona wanted for him?

The Monday-morning drive to Buckford stirred memories, since it had been the pattern of her week when she was researching the articles. And the time warp persisted as, having parked the car, she made her way through the narrow streets to Market Square. It seemed the Family History and Archive Centre was housed in a building directly opposite the library, so she must have passed it many times.

She was directed into a large room filled with screens and keyboards, at which people sat intently scrolling through micro-fiches. A member of staff located the machine reserved for her, explaining it would first be necessary to check the borough ward in which the address she wanted was located. That done, Rona selected the fiches for 1979 and returned to her machine with rising excitement.

There were two columns to each page, and she scrolled rapidly until she came to Elton Road, the address given on Zara's birth certificate, then down again to number thirty-seven. The names given for that property were Bradley, John; Bradley, Margaret – presumably the couple in the ground-floor flat – Grant, Gemma and O'Toole, Selina.

Rona sat back, frowning at the screen. Selina O'Toole . . . The name seemed familiar; she was sure she'd heard it recently, but couldn't place it. Perhaps it would come back to her. Scrolling further down the page, she made a note of the neighbours on either side, and also of those in two of the houses opposite, though it was doubtful if any of them still lived there.

On the principle of leaving no stone unturned, she also looked up the address given on Gemma's birth certificate, to see if her mother was still listed at the time of the murder. She was not. Either she'd sold the house when she moved to South Africa, or the names given were tenants.

And that was all she could do; a five-hour round trip, for

half an hour in front of the screen. Still, she'd found the information she wanted; too bad it hadn't been available at Stokely.

Rona collected her things, signed off at the desk, and emerged on the leaf-strewn pavement. Over to her left was the little café she'd frequented in the summer, and she decided to have an early lunch before setting off for home. But she had taken only a couple of steps when she heard her name called and saw Lois Breen, the vicar's wife, hurrying towards her.

'Rona – I thought it was you! What are you doing here?'

'Hello, Lois. I needed to check some registers for my new project.'

'Ah – we're old hat now, are we?'

Rona smiled. 'No, the articles are ongoing.'

'Oh, I know; I'm assiduously collecting them. Have you time for a coffee?'

Rona looked at her watch. It was almost midday. 'Actually, I was going for an early lunch. Will you join me?'

'At the Coffee Shop? Why not? Gordon's at an all-day meeting, so my time's my own.'

She linked her arm through Rona's and they walked together round two sides of the square to the little bow-fronted café, where they seated themselves at a window table. Rona liked Lois; a talented sculptor, she cared little about her appearance. As usual, she was dressed in working clothes, and – also as usual – her short blonde hair looked as though she'd just run her hand through it. However, her grey eyes were sharp and missed nothing, and her tongue could be astringent.

'Nuala said she'd seen you,' she commented, picking up the menu.

'Yes, that was the tale-end of the Buckford job. I dashed up with a photographer, just for the day.'

Lois smiled. 'You don't have to apologize for not contacting me, if that's what you were doing.'

Rona laughed. 'It probably was. I'm glad we've met now, though. How are things?'

'Oh, we've just about recovered from the hornets' nest you stirred up.'

Rona glanced at her quickly, unsure how to take the comment. 'I did rather, didn't I?'

'Gordon had his work cut out for a while, but things have settled down again.' Seeing her uncertain face, Lois added, 'You righted a wrong, my dear. If other people were hurt in the process, that was the price to pay. So –' she sat back in her chair – 'what's your latest project?'

'Looking for the birth father of a girl adopted as a baby.'

A waitress approached and they gave their order. As she moved away, Lois commented, 'I'm computer-illiterate, as you know, but I thought there were websites dealing with that sort of thing.'

Rona made a little grimace. 'Problem is, we don't know his name.'

Lois gave a bark of laughter. 'You don't go for the easy option, do you? How do you propose to set about it?'

'Well, as I said, I've been looking at electoral registers. They didn't live in Buckford, but with its being the county town, all registers except the current ones are kept here.'

'Did you get anywhere?'

Rona answered indirectly. 'Does the name Selina O'Toole mean anything to you?'

Lois pursed her lips thoughtfully. 'I've heard it, certainly. Who is she?'

'I was hoping you could tell me. I agree it sounds familiar, but at the moment all I know is that she was the flatmate of my subject's mother.'

'Who, presumably, you're also trying to trace?'

'Well, no.' Reluctantly, under Lois's piercing gaze, she related the circumstances of the case.

'Haven't you had enough to do with murder?' Lois demanded when she finished, startling the waitress who was setting down their meal. 'It's like Russian roulette, you know; there are only a limited number of times you'll escape unscathed.'

Rona shivered. 'I'm not looking into that side of it, honestly. All I'm trying to do is trace the father, and I reckon the flat-mate must have known who he was, even though she swore not at the time.'

'But surely he'd have been the prime suspect?'

'As it happens, no; he emigrated before Gemma knew she was pregnant.'

Lois sighed. 'Well, for pity's sake don't go in over your head. We don't want any more histrionics.'

Rona picked up her fork. 'Advice noted. Now, tell me what you've been up to. What are you working on at the moment?'

The rest of the meal passed in more mundane conversation, and when it was over, they parted amicably on the pavement outside, Lois to go to the library, Rona to return to her car. But as she left the town behind her, Lois's warning echoed in her head: *Murder's like Russian roulette.*

It was not an analogy she cared for.

The following day, Rona again made an early start, and this time, since it wasn't convenient to leave him with Max, she had Gus with her. She had phoned Tess Chadwick the previous evening and arranged to call in at the paper after her session at the town hall. She also hoped to have a look at the houses where both Gemma and her parents had lived, and if possible, approach any neighbours who might be home.

The drive to Stokely took only fifty minutes, and she arrived soon after ten o'clock. Having taken Gus for a quick walk and apologetically returned him to the car, she sought out the town hall, where she discovered that because of the Data Protection Act, a member of staff had to accompany her while she examined the register. As she'd expected, the Bradleys no longer lived at 37 Elton Road, nor did the names of the neighbours on either side correspond with those in the earlier registers. To her delighted surprise, though, two names did reappear – those of a couple living opposite.

Stanley and Doris Jones were still listed as residing at number forty-two.

Armed with this information and a street map she'd purchased at the information bureau, Rona collected Gus and set off on foot to view the scene of the crime. Elton Road was a good twenty-minute walk from the town centre, a row of between-the-wars semis that had seen better days. Most of the front gardens were concreted over, and an assortment of cars and motorbikes filled the spaces once occupied by lawns and flowerbeds. Paint was peeling on the front doors, and dirty net curtains hung crookedly at several windows.

Having located number thirty-seven, Rona stood on the opposite pavement, staring across at it, but the bland frontage gave no hint of the traumas that had taken place within its walls. With accelerated heartbeat, she crossed the road and walked up the short path. Two bells beside the front door showed the house was still divided into flats. Rona pressed one, then the other, but neither was answered. Presumably the residents were out at work. She met a similar lack of response at the houses on either side, and it was without much hope that she returned across the road to ring the bell at number forty-two. But once again, the Joneses proved to be her sole success.

The door opened to reveal an elderly woman in a home-knitted cardigan, who peered at her uncertainly over the top of her glasses.

'Yes?' she said querulously.

'Mrs Jones?'

'Yes?'

'My name is Rona Parish, and I'm trying to trace someone who used to live across the road.'

The old eyes surveyed her suspiciously. 'Who would that be?'

Rona took a gamble. 'Selina O'Toole?'

The woman looked surprised. '*She* shouldn't be hard to find, surely?'

It was an unexpected response, and Rona raised her eyebrows. 'Why is that?'

'Well, with her being on the telly, and all.'

Rona gazed at her blankly, and in return received a disbelieving stare.

'You're never saying you don't know who she is?'

Honesty, Rona reflected, would be the best policy. 'I realize I *should* know her, but stupidly I just can't seem to place her.'

'Well, she's on pretty regular.'

And at Rona's continuing blankness, Mrs Jones stepped aside and said resignedly, 'You'd best come in.'

Rona indicated Gus, who was hopefully wagging his tail. 'Is it all right—?'

'Yes, yes, I've nothing against dogs. Haven't had one in the house since old Pip died.'

Rona followed her down the hall to the back room, where an elderly man nodded by the fire. The room was uncomfortably hot, but it was newly swept and dusted and the horse brasses on the wall gleamed in reflected firelight.

'Take no notice of him,' Mrs Jones instructed, jerking her head towards her husband. 'Deaf as a post – you'd have to repeat everything twice. Sit down. Now, what's all this about wanting Selina?'

'You say she's on television; is she an actress?'

Mrs Jones clicked her tongue impatiently. 'No, not an *actress*. She does them documentaries, doesn't she, interviewing people in the news.'

So that's why both she and Lois had heard of her; and, with enlightenment, an image came to mind of a strong-featured face topped with spiky hair of an unlikely red. Gemma's old flatmate had certainly made the big time.

Mrs Jones was watching her astutely. 'I hope you're not thinking of raking that murder story up again?' She reached for a biscuit from the tin on the table and tossed it to Gus, who caught it in his mouth.

'Only in passing.' Rona hesitated, then added on impulse, 'Did you know Gemma's baby?'

The woman's head shot up, but since she didn't reply, Rona went on, 'I'm here on her behalf, really. She's trying to trace her father.'

The transformation was immediate. 'Little Amanda? She's – all right? Well, that's the best news I've heard this side of Christmas!'

Rona said carefully, 'Yes, she's very well. She's married now, and expecting a baby of her own.'

'Did you ever!' exclaimed the old woman delightedly. 'I used to babysit her, you know. Gemma often brought her over, when she wanted to go shopping and that. Bright little thing she was, with those big green eyes and copper-coloured hair. Gemma worshipped her. "I'm so glad I kept her, Mrs J," she used to say. "She's the best thing that ever happened to me."'

Her eyes filled with tears. 'And to think what lay in wait for her.'

Rona mentally crossed her fingers. 'Did you by any chance know who she was seeing?'

'That got her in the family way, you mean? No, she never let on. Said she'd tell me when the time was right.'

'And she stuck to that, even when he left the country?'

Mrs Jones shook her head sadly. 'Broke her heart, him going to *Aw*stralia, but she wouldn't name him, though we all thought he should help out. "They'd never find him out there," she said.'

She eyed Rona with grim-faced satisfaction. 'And if that's why you're looking for Selina, you can save yourself the trouble; she doesn't know any more than we do. After Gemma – died – we all thought Amanda should be with her dad, but we couldn't begin to look for him, not even having his name.'

Rona's heart plummeted. Illogical though it was, she'd been counting on Selina; now it seemed even that frail thread had disintegrated. They were silent for a while, watching the logs redden and collapse in the hearth. The old man stirred and muttered something in his sleep.

Eventually, Rona said tentatively, 'After he went, did Gemma go out with anyone else?' *Anyone who might have murdered her?*

'That's what the police kept asking, but I couldn't help them then, and I can't help you now.'

Rona rose to her feet. 'Well, thank you very much, Mrs Jones. I won't hold you up any longer.'

'Not what you wanted to hear, I'm afraid.'

'I'll just have to think of another angle.'

The old woman preceded her back down the hall and opened the front door. 'Give Amanda my love. She won't know who I am from Adam, but tell her I was fond of her mum.'

She bent to give Gus a farewell pat and closed the door behind them.

'To what do I owe this honour?' Tess Chadwick enquired, clasping her coffee mug with both hands. 'You were pretty cryptic on the phone.'

They were sitting in a little café next door to the offices of the *Stokely Gazette*. Rona, looking at her friend across the table, reflected that Tess's appearance hadn't altered in all the years she'd known her. She was dressed, as always, completely in black – polo-neck sweater, short skirt, leggings and boots, and her chestnut curls appeared to defy any comb to penetrate them. She must be in her forties, but looked at least ten years younger.

'I want you to do me a favour,' Rona said. 'I don't know how you can work it, but I'm sure you'll think of something.'

'Go on.'

'Do you remember that murder back in '79, when a girl was strangled in her bath while her baby cried in the next room?'

'Gemma Grant,' Tess said promptly. 'Of course I remember it; it was the first case I covered for the *Gazette*.'

'Well, that baby has asked me to trace her father.'

Tess sat back in her chair. 'And how many impossible things do you usually do before breakfast?'

'That bad?'

'You must know it is.'

Rona toyed with her spoon. 'I wondered if perhaps you could run a para or two asking for information? Say, under a heading "Did you know Gemma Grant?" or "Murdered girl's baby seeks father"?'

Tess raised an eyebrow. 'You wouldn't by any chance like to write it for me?'

Rona smiled. 'Sorry. Just trying to be helpful.'

'I think I can manage, thanks.'

'But could you do it?' Rona pressed.

Tess considered. 'Will there be a follow-up?'

'I hope so; I'm intending to write one for *Chiltern News*. It's a different readership, though, so it shouldn't be a problem.'

Tess sipped her coffee. 'You'd get a lot of cranks replying, and we'd have no means of vetting them.'

'I wouldn't expect you to.' Rona hesitated. 'Without wanting to teach my grandmother, there are two particular points I'd like covered.'

'Shoot.'

'Well, "Amanda", as she was then called, was born in November '78, so her father would have emigrated in the spring of that year. I'd like to know if anyone remembers a local family leaving for Australia around that time. It might at least give us something to work on.'

'True. And the other point?'

'Any memories of Gemma herself. Her daughter knows nothing whatever about her.'

'Folks might be a bit chary on that one, for obvious reasons.'

Rona shrugged. 'We can but hope.'

'I'll see what I can do.'

'Thanks, Tess, you're a star. How soon could you run it?'

'Provided I get the OK, it should squeeze in this week.

Thursday's press day and the paper's out Friday. What about a name or number for contact?'

'No name, on Max's instructions. I thought I'd use my email. That way the information would be written down, and I could follow it up at my leisure.'

Tess chewed her lip. 'One drawback – not everyone's on the Internet. If the only means of contact is by email, they mightn't bother. If I were you, I'd go for your mobile.'

'Good point. I hadn't thought of that.'

'We'll sort it out when we've finished here. What else have you tried?'

'Not much; I only embarked on it last Friday. All I've done so far is look at registers and track down ex-neighbours. I hadn't realized her flatmate was Selina O'Toole. She's the one I'd really like to speak to.'

'I warn you, she's very prickly on the subject. Her standard reply is, "No comment."'

Rona, about to take a drink, put down her mug. 'You *know* her?'

'I did, when she lived here. Not well, but we often found ourselves covering the same story, she for radio, me for the *Gazette*.'

'Are you still in touch?'

'The odd phone call now and then, but she's far outstripped me professionally; I'm still a local hack and she's on prime-time TV.' Tess surveyed Rona sceptically. 'And now I suppose you're going to ask for an introduction?'

'Tess, I'd be so grateful.'

'I can't guarantee anything. As I said, she's sensitive on the issue. You can mention my name, and I'll give you her private number if you swear not to divulge it, but that's as far as I can go. Believe me, you'll need all your powers of persuasion on this one.'

'Have you got her number on you?'

Tess shook her head. 'I don't use it often enough to carry it around. I'll give you a buzz this evening.'

'You're a gem.'

'And if she gives you an interview, you can buy me a meal on the strength of it.'

'It's a deal.'

The conversation switched to more personal matters. Tess asked after Max, and Rona, rather cautiously, after Tess's latest partner. It was seldom the same from one of their admittedly infrequent meetings to the next, and, as she'd expected, a different name came up this time.

'I lose track!' she confessed. 'All I ask is, don't get yourself murdered; it would be a case of *cherchez les hommes*, and there'd be so many, they'd never find the right one!'

'I'll bear it in mind,' Tess replied.

'I received two letters this morning,' Max announced on the phone that evening, 'both of them addressed to you, and one on House of Commons stationery. No prizes for guessing who that's from.'

'And the other?'

'Again, a typed envelope, thick and creamy. Expensive-looking.'

'How intriguing. Open them for me, will you?'

'Both of them?'

'Certainly; I can't bear the suspense.'

There was a pause, and the sound of tearing paper reached Rona down the phone. 'This is James's: "Dear Ms Parish, Many thanks for the copy of my youthful manifesto, which I read with great interest. It shows a touching faith in the ability of politicians to perform miracles: more a question of *If I Ruled the World*.

'"However, I'm advised it contains nothing politically inappropriate, so by all means make whatever use you will of it. I enjoyed meeting you at the constituency evening, and trust that the pleasure will soon be repeated.

'"With regards to yourself and Max, Yours ever, James Latymer."'

'Good,' Rona said with satisfaction. 'That means I can complete the final Buckford article and get it off to Barnie. What's the other letter?'

More paper-tearing, then: 'As we might have guessed from its being sent here, another Latymer missive, this time from the lady, and in the form of a printed invitation. "Mrs James Latymer at home for luncheon. Thursday, 14th October at twelve noon. RSVP." You *are* honoured!'

'Just me?'

'It seems so. Must be ladies only.'

'She mentioned wanting to discuss my books, but I wasn't expecting a full-blown lunch.'

'Luncheon,' Max corrected slyly.

'I beg your pardon – *luncheon*. If it's a load of Conservative ladies in twinsets, I shall be out of my depth.'

'Nonsense, you'll enjoy seeing how the other half live. So, what have you been up to today?'

She sketched in her visit to Stokely. 'Tess Chadwick agreed to run a para for me,' she told him. 'And what's more, she knows Gemma's ex-flatmate, who turns out to be an eminent TV journalist, no less. Tess has her private number, and if she agrees to meet me, I'll dash off to London post-haste.'

'Not this week, if you've any sense.'

'Why not?'

'There's a threatened rail strike, remember.'

'Talks are continuing, aren't they?'

'Yes, but not making much headway.' He paused. 'I trust you didn't include your name in these newspaper snippets?'

'Don't worry, I shall be completely anonymous.'

'Mind you keep it that way,' he said.

Tess phoned half an hour later with the required number, and as soon as she rang off, Rona called it. The ringing continued for several minutes, and she'd just decided Selina must be out, when a husky voice in her ear said, 'Hi.'

'Selina O'Toole?'

The voice sharpened. 'Who's that?'

'My name is Rona Parish,' Rona said quickly. 'Your number was given to me by Tess Chadwick of the *Stokely Gazette*.'

No response.

'I hope you'll forgive my contacting you, Ms O'Toole, but I should very much like to meet you.'

'Why?'

Not much encouragement there. 'I want to speak to you about Gemma Grant—'

'Now look,' Selina broke in angrily, 'if I find Tess has passed my number to some tin-pot journalist who's—'

'—on behalf of Gemma's daughter,' Rona finished, raising her voice over the other woman's.

There was a silence, then Selina said, 'Would you repeat that?'

'Gemma Grant's daughter contacted me. She wants to trace her father.'

'*Amanda* contacted you?'

'She has a different name, but yes.'

There was another silence, longer than the first. Then: 'I don't *know* who her father is, as I've been telling everyone for more than twenty years.'

'Could we meet? Please?'

'Who did you say you are?'

'Rona Parish. I live—'

'The Rona Parish who writes for *Chiltern Life*?'

'Yes,' Rona admitted with surprise.

'I subscribe to the magazine,' Selina said shortly. Then, 'I apologize for calling you tin-pot.'

'Apology accepted. But will you see me?'

'It would be a wasted journey. I really—'

'If nothing else, I'd like to talk about Gemma, try to get to know her, so I can tell – her daughter. Now she's pregnant herself, she feels the need to learn about her real parents.'

'Oh God,' Selina said flatly. 'And there was I, congratulating myself that I'd put it all behind me.'

'I'd be so grateful,' Rona pressed.

A sigh came down the phone. 'Well, I suppose I could stretch it just one more time. For Amanda's sake.'

'Thank you so much.'

Having reached her decision, Selina swiftly finalized the

details. 'Six thirty on Friday, the Grapes Wine Bar in Campion Street?'

'I'll be there. I look forward to meeting you.'

'Goodbye, Rona Parish,' said Selina, and broke the connection.

Eight

Rona spent the next morning finishing her article on education by inserting the sentences she'd already earmarked from James Latymer's manifesto. And this, she thought as she slipped it into an envelope, finally drew the line under her Buckford assignment. It was a relief, but she was also aware of regret for the friendships she'd made there which would, in the nature of things, now lapse.

'Walk, Gus!' she called as she went downstairs, and heard the answering patter of his paws as he lolloped up from the basement.

Out on the street, the chill breeze stung her cheeks and lifted her hair, but she welcomed its freshness. She'd spent most of the last two days in the car, and a little exercise was welcome. After delivering the article and buying the few household items she needed, she intended to take Gus for a brisk run in the park.

As usual, Polly, the receptionist at *Chiltern Life*, relieved her of him, enabling her to visit Barnie without the danger of a waving tail unbalancing the piles of papers in his office.

'So this is it, then?' he commented, sliding the sheets out of the envelope she handed him. 'End of story?'

'It's the last to be written, yes, but you already have the one that'll appear last, pulling all the threads together.' The articles were scheduled to spill over into the new year, when the octocentenary officially began.

Barnie nodded, running his eyes down the topmost page. 'It was a good idea, Rona; we've had a lot of positive feedback and circulation is up again this month.' He regarded her over the top of his glasses. 'Probably coincidence, mind!'

'No doubt.'

He eyed her more closely. 'How goes this harebrained scheme you've embarked on?'

'Slowly but surely.'

'You put the wind up Dinah, you know; she's quite worried about you.'

'Sweet of her, but she needn't be. How are the family?'

He held her gaze a moment longer, to show that he'd registered her swift change of subject. 'The same as when you saw them.'

'You must all come to us one weekend.'

'As long as you're prepared to have your home wrecked. It'll be too cold to be outdoors and Sam moves like greased lightning.'

'I'm sure we can cope.' She stood up. 'I'll be in touch. Love to everyone.'

Back in the foyer, Rona had a quick word with Polly, retrieved Gus, and, leaving the building, turned in the direction of Guild Street to do her shopping. She had taken only a few steps when a voice behind her called, 'Lindsey!' and, as she instinctively turned, 'That's a bit of luck! I was afraid we—'

The man who had spoken broke off as Rona faced him. 'Oh! You're not . . . but good God, you almost are!'

She laughed and held out her hand. 'Rona Parish. The other half.'

He took her hand, smiling ruefully. 'I do apologize. Jonathan Hurst – a colleague of your sister's.'

So this was the new man in Lindsey's life. Rona regarded him more closely. He was older than she'd expected – late forties, she guessed – and, his equilibrium restored, there was an easy self-assurance about him. His hair was fairish, thick and over-long, his grey eyes deep-set, his jaw firm, and he was regarding her with a half-smile, as though wondering how much she knew about him.

'Lindsey's mentioned you,' she said, deliberately with-holding the extent of her knowledge.

He gave a little nod, acknowledging her prevarication. 'And you to me, obviously. I'm delighted to meet you. You're uncan-nily alike, aren't you?'

'It goes with the territory.'

Hurst looked down at Gus, who was sniffing at his trouser leg. 'Handsome animal,' he commented. 'I have a bassett hound myself. Takes a lot of exercising, as I suppose this fellow does.'

'Yes; we're going up to the park shortly, for a run before lunch.'

'I envy you; I'm on my way back to the office and sand-wiches at my desk. Apologies again for accosting you. I'll be more cautious next time.'

Not wishing to walk with him, Rona, with a murmured goodbye, turned into the doorway of the adjacent building and waited there until Hurst had crossed the road and rounded the corner on to Guild Street.

He was not the office Lothario she'd expected, being alto-gether more – established, she thought, not pleased with the adjective but unable to think of a better. He gave the impres-sion of a settled family man – with a bassett hound, for heaven's sake – who belonged to the golf club and took his children to the zoo at weekends.

What was it he'd said before he realized his mistake? *I was afraid we—* We what? What had he wanted to speak to Lindsey about? Rona hoped profoundly that her twin was not serious about this man; she was convinced he'd be unwilling to disturb his pleasant lifestyle with anything as traumatic as divorce.

Rona mentioned the meeting to Max over supper.

'What did you think of him?' he asked.

'A smoothie. I'd say his intentions are strictly dishonourable.'

'She does pick them, doesn't she? She might just as well take Hugh back, and have done with it.'

'I'm not sure that's still an option.'

'Have you seen him at all?'

'No, which is odd, come to think of it, when he's working and presumably living here.'

'Keeping a low profile, perhaps.' Max suggested absently.

Rona glanced at him. 'You seem a bit preoccupied. Anything wrong?'

He met her eyes, then looked away. 'No, not really.'

'Which means "yes". Come on, what is it?'

He smiled wryly. 'Promise not to fly off the handle?'

Rona raised her eyebrows. 'Do I ever?'

'Frequently!'

'All right, I promise.'

'Well, it's probably nothing, as I said. Just that Adele didn't turn up at class this afternoon.'

Rona held back an instinctive retort. 'And that's a cause for concern?' she asked instead.

'Let's say it's never happened before. Oh, sometimes she can't make it, but she always phones to cancel.'

'And this time she didn't?'

'No.'

'Well, perhaps one of the children was taken ill, and it just went out of her mind. There are hundreds of possibilities.'

'I know.'

Rona regarded him steadily. 'But you're wondering if Philip's been beating her up?'

Max's head reared.

'Admit it; that *is* what you're wondering, isn't it?'

He looked at her mutely.

'Max, hard though it is to accept, it's really none of our business. It's not as if she's a child; the solution's in her own hands.'

'From what I hear, though, women in that position seldom do anything about it.'

'If they've no money, or are dependent on their husbands, perhaps not. But I doubt if Adele's in that bracket.' Rona took a deep breath. 'You want me to phone Lindsey and ask her to go round.'

111

He reached for her hand. 'Would you?'

'I can't promise she'll oblige.'

'Worth a try, anyway.'

'I hear you met Jonathan,' Lindsey said at once.

'I did indeed.'

'What did you think of him?'

Rona toned down her impression. 'Attractive, certainly. Affable.'

'*Affable?*'

'Heavens, Lindsey, what do you want me to say? We spoke for about two minutes. Anyway, that's not why I'm phoning. You're not out of sugar, by any chance?'

'*What?*'

'Adele didn't show at the class today. Any chance of your popping round with some excuse?'

'God, Rona, what is this? I've already had her to tea at your husband's request. There is a limit, you know.'

'Just this once? Please?'

'And then what? Report back to you?'

'Please,' Rona said again.

Lindsey sighed gustily and rang off.

Half an hour later, she phoned back. 'She wasn't overjoyed to see me, but she seemed OK.'

'What excuse did you make?'

'Told her my phone wasn't working and asked if hers was.'

'Brilliant. And she was all right?'

'Well, she seemed a bit harassed, but the children were running round in their pyjamas and she was obviously trying to get them to bed. She did at least try the phone, which, not surprisingly, was working, and offered to report mine as being out of order. I told her I'd do it on my mobile.'

'Thanks, Linz, that'll set Max's mind at rest.'

'My mission in life, as you know.'

The threatened rail strike had not materialized by the time Rona parked her car at the station on Friday afternoon. The prospect of arriving in London at the height of the rush hour was not appealing, but she'd have put up with far more inconvenience for the chance of meeting Selina O'Toole. Reference to the A-Z had revealed that the nearest tube station to Campion Street was Sloane Square, and she accordingly made her way there, thankful that a large portion of the home-going crowd was travelling in the opposite direction.

The volume of conversation from the Grapes Wine Bar spilled out on to the pavement, enveloping her even before she set foot inside. How, she wondered despairingly, could she hope to find Selina among this seething mass of people? But along the right-hand side ran a raised area approached by a couple of steps, and, seated at a table there, she caught sight of the inimitable red hair and made her way thankfully towards it.

'Rona Parish, I presume?' Selina said, reaching up a hand.

Rona took it. 'Yes. Thanks so much for agreeing to see me.'

She sat down, taking stock of her companion. It was not only Selina's hair that was red, she noted; her lips and fingernails were the same vibrant colour, and her eyes were heavily mascara'd. Television make-up? Rona wondered. For the rest, she was wearing a trouser suit in bottle green, gold hoop earrings, and an enormous topaz on her right hand. No wedding ring was in evidence, though a brief check had revealed she'd been married twice.

'Right,' she said, in her distinctively rasping voice, 'now we've sized each other up, let's get down to business. I've ordered tapas, by the way, and a bottle of red. OK?'

'Fine. Thanks.' Too bad she couldn't use her tape recorder, but the background noise would render it useless.

Selina took a pack of slim cigars from her handbag, offered it to Rona, who shook her head, and selected one for herself. 'I don't know what you're expecting me to tell you,' she went on, as she proceeded to light it. 'Everything I know is on record, but that doesn't stop someone crawling out of the woodwork every three or four years to ask the same old questions.

I might tell you I only agreed to this because of Amanda. I want to hear all about her. You say she's changed her name?'

'Yes, though I'd rather not reveal it at this stage.'

Selina gave a twisted smile. 'You're talking to a journalist, babe.'

A young man approached the balustrade beside them and handed up a tray laden with plates, glasses and a bottle of wine. 'Food will follow shortly,' he assured them. Rona hid a smile. Dino's this was not.

Selina removed the items from the tray. 'It's largely DIY here, as you'll have gathered,' she remarked, seeming to read Rona's mind, 'but it suits me. No one gives me a second glance, and it's just round the corner from my flat. Now – Amanda. Give.'

'She's happily married, and about four months pregnant. That's why she's so keen to find out about her parents.'

'But she's been happy with her adopted family?'

'Very. I've met them, and they're a pleasant couple. A little dubious about the search, though.'

'With reason. What's her job?'

'Primary school teacher.'

'Good for her. She must have more patience than I have.'

'So tell me about Gemma,' Rona prompted. 'How long were you flat-sharing?'

Selina poured a generous amount of wine into the two glasses, and raised hers in a silent toast. Rona responded, also in silence, and they both drank.

'Three years,' Selina said then. 'She was an odd girl in some ways. She'd adored her father, and when he died, I gather she went a bit haywire. Not particularly close to her mother. She was just seventeen when she replied to my ad, and Mrs Grant was still living locally.'

'You didn't meet through County Radio, then?'

'God, no. She was working in some office or other, but having decided my job was the height of glamour, she wangled her way in on the ground floor. Proved a quick learner, too; within a year she was covering village fêtes and suchlike.'

The waiter appeared below them again, this time armed with bowls of tapas which were duly transferred to their table.

To Rona's relief, Selina stubbed out her cigar. Unused as she was to smoking, the pungent aroma had been tickling her nostrils.

'Did you get on well?' she asked.

'Well enough. She was a year or two younger, of course, and a bit naïve, but she pulled her weight, taking turns with the cooking and cleaning and so on, and we had some good times together.'

'Did you meet any of her boyfriends?'

'Ah, the million-dollar question! Several, yes. We used to go round with a crowd from the tennis club. I was a member, and though Gemma didn't play, she always came with us. The gang called us the Reds, because of our hair. God, fancy remembering that! She was very pretty, and several of the lads lusted after her.'

'Did any of them emigrate to Australia?' Rona asked with a smile.

'Absolutely not.' Selina popped a cube of tortilla into her mouth. 'But Australia apart, I'm sure it wasn't one of the gang. Granted, she flirted with them, but she didn't take them seriously. On the contrary, she used to regale me with everything they'd said to her, hamming it up till we fell about laughing.'

She emptied her glass, and refilled Rona's along with her own. 'Then, suddenly, everything changed. She made excuses not to come out with us, and she stopped confiding in me. It was pretty clear she was in love, but I'd no idea with whom, and she refused point-blank to tell me. She used to meet him on average once a week, and every so often she'd ask if I'd mind vacating the flat for the evening, so he could come round. I protested at first, demanding at least to meet him, but she said I would when "the time was right".'

Selina smiled into her wine glass. 'I hid round the corner a couple of times to keep watch, but it didn't do me any good.'

'You never saw him?'

'Not close to. It could have been anyone.'

'How long did the affair last?'

Selina shrugged. 'Six months? Thereabouts, anyway.'

'Then what happened?'

She drew a deep breath and let it out in a sigh. 'One evening she'd been out as usual and I was asleep when she got back. Next morning when I left for work she was still in bed, complaining of a headache, and told me not to wait for her. Later, she rang in sick, and when I got home I found her lying on the bed, sobbing her heart out. She wouldn't say what was wrong, and I thought it was just a lovers' tiff. Then, finally, she told me her boyfriend's family was emigrating to Australia at the end of the month, and he was going with them.'

'Rather short notice, surely?'

'That was my reaction. It seemed she'd always known the family was moving, but he'd kept quiet about going himself. Wanted to avoid the hysterics, I suppose. Anyway, to the best of my knowledge that was the last time she saw him.'

'And when did she realize she was pregnant?'

'About six weeks later. She couldn't decide whether to keep it, and kept dilly-dallying until it was too late to do anything.'

They ate in silence for a few minutes, picking delicacies from the selection of dishes – marinated sardines, anchovy-stuffed mushrooms, prawns in Filo pastry. Then Rona said, 'If you never knew his name, how did she refer to him?'

'She always called him Morrison. It was a private joke, apparently.'

'And even after he'd gone, she wouldn't say who he was?'

Selina shook her head, confirming what Mrs Jones had said. 'Still, she perked up eventually, and when Amanda was born she changed yet again, becoming altogether more responsible, and determined the child would lack for nothing.'

'Had her mother gone to South Africa by this time?'

'Oh yes, long since.'

'Were they still in touch?'

'Spasmodically. She sent a silver bracelet for the baby.'

There was another silence. Then, bracing herself, Rona said tentatively, 'You found her, didn't you?'

Selina sighed and nodded.

'Do you mind talking about it?'

'My dear, I've gone through it so often, all the emotion has leached out of it.' She signalled to someone on the floor below to bring another bottle. Rona didn't want it – she had to drive home from the station – but this was not the moment to protest.

'That particular evening there'd been a leaving party, so I was later than usual getting home. Gemma was still on maternity leave – the baby was only a couple of months old – and since I always arrived back with my arms full of shopping bags and other clobber, she used to leave the door on the latch for me, to save my juggling with the key.

'It was just after eight when I got there, and I knew Amanda would be bathed, fed, and in her cot. Once she'd got her down, Gemma often had a bath; it helped her to relax – soaked the tiredness out of her, as she put it – so I wasn't surprised to see the bathroom light on. What *did* surprise me was that Amanda was crying, and obviously had been for some time. And Gemma never – but *never* – left her to cry.

'I went to the baby first. She was very hot and the sheet under her head was soaked with tears. I lifted her over my shoulder, and she immediately released some wind – which, no doubt, had been part of the trouble. I carried her to the bathroom door, knocked, and called, "Gemma, have you gone deaf? Amanda's crying."

'There was no answer, so I pushed the door open – we never bothered to lock it – and . . . then I saw her.' Selina stared down into her glass. 'For as long as I live, I'll never forget standing there, Amanda's warm little head on my shoulder, staring down at Gemma with her tights round her neck.'

Not all the emotion had leached, Rona thought. After a minute she said, 'Was it the tennis crowd you'd been with?'

Selina, lost in her memories, looked at her blankly. 'Oh – no, I told you; it was a leaving party. For someone at work.'

Rona said carefully, 'So although none of the crowd was Gemma's lover, one of them *could* have killed her. Jealousy, perhaps? Resentment at being rejected?'

'Don't think that wasn't considered,' Selina said harshly, nodding to the waiter who was handing up a fresh bottle of wine. 'We were grilled mercilessly – everyone who'd ever known her, as far as I could see – but there was absolutely nothing to point at anyone. We were all just – numb.'

She poured the wine and Rona did nothing to stop her, resolving simply not to drink hers. And into their silence seeped an increased volume of sound from below. People were leaning from one table to another, seemingly passing on an item of news. Several stood up, looking at their watches, and others took out their mobile phones.

'What is it?' Selina called down to someone passing.

'The rail talks have collapsed. The guards called a lightning strike and walked out, so there are no bloody trains.'

'Oh, God!' Rona said.

'Don't even think buses,' Selina advised. 'There'll be queues to kingdom come, and the same goes for taxis.'

'I'd better go. I'll have to try to book in somewhere.'

'Along with the world and his wife.'

'Then what do you suggest?' Rona snapped, resenting Job's comforter.

Selina calmly sipped her wine. 'I can put a sofa at your disposal, if that's any help.'

Rona stared at her. 'But I couldn't – I mean . . . '

'What's the alternative? God knows how long it'll take for things to get back to normal; if it's a wildcat strike, all the trains will be in the wrong places. Added to which, it so happens I'm driving up to Buckfordshire tomorrow, so I could drop you off.'

It was a lifeline, Rona thought, watching as half the clientele impatiently queued at the cash desk. 'It's awfully good of you,' she said hesitantly. 'I'd be extremely grateful.'

'That's settled, then. So now you can relax and enjoy that wine you've been sitting looking at.'

Rona laughed and, as she met the other woman's eyes, the last of the restraint that had lingered between them dissolved.

'I'm not as black as I'm painted, you know,' Selina observed

118

mildly, 'though I don't advertise the fact. My bad press is very dear to me – hard-nosed interviewer, bolshie bitch, and the rest. You're lucky I like you, mind; I've been known to reduce people to tears.'

'So I believe,' Rona replied, drinking her wine as instructed.

Selina glanced at her wedding ring. 'Hubbie expecting you home?'

Unwilling to embark on their domestic arrangements, Rona merely said, 'Yes; I'll give him a ring in a few minutes.'

'Wait till we get to the flat, where you can hear yourself think.'

'You really are driving up tomorrow?'

'I really am. It's my mother's birthday at the weekend. My parents still live in Chilswood. They complain I use their house as a depository, which is true: I hoard my excess baggage there, and it saves cluttering up my place.'

Selina's flat was located in the maze of similarly named streets behind Sloane Square. It comprised only one bedroom, one living room, kitchen and bathroom, but all the rooms were large and airy, and Rona was entranced with it.

'I bought it after my first divorce,' Selina informed her. 'It took all the settlement and then some, and I was on starvation rations for weeks. Now, it's worth a king's ransom.'

While she busied herself cooking spaghetti, Rona phoned Max.

'What did I tell you?' he greeted her. 'Now I suppose you're stuck there?'

'Selina's very kindly putting me up for the night, and as luck would have it, she's driving to Chilswood tomorrow and will give me a lift.'

'Trust you to land on your feet. So Gus and I are on our own tonight?'

''Fraid so. And would you be an angel and collect my car from the station? The parking ticket will have run out by morning, and I'd rather not leave it there overnight.'

'OK; we'll make that our evening stroll.' He paused. 'Did what's-her-name come up with the gen?'

119

'We had a very interesting talk,' Rona said, aware of Selina's proximity, though she had tactfully switched on the kitchen radio. 'I'd better go. Thanks, love, and I'll see you tomorrow.'

She had cast an anxious glance at the sofa when she first came in, relieved to see it was both wide and long and that the cushions looked soft. The furniture throughout was in pale wood, the dining table being protected by a sheet of glass. On this, the royal-blue crockery lent an exotic air, enhanced by the stubby blue candles in their squat glass holders. All this, she marvelled, within a ten-minute walk of the square and tube station. She'd never wanted to live in London, but she admitted she could just about come to terms with this.

'Are you still in touch with the tennis-club crowd?' she asked over coffee.

'Not really, we've all dispersed now. Occasionally I run into one or other of them, or see their names in the paper. No doubt you've heard of Penelope Jacobs, the actress? She was one of us, and I actually interviewed her for an arts programme. It was a novel experience, I can tell you.'

'It would have been interesting to have met them,' Rona said reflectively. 'How many of you were there?'

Selina topped up her coffee. 'A hardcore of eight, but others came and went. We were all in our early twenties, and some were at university. They joined us in the vacations.'

'Did you go out with any of them yourself? On a one-to-one basis, I mean?'

Selina smiled reminiscently. 'I ran through most of them, yes. Philip Yarborough lasted the longest.'

Rona stiffened. 'Philip Yarborough? The sales director at Netherby's?'

'Quite possibly. When I knew him, he was something lowly in the Stokely store.'

Rona's mouth was dry. Philip Yarborough, whom Max suspected of maltreating his wife, had been a friend of the murdered Gemma Grant.

'I gather you know him?' Selina prompted, surprised by her continuing silence.

'I've met him. He and his wife live near my sister.' She hesitated. 'It never occurred to me, but I might know some of the others, too.'

'Quite possibly. You live in Marsborough, don't you? Stokely's not a million miles away, and as I said, we've all dispersed. Let me think, now: there was Judith Perry and her brother Gordon; Penny Jacobs, as I've said, and Philip, and Susanna Martin, and – oh, what was his name? Steve Deacon.'

She raised a questioning eyebrow, but Rona shook her head. 'What about those at university?'

'That's more difficult. There was one chap whose name I can't remember – he only came a couple of times – and Frances – Kendrick, I think, and Russ Blakison. Oh, and Jonathan Hurst.' She looked up at Rona's convulsive movement. 'Ring another bell?'

'I've met Jonathan Hurst,' Rona said aridly.

'Well, it's a small world! What's he up to these days?'

That would be telling! Rona thought. Aloud, she said, 'He's a solicitor. In my sister's firm.'

'The same sister who lives near Philip?'

'I've only the one.'

'Odd, that she should be linked to both of them. Jon was always very laid-back. Is he still?'

'Oh yes. Very.'

'Well, give him and Philip my regards, next time you see them.'

Rona nodded, though she'd no intention of doing so. Their friendship with Gemma had no doubt been innocuous, but at this stage she'd prefer them not to know she was aware of it. Had the two of them kept in touch? she wondered. They worked within a few hundred yards of each other.

'One last question: did the police ever come up with a motive?'

'No, that was the stumbling block all along. The drawers in Gemma's room had been gone through, and so had her handbag, which was on the kitchen table, but nothing seemed to have been taken. All her money, credit cards and jewellery were there.'

121

'So whoever it was, was looking for something?'

'That was the inference. But for what, no one knows.' Selina glanced at her thoughtful face. 'Well, was our meeting worth the journey, hazardous though it's proved to be?'

Rona smiled. 'Most certainly. You've been very frank with me, and I'm grateful. I've a much clearer understanding of the background now.'

'Happy to oblige,' said Selina O'Toole.

Joyce Cowley sat immobile at her dressing-table, staring at her reflection in the mirror and the looking-glass world behind her. The room looked entirely different that way round, she thought inconsequently; but then at the moment everything *was* different, whichever way she looked at it.

Despite herself, her eyes dropped to the paper on the floor beside her, and the black headlines that had screamed in her head all day.

MURDERED GEMMA'S DAUGHTER SEEKS DAD.
CAN YOU HELP?

She gave a little moan and covered her face with her hands. Gemma's daughter – the baby she'd called Amanda – her own granddaughter. God, she'd hoped this nightmare was behind her. Would it never go away?

The lavatory flushed in the en suite, and a minute later Nigel come into the room. She felt him approach, put his hands on her shoulders.

'Come to bed, love,' he said gently. 'We can talk about it again tomorrow.'

She let her hands fall and regarded him in the mirror. 'It's not just Amanda, it's the whole, horrible business of Gemma,' she said miserably.

'I know.'

'I keep wondering if I'd stayed here, not gone to Cape Town, would she still be alive.'

He bent and kissed the top of her head. 'There's no point

in torturing yourself like this. It's not as though she was living at home and you went off and left her. She'd already left *you*. Anyway,' he added, trying to lighten her mood, 'if you hadn't gone to Cape Town, you'd never have met me!'

She continued as if he hadn't spoken. 'I'd have been there to help her; she could have confided in me, and perhaps avoided what happened. She must have felt so alone, all by herself with a new baby, and no one to turn to but that girl she shared with.'

She turned on the dressing stool, looking up into her husband's face. 'What do you think I should do, Nigel?'

'Sweetheart, we've been discussing this all day. It's not a question of what *I* think, it's what feels right for you.'

'I'll have to see her, and she'll ask all sorts of questions, and then God knows what she'll think of me.'

'What could she possibly think, except that she's found her grandmother?'

'That I should have taken her in myself?'

Nigel Cowley pursed his lips. 'That's what's really worrying you, isn't it?'

Joyce nodded. 'I've been asking myself ever since if I did the right thing. But God, after Harry's illness and death, and the rows with Gemma culminating in her leaving home, and every-thing being generally foul, I was just getting my life back – in a different country, meeting new people, and at long last starting to enjoy myself again.'

'Darling, you don't have to convince me.'

'The last thing I wanted was to be saddled with a baby.' She glanced at her husband's concerned face. 'Did I tell you I learned of her birth in a Christmas card? Gemma hadn't even told me she was pregnant. That's how close we were. She was always a daddy's girl.'

Nigel took her hand and drew her gently to her feet. 'Have you any sleeping pills?'

She shook her head.

'Then come to bed and I'll massage your neck and shoul-ders – the muscles are all knotted and tight. That'll make you drowsy and help you to sleep. And tomorrow we'll come to a decision. Together.'

She reached up and kissed him. 'What would I do without you?' she said.

Nine

Rona had an excellent night on the sofa, and awoke to sounds of Selina preparing breakfast. After a quick shower, she joined her in the kitchen for fresh orange juice, croissants and filter coffee.

'Any news on the strike?' she asked, nodding towards the now silent radio.

'It's for twenty-four hours, so no trains till this evening. Just as well it's the weekend.'

'I really am grateful for your help.'

'No problem. It's good to have company for a change.'

With cars and buses the only means of transport, the London roads were even more congested, but once out of the centre they had a clear run, reaching the outskirts of Marsborough just before midday. Selina insisted on taking Rona to her door, but declined the invitation to go in.

'The parents are expecting me for lunch,' she said. 'Good to meet you, Rona. If there's anything else I can help with, give me a bell.'

Gus came hurtling up the basement stairs as she went in, followed more slowly by Max.

'Welcome home, intrepid wanderer,' he said as he kissed her. 'Judging by reports on the radio, you got off very lightly.'

They went down to the kitchen, where the syndicated local paper lay spread on the table, open at an inside page.

MURDERED GEMMA'S DAUGHTER SEEKS DAD,

Rona read.

'Not in line for the Pulitzer Prize,' Max commented, 'but I thought you'd want to see it.'

She picked up the paper and scanned the paragraph. As suggested, it mentioned families emigrating in '78 and incorporated a plea for anyone who'd known Gemma to get in touch, *to help Amanda (not her present name) build up a picture of her mother.* Fleetingly, Rona wondered if Gemma's killer would read it.

'It's eye-catching, you have to admit,' she said. 'Tess has done me proud. Now all I can do is wait to see if it bears fruit.'

Max poured a creamy mixture into a pastry case and scraped the bowl. 'So, tell me about the acerbic interviewer. What was she like in person?'

'A pussy cat,' Rona replied. 'Very helpful, in fact. And here's an item of information for your ears only: both Philip Yarborough and Jonathan Hurst knew the murdered girl.'

'Jonathan Hurst?'

'Lindsey's new man.'

'Hm.' Max slid the quiche into the oven. 'Interesting about Yarborough, though.'

'It's interesting about both of them,' Rona said.

He turned to look at her. 'You're not planning to beard them in their respective dens?'

'Not for the moment.'

He shook his head despairingly. 'Promise me your next job will be a biography of someone who died in his sleep at least a hundred years ago.'

'I'll see what I can do,' she smiled.

Avril stood at the sink in what seemed to be her permanent position, peeling potatoes. Out in the garden she could see Tom sweeping up leaves. This time last week, she'd been lunching in Netherby's with Lindsey – and a waste of time and money that had proved to be.

She tried to remember what she'd been thinking when, encouraged by her daughter, she had bought the new clothes and make-up. What exactly had she hoped to achieve? A lessening of depression? A feeling of well-being? More attention from her husband? All three had been of short duration. Certainly Tom had professed approval of her changed appearance, but he'd not spent any more time with her.

He's an attractive man, Lindsey had said of her father, and it had sounded like a warning. Did she know something Avril did not? Could he – impossible thought – be *seeing* someone?

Avril's mind skittered rapidly through their friends, remembering a warm greeting from one woman, a compliment to another. But no, Tom wasn't like that; he'd never given her cause for jealousy. Nonetheless, despite her prompting, he'd made no move on the proposed round-the-world trip, and his retirement was only a couple of months away.

Mechanically, slouched over the sink, she moved from the potatoes to the carrots, looking up at a sudden noise outside. But her eyes rested not on her husband, starting up the mower, but on a pale reflection of herself against the dark bole of a tree: hair bedraggled once more, shapeless jumper and skirt – for, as hope had faded, she'd already begun to revert to her old ways.

And suddenly, remembering the uplift her changed image had given her, she was filled with a scalding self-disgust. She would *not* let herself go again, when Lindsey had shown her an alternative. On the contrary, she'd have her hair restyled, something she'd baulked at last week; not for any impression it might make on Tom, but for her own satisfaction, and so that Lindsey would never again have to look at her as she had last week.

We used to be so proud of you, she'd said. And they would again, her smart, sophisticated daughters. She'd make sure of that, and her husband could take it or leave it as he chose.

That afternoon, Max, Rona and Gus went up to the park. It was a mellow autumn day, with the trees just beginning to change colour, and below them the distant roofs and steeples of the town winked and glinted in the thick sunshine. They had brought Gus's frisbee, and as they walked, Max constantly threw it ahead, only to be immediately re-presented with it. In the distance, other dog walkers performed similar exercises, and Rona's eye was caught by a family group with their bassett hound.

Her eyes narrowed suddenly, and she looked more closely. 'Max,' she said, touching his arm, 'see that man over there? That's Jonathan Hurst.'

Max turned to study the fair-haired man and his dark wife, the two children running with the dog. 'Happy family scene,' he commented drily. 'I hope to God Lindsey knows what she's doing.'

But it was not of her sister Rona was thinking. 'I wonder how well he knew Gemma,' she mused.

They were relaxing with tea and crumpets when Rona's mobile rang. 'Good afternoon,' said a hesitant female voice. 'Am I speaking to Amanda Grant?'

Rona straightened. 'No, but I'm – acting on her behalf.' Only partially true. 'Can I help you?'

'My name is Joyce Cowley,' the caller informed her, 'and I believe I'm Amanda's grandmother.'

Rona's heart jerked. 'Cowley?' she repeated.

'Formerly Grant. Gemma was my daughter.' A pause. 'To whom am I speaking?'

'My name is Rona Parish, Mrs Cowley.'

'And what's your connection with my granddaughter?'

'She asked me to find out what I could about her parents.'

'You work for a tracing agency?'

'No, I—' Rona broke off, realizing the impression she was about to give, and tempered her reply. '*Chiltern Life* is considering a series about people searching for their birth parents.'

Her strategy was in vain. 'You're a journalist?'

'Not for a newspaper.'

'But you inserted the paragraph in the *Gazette*?'

'I requested it, yes.'

'Then I'd like you to put me in touch with her, please.'

'Of course; if you let me have your number, I'll pass it on. I'm sure—'

'I'd prefer to have hers.'

'Unfortunately the approach has to come from her, but I'm sure she'll contact you. In the meantime, I'd be very grateful for a word with you myself.'

'I'm sorry,' Joyce Cowley said coldly. 'I don't talk to the press.'

'But your granddaughter specifically—'

'She can question me herself.'

'It was because she felt that might be difficult that she asked me to handle initial inquiries,' Rona persisted, ignoring Max's raised eyebrows. 'As I said, I'm sure—'

'I'm sorry, Ms Parish. If you insist the only way I can reach Amanda is by giving you my number, I have no option but to comply, but I've no intention of granting you an interview.'

Rona bit her lip. 'That of course is your privilege. If I could have your number, then?'

Max passed across pad and pencil and she noted it down. 'Thank you,' she said into the phone. 'I'll see she gets it.'

'Oh dear,' Max commented as she rang off. 'First hurdle?'

'She sounded a right old battleaxe. No wonder Gemma left home.'

Max smiled. 'Eat your crumpet – it's getting cold.'

Rona took a bite. 'Damn her!' she said indistinctly. 'I need to see her, Max. She might know more about the missing father than she thinks, and Zara's too emotionally involved to ask the trigger questions.'

Max shrugged. 'You can't force her, love. What now?' As Rona lifted the phone again.

'I must tell Zara,' she said.

It was Tony Crane who answered, and Rona requested a word with his wife.

'Yes – yes, of course. She's right here.'

There was a murmured exchange, then Zara's eager voice. 'Rona? You've found something?'

129

'I've just had your grandmother on the line.'

Zara caught her breath. 'However – oh, because of that bit in the paper?'

'Yes; she wants to see you. I didn't give her your name or number, but I have hers, if you've a pencil to hand. She's married again, by the way; her name is now Joyce Cowley.'

Zara took down the number. 'Where does she live?'

'I didn't ask, but it's a local code.'

'What did she sound like?'

Rona hesitated. 'At first, when she thought I might be you, she was nervous. After that – well, she doesn't approve of the press.'

'How do you mean?'

'She refused to see me.'

'But that's nonsense!' Zara's voice rose. 'You'll have to come with me! I'm certainly not going alone – not the first time, anyway.'

'But surely your husband—?'

'Tony's away on a course all next week. Please, Rona!'

Rona took a deep breath. 'Look, give her a ring. Talk to her. You might change your mind.'

'No way. She'll have her husband there to back *her* up, and it's not even as if he's my grandfather.'

'Back her up?'

'When she makes excuses for not taking me in herself.'

That angle hadn't occurred to Rona, but Mrs Cowley might be anticipating it.

'You do want to see her, don't you?'

'Of course I do. But not alone.'

'Then speak to her, and see what she says.'

Twenty minutes later, when they were up in the sitting room, the phone rang again and Rona went to answer it.

'I should have checked with you first,' Zara said without preamble, 'but is four thirty on Monday OK?'

Yes! Rona thought exultantly. 'She agreed to my coming?'

Zara giggled. 'It took a bit of doing. She asked if you'd "put me up to it"!'

'Where does she live?'

'The address is Oakleigh Farm. It's out in the sticks somewhere. She says the nearest village is Shellswick.'

'I'll check on my road map.'

'It's OK then? You'll come?'

'Oh, I'll come. I'll be very interested to meet your grandmother.'

As arranged, Rona picked Zara up outside the school on Monday afternoon. 'How was she on the phone?' she asked, as they drove out of town. 'Did she have a lot of questions?'

'Masses, mainly about my early life. If I was happy with my adoptive family, where I went to school – that kind of thing.' Zara smiled. 'When I told her my change of name, she said, "So you've gone from A to Z".'

'And what did you ask her?'

'Nothing, really; I decided to wait till we saw her. Oh, and she wanted to know how I met you, and why I decided to ask for your help.'

It would be politic, Rona decided, not to enquire as to Zara's reply.

Shellswick proved to be some ten miles south-west of Marsborough, a small, undistinguished village composed of a few smallholdings, a general store and a green with a duck pond at its centre. The farm itself lay a couple of miles farther on, and, as was immediately apparent, was considerably more affluent. The house was built of stone with a slate roof, deep mullioned windows bearing witness to the thickness of its walls. The yard by which it was approached was immaculate and the outhouses – stables, byres and an old barn – looked neat and well furbished. As Rona switched off the engine, the monotonous hum of a tractor reached them from an adjacent field.

'A gentleman farmer,' Zara opined. 'Bet all he does is sit back and go through the accounts.'

131

Rona threw her a glance. 'Better not to form an opinion till you've met him,' she advised.

It seemed, though, that at least the first part of Zara's assumption was correct. As they got out of the car, a man emerged from the house and came towards them, neatly dressed in slacks and sweater. Of medium height, he was stockily built with iron-grey curly hair, and the blue of his sweater exactly matched his eyes. He was, Rona noted, deeply tanned.

After giving her a quick nod, his eyes fastened on Zara, though he addressed them both.

'Good afternoon, ladies. I'm Nigel Cowley. My wife's expecting you; do please come in.'

They went in silence through the low doorway into a passage smelling of beeswax and, at their host's direction, turned left into the sitting room. The sun was streaming through the windows, and for a moment Rona was almost blinded. Then, as she moved further into the room, her vision cleared and she registered the low, beamed ceiling, the handsome fireplace with an inglenook on either side – and the woman standing motionless by a laden tea trolley.

Marginally taller than her husband, Mrs Cowley was equally tanned, with the muscular arms and legs that resulted from a lifetime of sport. Her hair, like her husband's, short and tightly curled, was pepper-and-salt, but could once have been red. She must, Rona reckoned, be in her seventies; her face was lined but she stood tall and straight and her eyes, as vividly green as her granddaughter's, were shrewd and assessing.

She held out a hand to Zara, who went to her and awkwardly accepted her kiss.

Rona, hoping to break the ice, smiled brightly. 'Good afternoon, Mrs Cowley. I'm Rona Parish. We – spoke on the phone.'

'Indeed,' Joyce Cowley acknowledged, her eyes still on Zara. 'You appear to have had your way, don't you?'

Behind them, Nigel Cowley cleared his throat. 'Do sit down, everyone. We thought a spot of afternoon tea might help to ease things.'

When Zara remained silent, Rona said, 'That would be lovely. Thank you.'

'I'll put the kettle on.'

As he went out of the room, his wife said, 'This isn't at all the meeting I'd envisaged. I – don't know what to say to you.'

Zara flung an anguished look at Rona, who reluctantly came to her aid. 'We were hoping you could give us some information about Zara's father,' she said.

Joyce Cowley threw her an impatient glance, but after a moment replied, 'I've none to give. They met after I'd gone to South Africa.'

Rona's heart sank. 'But Gemma must have mentioned him, surely? I mean, you kept in touch.'

'Barely.' There was bitterness in her voice. 'Oh, I wrote to *her* often enough, but I had only one reply – a Christmas card, telling me she'd had a baby. I phoned at once, naturally, frantic to hear all the details. She told me she wasn't married and had no prospect of being, and when I asked about the father, said he'd emigrated and didn't know about the baby. She never mentioned his name, and I was too upset at the time to think of asking.'

She stared down at her knotted hands. 'However, we did establish some kind of rapport, for which I was grateful later, and I sent Amanda – you,' she amended, with a glance at Zara, 'a silver bracelet.'

'I still have it,' Zara said softly. 'It was the only thing that came with me into my new life.'

Joyce Cowley's eyes filled with tears, and Rona was relieved to see her husband return with the teapot. The pouring of tea and handing round of sandwiches was a welcome diversion, and while they ate and drank, the conversation remained on a determinedly light level. As they were finishing, however, Nigel Cowley prompted gently, 'Didn't you look out some photograph albums, darling?'

'Oh!' Zara exclaimed. 'I'd love to see them!'

Cups and plates were collected and stacked on the trolley

as Joyce produced two or three small albums and seated herself on the sofa.

'Come and sit next to me,' she instructed Zara, patting the cushion beside her, and, though uninvited, Rona also moved across and stood looking over her shoulder. The earliest pictures were of Gemma as a baby, though occasionally a young Joyce, or the dark man who was then her husband, also featured in them. They became more interesting as Gemma grew, and Rona found herself looking for family likenesses, as Zara must also be doing.

'She was always wilful, even as a baby,' Joyce said reflectively, staring down at the faded past. 'Not an easy child, by any means.'

Too like her mother, perhaps, Rona thought; two strong personalities, destined always to clash and strike sparks off each other.

The last photograph, entitled *Gemma's sixteenth birthday*, showed an attractive, long-legged girl standing in a garden with her arm round a frail-looking man. With a shock, Rona realized this almost unrecognizable figure was her father, who must have died soon afterwards. The rest of the pages in the album were poignantly blank.

'She adored Harry,' Joyce said sadly. 'He was the only one who could do anything with her, and when he died she went completely off the rails. She left school at the end of that year and took some petty little job in an office. I hadn't the strength to argue with her; having nursed my husband through eight months of deteriorating health, I was at my lowest ebb. I couldn't even stop her moving out to share a flat with some girl she didn't even know.'

'When did you go to South Africa?' Zara asked.

Joyce threw her a sharp look. 'I didn't abandon her, you know; she'd already abandoned me.' Had they known it, she was quoting her husband.

Zara said nothing, awaiting her reply. After a minute, Joyce went on, 'At the time, I was on the verge of a nervous breakdown. My doctor advised me to take a long break, and I remembered a school friend who'd married a South African, and who'd kept inviting us to go and stay with them. Eventually I summoned up the strength to contact her, and it was all arranged.'

'How long was that after Gemma left home?' Rona asked.

Joyce started and half-glanced over her shoulder. It was clear she'd forgotten Rona's presence. 'About eighteen months,' she said.

And she had still been there when her daughter was murdered, two and a half years later. An accommodating school friend indeed.

As though to correct her assumption, Joyce went on, 'I liked it out there, and as there seemed no reason to hurry home, I rented a small apartment and started to make friends of my own.' She smiled across at her husband. 'Nigel among them.'

Zara asked the question Rona dared not. 'And how long did you stay after Gemma died?'

Joyce bit her lip. 'Five more years. I flew home, of course, as soon as I heard the news, but with all the police and media attention, it was bizarre and utterly horrible. The Stokely house was rented out, so I'd no real base, and an English January was poor exchange for high summer in Cape Town. When I learned they were delaying the funeral in case – in case a second post-mortem was required, I fled thankfully back to South Africa, only returning when it finally took place three months later.'

'If you liked it so much, why did you come back here?' Rona asked, before she could stop herself.

It was Nigel Cowley who answered. 'By then she'd met and married me, and I'm also English. I have a son and daughter from my first marriage, and I decided I'd been away from them long enough. By a strange coincidence, my daughter lives in Buckfordshire, so we decided to settle here – oh, twenty-odd years ago.'

'And you never—' Zara began, then broke off, colouring.

Joyce completed the question. 'Made any attempt to find you? No, I'm afraid I didn't. It would have evoked too many painful memories. I had a new life by then, and I was sure you had, too. I didn't see that stirring things up would be to anyone's advantage.' She paused, then asked more gently, 'Why did you decide to dig up the past, Zara?'

'Because of my own baby. I realized I'd no idea who my parents were or what they were like – where I'd come from, in fact. I still don't know much.' Her eyes dropped to the album. 'For instance, was Gemma allergic to peanuts, like I am? Was she afraid of thunder? Which subjects was she best at? What kind of books did she read?'

'Oh, my dear!' Joyce said helplessly, and spread her hands. It occurred to Rona there had been even less closeness between mother and daughter than she'd supposed.

Zara seemed to have reached the same conclusion, because she suddenly passed back the album she'd been holding and got clumsily to her feet. 'We really should be going,' she said shakily. 'Tony will be home soon.'

Rona looked at her in surprise, aware that he was in fact away for the week, but she moved with her to the door, adding her thanks to Zara's. The Cowleys came out to see them off, and as the farmhouse dwindled into the distance in the rear-view mirror, Rona breathed an unconscious sigh of relief.

She glanced at Zara, about to make a flippant comment, and saw to her consternation that she was crying.

'I had to get out,' she gasped. 'I couldn't hold back any longer.'

'Was it seeing the photographs?' Rona asked gently.

'Partly. I don't even *look* like Gemma, do I?'

'You have her colouring, and so does Mrs Cowley.'

Zara's sobs intensified and, feeling she needed the release they brought, Rona didn't try to stop them. Eventually she hiccupped to a halt, blew her nose, and said brokenly, 'I didn't feel *anything* for her, Rona – nothing at all! You'd think I'd have felt *something*, wouldn't you, but I'm not even sure I liked her! When she talked about coming back after the murder, it was all about how horrible it was for *her*, not a word about shock and sadness for Gemma – or me, for that matter.'

'There's one thing you can be thankful for,' Rona commented.

Zara turned her tear-stained face towards her. 'What?'

'That she *didn't* want to bring you up!' Rona answered, and was rewarded by a strangled little laugh.

Back at Grosvenor Terrace, Rona insisted on going inside with Zara, making some more tea, and waiting until she'd recovered her composure. To help the process along, she told of her meeting with Selina.

Zara listened avidly, asking a string of questions. 'I'd love to meet her,' she said, when Rona came to an end. 'Do you think she'd agree?'

'She might. She asked a lot about you, too.' Rona glanced at her watch and rose to her feet. 'I must be going. Are you sure you'll be all right now?' It was too bad Tony Crane wouldn't be back that night.

'I'll be fine,' Zara assured her. 'Thanks for staying a while, and for all you're doing.'

'You're not sorry you embarked on this? There might be worse to come.'

Zara wrinkled her nose. 'Impossible!' she declared, and they both laughed. 'Yes, of course I want you to continue.' She paused. 'Will you write all that up?'

Rona shook her head. 'It's the father search that's my main priority,' she said. 'It's not as though you found Gemma herself.'

'Only her ghost,' Zara said sadly.

For a reason she couldn't explain, Lindsey always drew the bedroom curtains, shading the room from the full light of midday and affording a nebulous sense of privacy. Not that anyone could have seen inside, the flat being on the first floor, but it seemed more appropriate, somehow.

The first time, Jonathan had laughed at her. 'Such prudery!' he'd teased.

'It's just that love in the afternoon seems a bit . . . decadent.'

'So much the better!' he'd retorted.

The arrangement had started a month ago, largely unpremeditated. On hearing that Lindsey would be working from home the next day, he'd suggested going over during his lunch hour, and they had enjoyed their most relaxed and pleasurable lovemaking to date.

'Why didn't we think of this before?' he'd demanded, as he lay beside her in the aftermath of passion. 'A *bed*, forsooth! Such luxury!' Until then, their hurried comings together had taken place either in his car or in some distant field, always on the alert for intruders.

Lindsey had taken to making smoked salmon sandwiches, which they shared, accompanied by a bottle of wine, before Jonathan showered, dressed, and returned to the office. The snack meal, in place of the lunch he'd forfeited, took on the ambience of a picnic and had become an enjoyable part of the routine.

That Tuesday was the first time they'd exchanged more than a quick comment since Jonathan's meeting with Rona, and as they sat in bed partaking of their sandwiches, he remarked, 'You're very alike, aren't you, you and your sister? What was it you said she did?'

'Basically, she's a writer. She's published several biographies and she also does articles for magazines. Do you read *Chiltern Life*?'

'Only at the dentist.'

'Well, they're running her series on Buckford at the moment – part of the build-up to the octocentenary.'

'So that's what she's working on at present?'

'No, she's just finished, I think. She's now involved with some girl who was adopted and wants to trace her birth parents. And as you might know when Rona's involved, her mother was murdered.'

Jonathan gave a short laugh. 'You mean she's come across murder before?'

Lindsey sipped her wine. 'Twice.'

'Ye gods! So who *was* this girl's mother?'

138

'Gemma someone. She was murdered in Stokely when the girl was a baby.' She was reaching for a sandwich, and didn't notice Jonathan's sudden stillness.

After a moment he asked levelly, 'And is she making any progress? Your sister, I mean?'

'I don't know; we haven't discussed it recently.'

'I hope—'

But what he hoped, Lindsey was never to know, for at that moment, to her incredulous horror, the doorbell sounded. They both froze, turning to each other with widening eyes.

'Ignore it,' Jonathan advised after a minute.

'I'll have to! There's no way I can answer the door in my present state!'

They waited, unmoving, for the bell to sound again, yet still jumped when it did. Lindsey slid out of bed and padded to the window, cautiously peering outside.

'Oh, my God!' she exclaimed, recognizing the car in the drive. 'It's my mother!'

In confirmation, the letterbox rattled and a voice called through it, 'Lindsey! Are you there? It's Mum!'

She gazed at Jonathan, stricken. 'What shall I do?' she whispered in panic.

'I told you, ignore it. She'll go away.'

'But I can't – she must know I'm working from home, or she wouldn't have come. I'll have to let her in. Stay where you are – she won't come in here.'

'For God's sake, Lindsey, get rid of her! Time's getting on! I've an appointment in forty minutes!'

Ignoring him, she ran naked on to the landing and leaned over the banisters. 'Sorry, Mum!' she called down. 'I'm washing my hair. Hang on – I'll be down in a minute.'

She seized her dressing gown from the back of the door, ran into the bathroom and, bending over the bath, briefly switched on the shower. As she wound a towel round her dripping hair, she caught a glimpse of her reflection, cheeks flushed and eyes still bright from love-making.

Without glancing at Jonathan, still on the bed with a

half-eaten sandwich in his hand, she pulled the door shut, ran
breathlessly down the stairs and pulled open the door. Avril
stood smiling on the doorstep.

'So this is how you "work at home"!' she said. And then,
as Lindsey pulled the sash on her gown closer, 'Aren't you
going to ask me in?'

'Yes, of course, but I'm afraid I can only spare a minute.'

She stood aside for her mother to precede her up the stairs,
praying that Jonathan hadn't left anything in the sitting room.
'I had an urgent case to prepare,' she explained belatedly,
'which is why I postponed my shower till lunch time.' True
as far as it went, though the shower had been taken before
Jonathan's arrival. 'Also, I'm expecting an important call at –'
her eyes flicked to the clock – 'a quarter to two, and I've not
finished preparing for it.'

Looking at her mother properly for the first time, and primed
by her expectant expression, she suddenly registered the new
hairstyle.

'Oh, Mum – you've had your hair cut! It looks super!'

'I wanted you to be the first to see it,' Avril said. 'I went
straight to the office from the hairdresser's, but they said you
were working at home, so I came on here. You really do like
it?'

'It's great!' Lindsey assured her sincerely, studying the style
as Avril slowly rotated for her. 'You look about ten years
younger – really with it!'

Avril laughed in pleased embarrassment. 'I'm glad you
approve.'

'It'll certainly stop Pops in his tracks!'

Avril's smile faded. 'I did it for my own satisfaction, not
your father's,' she said, and Lindsey's heart sank. Desperately
she glanced at the clock again. Jonathan would be getting
increasingly restive, and there was no way he could shower
while Avril was there – the running water would be a give-
away. As the thought formed, the phone rang suddenly, startling her.

'Lindsey Parish,' she said into it.

'Get her the hell out! Now!' said a low voice in her ear. Jonathan, on his mobile.

'Yes, yes of course,' Lindsey murmured, heart pounding. She turned pleadingly to her mother. 'Sorry, Mum,' she whispered, her hand over the receiver. 'He's a few minutes early.'

'I'll let myself out,' Avril whispered back, and, with a small wave, she ran down the stairs and pulled the front door shut behind her. Immediately the shower sounded in the en suite.

Shakily Lindsey replaced the phone, went through to the bedroom, and tidied the bed. When Jonathan emerged from the bathroom, she was drying her hair.

'Narrow squeak, or what?' she said.

'Too narrow by half. Does she make a habit of that?'

'Believe it or not, it's the first time ever.'

'Just my luck.' He dressed quickly, standing at the mirror to tie his tie.

'She only delayed you by five minutes,' Lindsey said in mitigation.

He glanced at his watch and nodded. 'No big deal, fortunately.' He kissed her quickly. 'See you,' he said, and was gone.

Ten

In the days following the newspaper insertion, Rona had received about a dozen calls on her mobile, equally divided between people claiming to have known Gemma, and those recalling families who had emigrated. All of them, to Rona's relief, could be dealt with over the phone.

The ones regarding Gemma described her variously as 'pretty', 'moody', 'good fun' and 'difficult', depending on the perception of the caller, but nothing significantly new emerged. On the emigrating families, four names came up, two of them more than once, and included several young men who were confidently asserted to be the father of her baby. However, since the rider: 'as I told the police at the time' was invariably added, it was clear Rona could discount them. As to the departing families, their destinations varied and emigration dates were vague – 'It must have been either '78 or '79' being the closest they came. She'd follow them up as a matter of course, but she was not hopeful.

And that seemed to be that, she thought, discouraged; the newspaper hadn't been much help after all. Admittedly she still had pointers to Jonathan Hurst and Philip Yarborough, neither of whom she was anxious to pursue. An added worry was how could she alert Lindsey to Jonathan's connection without arousing her antipathy.

On impulse, she phoned her. 'We mentioned a foursome,' she began. 'Any chance of it coming off?'

'Could be tricky,' Lindsey replied. 'Incidentally, Mamma nearly caught us *in flagrante* yesterday! She called at the flat while Jonathan was on one of his lunch-time visits.'

'I didn't know he made lunch-time visits,' Rona said mildly.

'He does when I'm working from home. Anyway, Mum has a new hair-do to go with her altered image, and she called round for my approval.'

'What's it like?'

'Very chic, actually, but she bit my head off when I said Pops would approve, insisting she'd done it for her own benefit.'

'Sounds as though things are no better, then. But about Jonathan – what do you think?'

'Well, weekends are out, naturally. Whether or not he could swing a 'business dinner' on Friday, I don't know.'

'Like to ask him?'

'Yes, I will. Thanks, Ro. Are you free for lunch, by the way?'

'Sorry, I'm off to Hester Latymer's in an hour or so.'

'Name-dropper!' Lindsey retorted. 'Enjoy yourself, and I'll get back to you about the meal.'

As Rona replaced the receiver, she thought back to the family group in the park, the children running happily ahead, the parents strolling after them. They'd not looked like a couple in the process of divorcing, she reflected uneasily, and yet again found herself fearing for her sister's happiness.

Tom sat at his desk, restlessly tapping his pen. This week, there'd been another notch-up in Avril's self-improvement programme. He admitted to himself that he'd not expected it to last, and by the end of the previous week it had seemed he was right. Now, though, with her ultra-modern haircut, she looked like an executive of a multinational.

Her manner was different, too. Last week she'd seemed uncertain and vulnerable, anxious for his approval. Yesterday, there'd been a take-it-or-leave-it air about her, and when – since he could scarcely ignore it – he'd complimented her on the new style, she'd merely shrugged and turned aside with a careless, 'Glad you like it', as though his opinion were of no consequence.

Irritably, he wished she'd at least be consistent. For years now her drab appearance had gone hand in hand with constant sniping at himself and, to a lesser degree, the girls. Consequently, her sudden smartening up had startled him, as had her palpable effort to be pleasant. Admittedly this latter was of short duration – possibly, he thought uncomfortably, because he'd not met her halfway – but instead of reverting to type, she'd changed again, acquiring a hard gloss that, intentionally or not, seemed to exclude him. And after briefly relapsing to supper on trays, they were again eating in the dining room. He no longer knew what to make of her, and the fact annoyed him. Whether or not her metamorphosis would make easier the parting he'd decided on remained to be seen.

The Latymers' constituency home was in Park Rise, a leafy avenue of substantial houses at the upper end of Furze Hill Park, much sought after for its high position and views over the town. Its paintwork, like that of its neighbours, was a dazzling white against the rose brick, but its exaggerated Dutch gables gave it a character of its own, emphasized by the nameplate, *Holland House*, attached to the gatepost.

The gates themselves stood open, but since the circular drive was already clogged with cars, Rona parked outside. Easier for a quick getaway, she thought guiltily.

She was admitted by a uniformed maid and shown into a large, airy room seemingly full of well-dressed women. Hester materialized beside her and handed her a glass of champagne.

'Rona – I hope I may call you that? – I'm so glad you could come. We'll all introduce ourselves shortly – I find it breaks the ice at these little gatherings – but in the meantime, come and meet one of James's colleagues, Lydia Playfair.'

The MP for Stokely, Rona remembered; she'd seen a

by-election poster on her last visit. The woman turned at the sound of her name, holding out her hand with a smile.

'Lydia, this is Rona Parish,' Hester said, and immediately excused herself to greet the latest arrival.

'Is this your first attendance?' Lydia Playfair enquired lazily, surveying Rona over a pair of large tortoiseshell glasses.

'Attendance?'

'At a Professional Women's Luncheon. Hester holds three or four a year.'

'Oh, I see. Yes, it's my first time; I only met her recently.'

'She always tries for new people, but occasionally – particularly if there's a cancellation – some of us are recycled.' Her mouth quirked. 'I'm on the reserve list. A word of warning, by the way: you'll be called on in a minute to give a brief spiel. We all will.'

'What about, for goodness sake?'

'Our life's work,' said Ms Playfair, and laughed at Rona's expression. 'No, not really. Just your name, and a brief account of what you do. No one knows each other yet, so it's a way of giving us a talking point.'

Rona was digesting this when someone tapped her shoulder, and she turned to find herself face to face with Magda.

'Hello, fellow Professional Woman!' she said.

'Magda – how good to see you!' Rona half-turned to Lydia Playfair. 'This is—'

But the two women were already shaking hands. 'I know who she is,' Magda said. 'Lydia patronizes my Stokely boutique – in fact, she performed the opening ceremony.'

'It made a change from supermarkets!' Lydia said with a smile. 'How long have you two known each other?'

'From my first day at primary school,' Magda replied.

Hester, reappearing in the doorway, clapped her hands, and the buzz of conversation died away.

'Now, ladies, if you would all find a seat, we'll have a brief introductory session before we go through for lunch.'

There was a pause, while everyone looked for somewhere to sit. Rona perched on the arm of a sofa next to Magda, and for the first time had a clear sight of her fellow guests, whose ages seemed to range from thirty to sixty.

'Lydia will start us off,' Hester announced, 'since she knows the drill, then each of you follow on in turn.'

Ms Playfair, now across the room from Rona, obligingly did so. 'I'm Lydia Playfair, Conservative MP for Stokely East.' She paused, and added, 'I think that says it all!'

There was general laughter. Lydia turned to the woman next to her, who said hastily, 'Cynthia Benson, managing director of Benson Landscaping and Garden Maintenance.'

They followed on in sequence and Rona tried to memorize names and occupations: Davina Medhurst, a surgeon at the Royal County; Beatrice Collins, head of the local sixth form college; Jacqueline Stone, a barrister. Then, after Magda, it was her turn, and her admission to being a biographer and freelance journalist elicited the usual interested murmurs.

'Right,' Hester said, 'now we all know each other, do come through for lunch.'

The table in the dining room across the hall was laid for eight, and there was a name card in each place. Rona found herself on her hostess's left, opposite Lydia Playfair and with Cynthia Benson on her own left. Magda, being on the same side of the table, was out of Rona's sight.

'Whose biography have you written?' Cynthia Benson enquired, as soon as they'd settled themselves. She was a small, dumpy woman in her fifties, but she'd an attractive smile and her eyes were alert and interested.

'Conan Doyle for one,' Hester answered, before Rona could speak. 'It was excellent, as was that on Sarah Siddons. And there's another, isn't there, Rona?'

'William Pitt the Elder,' Rona supplied. 'I chose him because he seemed less well known than his son.'

'That's right; but I learned a lot about him from your book.' Hester started to serve soup from the tureen in front of her. 'You really make your subjects come alive.'

'If you're into politicians,' Lydia remarked, passing the

filled bowls down the table, 'you should do one of James. I'm sure he'd love it! Has he any odd little foibles, Hester?'

'None printable! Except, perhaps, a penchant for quoting A. A. Milne. "The more it snows, tiddly-pom", and so on.'

Lydia gave a hoot of laughter. 'From now on, I shall address him as Pooh!'

'I shouldn't advise it! Seriously, though,' Hester added, turning back to Rona, 'how do you go about choosing your subjects?'

'I think of someone I'd like to know more about myself, then find out if anyone has written his or her biography recently. I say "recently", because it's virtually impossible to find anyone of note who *hasn't* been written about at some stage, but if it's a while ago, you can be lucky in unearthing new information.'

'Are you working on one now?' asked Davina Medhurst, who, sitting next to Lydia, had been listening to their conversation.

'No, I'm wearing my journalistic hat at the moment.'

'She did the Buckford series in *Chiltern Life*.' Hester seemed to have appointed herself publicity agent, but Rona, feeling she'd had more than her share of attention, didn't elaborate. Even so, the subject wasn't allowed to drop.

'You're still working on it?' Cynthia Benson pursued.

'No, I'm – actually trying to find someone's birth parents,' Rona said reluctantly.

'There was something about that in last week's *Gazette*,' interposed Jacqueline Stone, adding astutely, as Rona bit her lip, 'Is that the one you're involved with?'

The whole table awaited her reply. 'Actually, yes,' she acknowledged quietly.

'The girl whose mother was murdered?' Cynthia again.

'Poor child,' observed Beatrice Collins. 'Imagine being all excited about finding your mother, only to discover she'd been killed.'

'Obviously it's her father we're looking for,' Rona said aridly. 'But that's enough about me and my work.' She turned determinedly to Cynthia beside her. 'Tell me about landscaping. I've only a tiny garden myself, but I've always been interested in it.'

Cynthia hesitated, sensing everyone's reluctance to let the subject drop, but politeness demanded an answer, and Rona was at last able to withdraw from the spotlight.

For the rest of the meal – salmon in pastry with green salad, followed by syllabub – the conversation remained reassuringly general, each woman in turn being quizzed on her speciality. Rona had to hand it to Hester – her method *was* a good means of getting to know people. She learned among other things that Cynthia's firm did landscaping for the borough council and had been responsible for the layout of several parks, as well as advising on private gardens; that Jacqueline Stone was defending a case at the Old Bailey, and that Davina had successfully separated conjoined twins. An interesting group, indeed.

Talk continued over coffee in the drawing room, where they sat chatting in small groups, and it was almost three thirty by the time the party broke up and people began to leave, promising each other to keep in touch. Rona wondered how many would follow through that transitory resolve.

She and Magda left together, and stood talking on the pavement beside Rona's car.

'You created a stir with your investigation,' Magda commented.

'Thanks to you!' Rona retorted.

'I?' Magda exclaimed indignantly. 'I never said a word!'

'You started it in the first place; if you hadn't admitted to knowing me at that office party, none of this would have happened.'

Magda conceded the point. 'Are you getting anywhere?'

'Well, we tracked down the maternal grandparents, but they're no great shakes. Zara didn't even like them.'

'Nothing yet on the father?'

Rona shook her head. 'Still, I said I'd give it six weeks, and I will. Whether or not I find him in that time is in the lap of the gods, but at least it won't be for want of trying.'

'You should join the Mounties,' Magda said with a smile. 'They always get their man! See you!' And with a lifted hand, she walked along the pavement to her own car.

When Rona reached home, there was a message from Lindsey to the effect that she and Jonathan would be delighted to come to supper on Friday. She broke the news to Max on his return, and he was less than enthusiastic.

'I'd been going to suggest the cinema; there's a good film on, and it's some time since we've been.'

'We can go on Saturday,' Rona said.

He glanced at her suspiciously. 'You're not going to tax him with knowing that girl, are you?'

She smiled. 'How well you know me, darling!'

'Well, I don't want sparks flying round the dinner table, it's bad for the digestion. Added to which, it would get Lindsey's back up.'

'I'll be the soul of tact,' Rona assured him.

Selina phoned the next morning.

'I wanted to thank you for the flowers,' she began. 'They were totally unnecessary, but much appreciated.'

'Just a small token,' Rona said. 'I'd have been really stuck without you. How did the birthday go?'

'Oh, a great success. The only drawback to the weekend was that I was requested to remove my boxes that have been cluttering up their spare room. I went through most of them – no point in carting them back here only to throw them out – and I came across some things of Gemma's.'

Rona stiffened. 'What sort of things?'

'Just odds and ends she'd had at the flat. With her mother out of the country – and seemingly not interested anyway – there was no one to pass them to, and they were of no value anyway. Quite frankly, I forgot about them.'

'You mean – clothes and things?'

'No, those were all disposed of at the time. These are just

149

a few personal items – cassettes of interviews she'd conducted, one or two letters and some odd bits of make-up. Pathetic, really, to think that's all that's left of her, but her daughter might like to have them.'

'I'm sure she would; thanks. No diaries, I suppose?'

Selina's rich laugh came down the phone. 'Now wouldn't that be handy? Sorry, definitely no diaries, and the letters were all from her mother, so nothing of interest there, either, which is no doubt why the police didn't take them.'

'Surely they'd have gone through the cassettes, though?'

'Well, yes they would, but the fact is they never found them. I didn't myself till I was leaving the flat about a year later; they were mixed up with our commercial tapes. I skipped through them, but it was just routine stuff – people opening fêtes, getting prizes at flower shows, that kind of thing. A couple had been taped over, because while she was on maternity leave, she used the recorder as an aide-memoire, still beginning each entry with the date, mind you, like she'd been taught at County. I used to tease her about it. Anyway, I left what there is with the parents, to save you trailing down here. There's no hurry about collecting it – just give them a ring first. If you've a pen handy, I'll give you their address and phone number.'

Rona made a note of them. 'Thanks very much, Selina. Incidentally, Amanda-that-was would very much like to meet you.'

'I was afraid of that. I can't tell her any more than I've told you.'

'But she'd ask totally different questions; much more personal, and I'm sure you could answer those. Her grandmother was of singularly little help.'

Selina sighed. 'OK, but let's wait awhile. Until you've finished your investigation, for preference. In the meantime, phone me next time you're in town, and we'll meet for a meal.'

'I'll do that,' Rona promised.

Yes, she thought as she returned to her work, Zara would

be delighted with the mementoes, but she'd have a good look at them herself first.

The re-emergence of the Gemma case produced a couple of letters in that week's *Gazette*.

Reading about it brought it all back, one began. *I didn't know Gemma Grant, but I remember the shock and horror when she was killed. She was the same age as me, and, like her, I was sharing a flat with a friend. We had extra locks fitted to all the doors and windows.*

The second was more factual: *Gemma's flatmate at the time was Selina O'Toole, the television interviewer. She found the body. Amanda might try contacting her.*

'Some people have long memories,' Rona commented to Max.

He shrugged. 'Local girl makes good. It's the kind of thing they would remember. Anyway, it's all grist to your mill, giving you a second bite at the cherry in the publicity stakes.'

Rona laughed. 'A gloriously mixed metaphor, if ever I heard one!'

'Never mind the critical analysis; make yourself useful by laying the table. I'm keeping this meal strictly informal, by the way. I don't see why we should lay out the red carpet for Lindsey's latest fly-by-night. How's that for a metaphor?'

'More apt, I grant you. What are we having?'

'Chilli, rice and green salad, followed by pears in red wine.'

'Admirable.' Rona took out the cutlery and laid four place settings, wondering as she did so how she could bring the conversation round to Gemma. Jonathan's reaction might well be enlightening.

Tom said flatly, 'Quite frankly, I don't know what the hell's going on.'

Catherine handed him a glass and settled herself opposite him. This was an unscheduled visit, on his way home from the bank, and he was clearly on edge.

'In what way?' she asked quietly.

'With Avril. She's a chameleon at the moment, not the same for three consecutive days.'

Catherine frowned. 'Moody, you mean?'

'No, in appearance. After taking no interest for years, she's suddenly had her hair styled and bought new clothes.'

'Well, good for her.' When he did not reply, she added uneasily, 'Or do you think it's an attempt to win back your interest?'

Tom gave a brief laugh. 'It might have started out like that, but it isn't now. She made it clear she doesn't give a fig what I think.'

'That's good, isn't it?'

'Oh God, I don't know.' He ran a hand distractedly through his hair. 'It doesn't make for a very comfortable existence, I can tell you that, but at least it's made up my mind on one thing: as soon as I retire, I'm moving out.'

Catherine was quiet for a moment. Then she said tentatively, 'Will you come here?'

'Good God, no! I mean – I'd hardly announce it like that, would I, without even consulting you? No, no; it might seem old-fashioned in today's climate, but I've no intention of compromising you. People accept young couples living together, but rightly or wrongly, they're harsher on older ones. So as soon as I've set the divorce in motion, I'll rent a flat somewhere until it comes through.'

'Have you told your wife?'

'Not yet, I've only just decided.' He tipped his glass, watching the liquid coat the sides. 'In spite of her criticizing,' he went on slowly, 'I've always felt she's been – dependent on me. Now, though, I'm sure she's quite capable of managing on her own. She'll have the house, and there won't be any money worries. It'll probably be a relief to be rid of me.'

Catherine leant forward and laid her hand on his. 'I'm not worried about what people might say, Tom. You're very welcome to come here if you'd like to.'

'Bless you, but no. It's better this way. We'll be free to spend time together, and it won't matter by then who sees us, but we'll sleep under different roofs. At night, anyway!' he added with a smile.

Since her only meeting with Jonathan had been brief, Rona was interested to see if, on further acquaintance, her impressions of him would hold or need amending. She also hoped, during the course of the evening, to assess not only his relationship with her sister, but his earlier association with Gemma Grant.

Two things struck her at once: his apparent ease of manner, though there was wariness at the back of his eyes, and his subtle distancing from Lindsey. It was as though he were saying: *If I'm being paraded here as a future member of the family, forget it.*

Lindsey, on the other hand, had no such reservations. She had pinned her hair up and was wearing a dress Rona hadn't seen before. She looked, Rona thought achingly, young, happy – and in love. The word 'darling' peppered her remarks to Jonathan, but was never returned. Rona wondered if she noticed.

On their arrival, they went into the sitting room for drinks, where, as before, Jonathan made a fuss of Gus.

'We have a bassett at home,' he remarked, forgetting he'd already told Rona. 'Name of Caesar.'

'Yes,' she answered casually, 'I think we saw you with him, up in the park.'

Jonathan shot her a quick look, but she had turned to offer Lindsey a dish of olives.

'Quite likely,' he said evenly. 'It's a favourite exercising ground – for the kids as well as the dog.'

'How old are they?' Max asked, unaware of Lindsey's bitten lip.

'Twelve and ten. Dominic started at Buckford College this term, as a weekly boarder. Tamar's still at Greenacres Prep.'

This information, over and above what was asked for, struck

Rona as defiance. He was fencing with them, showing her he didn't care if she'd seen him with his family – that he'd nothing to hide. Before he could proceed to his wife's interests, she said quickly, 'How long have you been with Chase Mortimer?'

He held her eyes for a moment, aware of her deflection and seemingly amused by it, damn him. 'Man and boy; my great-uncle was the original Mortimer.'

'You're a partner, then, like Lindsey?'

'I am indeed.'

And therefore even less likely to cause a stir by divorcing his wife. Solicitors, Rona felt sure, could be stuffy about affairs between partners. Surely Lindsey realized this? Whether or not, she obviously didn't care for the turn the conversation had taken, and changed it abruptly by saying, 'I was telling Jonathan about your work, Max.'

Jonathan smoothly took up her cue. 'Indeed, yes – I hadn't known of the connection. I went to the exhibition at the Beaufort Gallery – last year, was it? – and I particularly liked your portrait of that young girl.'

'Good of you to say so,' Max said briefly, and, though he disliked his work being discussed, he allowed himself to be drawn into a discussion on techniques, which safely distanced them from the previous topic and lasted until it was time to go down for supper.

Jonathan was genuinely interested in the house, commenting with enthusiasm on the alterations they'd made to it, particularly the yellow and blue kitchen overlooking the now moonlit patio garden.

'This is fabulous!' he exclaimed. 'I must say I envy you having a place like this, and in such a convenient position, too. I have a half-hour drive into work each morning, which can take twice as long if there's a traffic hold-up.'

It was as they were beginning their dessert that Lindsey said out of the blue, 'Did you see the letters in today's *Gazette*?'

'No?' Jonathan looked up. 'What letters?'

'Referring to Rona's insert last week about the girl who was murdered.'

'Gemma Grant,' Rona underlined, her eyes on Jonathan. She caught the involuntary tightening of his jaw, but he made no comment.

'One of them mentioned Selina O'Toole,' Lindsey was continuing. 'She's the one you went to see, isn't she?'

'Yes.' Rona paused, still watching Jonathan, who seemed intent on spooning wine sauce over his pears. 'I believe you knew her, Jonathan?'

His hand jerked, spilling some wine on the table, and with a muttered apology he wiped it with his napkin. 'Knew whom?' he asked, his voice for the first time not entirely under control.

'Both of them, actually. Selina – and Gemma.'

Max shifted uncomfortably. Lindsey was staring at Jonathan in disbelief. 'You *knew Gemma?*' she demanded.

He cleared his throat. 'As it happens, yes.'

'But – how? When? And why didn't you say so, when I mentioned her on Tuesday?'

After a minute he said quietly, 'It's something I've spent my life trying to forget. Quite frankly, it – was a shock, to have it suddenly spoken of again.'

I'll bet it was, Rona thought grimly. He looked up, finally meeting her eyes. 'What exactly did Selina tell you?'

'That you went round with Gemma, and were upset when she broke it off,' Rona replied, embroidering slightly.

Lindsey gave a little gasp and her spoon dropped on to her plate.

Jonathan paled. 'I assure you I was exhaustively questioned, as was the rest of our group.'

'Even so,' Rona said enigmatically.

He lifted a hand and let it fall, turning to Lindsey with a crooked smile. 'As to why I've never mentioned it, it would hardly be a good career move, would it, to let it be known I'd dated the victim of an unsolved murder?'

Lindsey, who looked on the verge of tears, didn't reply, so

Rona stepped in again. 'What was she like, Gemma? I'm trying to build up a picture of her.'

Jonathan took a long draught of wine and wiped his mouth on his napkin. Delaying tactics, Rona thought. 'I was at university at the time,' he said then, 'so I wasn't around as much as the others. But from what I remember she was good fun. Pretty, a bit flirty. Most of us went out with her at one time or another. Then, from one week to the next, she changed.'

'Changed how?'

'Stopped playing around, joining in the fun. And shortly after, she dropped out altogether.'

'No explanation?'

'Not from her, but Selina said she'd met someone and wanted to spend her time with him.'

'Any idea who it could have been?'

He shook his head. 'Not one of our crowd, that's for sure.'

'How did you all react? Those of you who'd been out with her, I mean?'

'Were any of us insanely jealous enough to kill her?' Jonathan asked bluntly. 'I'd say definitely not. We simply shrugged and moved on to someone who *was* available. None of us had had anything heavy with Gemma, it was all very light-hearted.'

Max stood up and refilled everyone's glass. 'I hope you don't think we invited you here to give you the third degree,' he said, with a look of reprimand at Rona.

'I'm sure he doesn't,' she said blithely. 'It was Lindsey who brought the subject up, not me. And actually, Linz, there's someone else we know who belonged to that crowd – Philip Yarborough. That's right, isn't it Jonathan?'

'Philip Yarborough?' Lindsey echoed, her voice rising. 'But – my God! . . .'

Rona sent her a warning look as Jonathan nodded. 'Yes, Phil was there.'

'Are you still in touch with him?'

'We meet occasionally, in the course of things, but we were

never that close. Also,' he added frankly, 'we remind each other of a period of our lives we'd both rather forget.'

'But he went out with Gemma too?' Lindsey pursued.

'For a while, though he was more involved with Selina.' He paused, allowing himself a faint smile. 'Now, there's someone who's made a name for herself.'

Max had been busying himself with the coffee, and they drank it in sporadic silence, thinking over what had been said.

Jonathan looked at his watch. 'The hypothetical Masonic dinner finishes at eleven,' he said. 'I should be making tracks.'

Max glanced at the clock. 'You're cutting it fine, if you're running Lindsey home first.'

'We came in separate cars for that very reason,' Lindsey told him. 'What's more, we had to park at the far end of the road. I'll walk back with you,' she added to Jonathan, getting to her feet as he did.

'Thanks for a delightful evening,' he said at the front door, adding with his crooked smile, 'though I could have done without the *This is Your Life* interlude!'

'It was all in a good cause,' Rona said equably.

Lindsey gave her a summary kiss and said tersely, 'I'll be in touch.'

'I rather think we'll be hearing from her before cockcrow,' Max observed, shutting the door behind them. And it was in fact barely half an hour later – presumably as soon as Lindsey had gained her own living room – that the phone rang.

Max, at the sink washing glasses, raised his eyebrows, and Rona, with a resigned shrug, picked it up.

'What the *hell* do you think you were playing at?' Lindsey's voice exploded in her ear. 'How *dare* you question Jonathan as if he were a criminal? And why in heaven's name didn't you *tell* me he'd known Gemma, not to mention Philip Yarborough? At least you needn't look any further for your murderer; it seems Max was right all along. Adele should be thankful he's only beaten her. So far.'

'Are you stopping for breath?' Rona enquired sweetly. 'If so, which question would you like answering first?'

'*Rona!*'

'All right, all right. I didn't tell you about Jonathan because I was afraid you'd react exactly as you are doing, and anyway I haven't seen you since I found out, and it's not something you can chat about on the phone. The same goes for Philip Yarborough.'

'Are you going to invite him to dinner, too?' Lindsey asked nastily.

'You're in a better position than I am to approach him.'

'Oh no! I'm not doing any more of your dirty work! I don't want to be found dead in *my* bath, thank you very much!' Her voice changed, became small. 'You don't really suspect Jonathan, do you?' she asked.

Rona bit her lip. 'I'm sure he's all sweetness and light,' she said. 'Now go to bed, sis, and stop worrying.'

Well, she thought as she broke the connection, she'd wanted to warn her sister about Jonathan's connection with Gemma. That she had most certainly done. It was now up to Lindsey to take any precautions that might be necessary.

Eleven

There had been a disappointing response to Rona's Internet search, but she'd expected little else. Not only had the murder been of only local interest, but it had happened a quarter of a century ago, and few of today's surfers would even have heard of it. Without the father's name, she thought despondently, there seemed little chance of tracing him. Admittedly she could try 'Morrison', but since it wasn't his real name – or Gemma wouldn't have disclosed it – it seemed a long shot.

There was, however, a development of sorts on the Monday morning, when Rona answered her mobile to find a male caller on the line.

'You were enquiring about Gemma Grant?' he said.

'Yes, I was.' She pulled pen and pad towards her and waited expectantly.

'I think I might have something to interest you.'

'Yes?'

'However –' long pause – 'I'm not prepared to tell you over the phone.'

Rona frowned. 'Who am I speaking to?'

'That's neither here nor there. Do you want to meet me or not?'

'If you could give me some idea—'

'Take it or leave it.'

'Look, I'm sorry, but I really—'

The phone clicked in her ear and went dead.

'Damn!' Rona said forcefully. A weirdo, no doubt; at least he didn't know who or where she was. Nonetheless, she felt oddly disturbed by the call and eventually, unable to concentrate on her work, she gave up and ran down the stairs, calling for Gus. It was after midday, and with luck Max would spare the time for a spot of lunch with her.

The sound of the Boston Philharmonic reached her before she even opened Farthings' front door, and she smiled to herself. It was for this reason that they had to work in separate establishments. She closed the door and directed Gus to the kitchen. As at home, he wasn't allowed upstairs.

'Good boy – wait there,' she told him, and started up the stairs. Useless to call out – the music would have drowned her voice as it masked her footsteps – and it wasn't until she'd rounded the stairhead that she realized Max was not alone. Immobile in a chair, his hands folded in his lap, sat James Latymer.

'Oh!' Rona came to an abrupt halt. Max had his back to her, but Latymer's reaction alerted him and he turned, switching off the hi-fi as he did so.

'I'm so sorry,' Rona said into the sudden silence. 'I'd no idea you had a sitting.'

'Good morning, Ms Parish,' James Latymer said, and, to Max, 'May I move?'

'Yes, of course. I was just about to suggest breaking for lunch.' He glanced at Rona, and she couldn't tell whether or not he was annoyed with her. It was rare for her to interrupt him when he was working, virtually unheard of to do so without notice. Which, she thought, proved how thrown she'd been by the phone call.

'Is there a problem?' Max asked her.

'It'll keep. Sorry to have butted in, I'll beat a hasty retreat.' She flashed an apologetic smile at James Latymer, who had stood up and was easing his aching muscles.

'Nice to see you again,' he said.

Max said a little ungraciously, 'You can join us for lunch, if you like.'

'Oh, I don't think—'

He grinned suddenly. 'Don't tell me that's not why you came!'

'Please stay,' Latymer urged. 'A little feminine company would go down a treat.'

'Then thank you; you've both talked me into it.'

They went together down the open staircase. The little table at the end of the sitting room was already laid. Max went to the kitchen for extra cutlery and Gus came trotting back with him, waving his frond-like tail. Latymer went down on his hunkers and Gus, accepting his overtures, tried to lick his face.

Max said drily, 'Make the most of him; there's no baby for you to kiss.'

Latymer laughed and stood up, still fondling the dog's ears. 'He's a great fellow. What do you call him?'

'Augustus. Answers to Gus.'

'Splendid name.' He ruefully brushed dog hair off his hands. 'Now I fear I'll need a wash before lunch.'

'The bathroom's through the kitchen,' Max directed him. As he left the room, Max glanced at Rona. 'Was it only lunch you were after?'

'A bit of company, really. I – had a rather odd phone call, and it unsettled me.'

He frowned. 'What kind of call? Threatening?'

'No, but – strange. A man said he had information about Gemma, but insisted he'd only give it to me in person.'

'You didn't agree?' Max cut in sharply.

'Give me credit for some sense.'

'And it was on your mobile?'

'Yes, the number that had been in the *Gazette*. No name or address, as you stipulated.'

'Thank God I did.'

'It was probably nothing, Max.'

'Well, if he rings back, hold your ground. Under no circumstances are you to arrange to meet him, OK?'

'OK,' she said meekly, smiling at James Latymer, who was re-entering the room. 'Thanks for letting me quote from your manifesto,' she went on, as Max excused himself to bring the lunch. 'It added a personal note to the article.'

161

'I'll look out for it. I hear you were at Hester's luncheon last week?'

'Yes, it was most enjoyable. They were an interesting group.'

Max returned and set an earthenware dish of fish pie on the table and they all seated themselves. 'Have we you to thank for this?' Latymer asked Rona, who shook her head.

'Max is the cook in our family.'

'Then he puts me to shame. I can barely find my way to the kitchen!'

He was very pleasant, Rona reflected, watching him surreptitiously as he and Max discussed the portrait. Critics maintained he was aware of his own importance, but so, surely, were all MPs, and there was no hint of condescension in his manner. The obvious enjoyment with which he tackled his lunch went some way towards explaining the rounded paunch beneath the expensively tailored suit.

Rona stayed for the fresh fruit and coffee that followed, enjoying the different slant of the conversation and reluctant to return to the empty house. However, by one thirty Max was looking at his watch, and she took her leave of them. James Latymer held her hand in both of his. A politician's touch?

'Delighted to see you again,' he said.

'And I you,' she replied. 'Please give my regards to your wife.' And, as Max started purposefully towards the stairs, she slipped on Gus's lead and let herself out of the house.

Lindsey was beginning to wish they hadn't come. The little pub was crowded, and the noise level was such that private conversation would be out of the question. Still, Jonathan had heard the food was good, and been anxious to try it out. There was also the advantage that, as the pub was a fifteen-minute run out of town, they were unlikely to see anyone they knew.

'Even if we do, it's no big deal,' he'd said. 'We're just two colleagues having a working lunch.'

She glanced impatiently at the queue at the bar. It didn't seem to be moving at all, and Jonathan was still four or five from the front. She stood up suddenly, spread her jacket over two chairs to reserve their places, and manoeuvred her way to the Ladies'.

When she emerged, it was to find herself entangled with men turning from the bar with brimming tankards, and she was weaving her way between them when, unbelievably, she found herself face to face with Hugh.

The shock was such that she stopped dead, someone cannoned into her from behind, and she in turn lurched forward into Hugh, spilling some of the drink he was carrying. It was clear he was equally startled.

'Lindsey – what are you doing here?'

'Having lunch with a colleague.' She nodded vaguely in Jonathan's direction, and saw that he had witnessed the meeting. 'And you?'

'The same.'

A smile and nod in passing was now all that was required, but they stood unmoving, rocks in the swirling tide of humanity that flowed around them, their eyes locked on each others'.

'How are you?' he asked.

'Fine. You?'

He nodded. 'Are your parents –' he broke off, flushed, and finished limply – 'well?'

Lindsey frowned. 'Yes. Why?' It hadn't sounded a perfunctory enquiry.

'I just – wondered.' But his discomfort was obvious. 'Give them my regards,' he added quickly, 'and Max and Rona, too.' And with a quick nod, he finally turned and forced his way through the crowds to his table.

Lindsey reached hers at the same time as Jonathan, who gave her a searching look as he set down the glasses. 'What was that all about?' he asked.

'He's my ex.'

'God! Did he see me?'

'I've no idea. I said I was lunching with a colleague. That's the party line, isn't it?'

'Yes, but—'

'You think he'll assume any man I'm with must be my lover?' Lindsey asked dangerously.

Jonathan said curtly, 'You're putting words into my mouth.'

It was the closest they'd come to a quarrel, and they realized it simultaneously and exchanged sheepish smiles. 'They'll call our number when the food's ready,' he said after a minute, and the subject dropped.

For the rest of that day, though, Lindsey's mind kept returning to the meeting with Hugh, and in particular his query about her parents. Did he know something she didn't? She was tempted to phone him and demand an explanation, but she'd only his office number. Also, it might look as though she were trying to re-establish contact. Which, she reminded herself, she wasn't. Nevertheless, seeing him had jolted her more than she cared to admit. It was depressing to realize that, even in the midst of a new affair, her pulses still quickened in the presence of her ex-husband.

'I've decided to go back to work,' Avril announced.

Tom, about to take a beer out of the fridge, turned to stare at her. 'What brought that on?'

'Boredom,' she said succinctly, continuing to stir whatever was in the pan. 'Also, it will stop us getting under each other's feet when you retire.'

He let that pass. 'A full-time job?'

'No, I can still do my stint at the charity shop and play bridge; but I'll be working mornings at the library four days a week, and on alternate Saturdays.'

He poured the beer carefully into a tankard, digesting what she'd told him. 'When do you start?'

'A week today. I had the interview last week, and it's just been confirmed. They're short of staff and glad to take me on.'

'But – don't you need special qualifications?'

'Not for the work I'll be doing, though I'll have to take a computer course. That'll be done in library time – an hour a day, I think.' She paused. 'It won't pay much, of course, but it'll be good to have some money that's totally mine.'

Was that a criticism? Their joint bank account was surely in her favour, since she'd contributed nothing to it since leaving work when the twins were born.

'Well – good for you,' he said, echoing Catherine. He was tempted to tell her of his own decision, hating the duplicity of keeping silent, but he reminded himself of Catherine's advice. It would not, after all, be for long, and it was undeniable that his retirement and all the events leading up to it would pass off much more smoothly if he and Avril were still together.

Feeling more was expected of him, he added, 'Is it the main library?'

'No, the local branch, on the parade. Within walking distance, which is another advantage.'

'Good for you,' he repeated, and, clutching his beer, escaped to the sitting room and the evening paper.

'Ro? You'll never believe it, but I bumped into Hugh at lunchtime!'

Rona sighed, supposing it had only been a matter of time. 'And how did that come about?'

'Jonathan and I drove out to the Watermill for lunch. Do you know it? It's on the Merefield road. Anyway, he was there.'

'You didn't *talk* to him, with Jonathan in tow?' It would be just like Lindsey to score points.

'Jonathan wasn't "in tow", as you put it, he was queuing at the bar. But what was odd was that Hugh asked after the parents.'

'What's odd about that?'

'The way he did it. As though he'd started to ask something else.'

'What did he say, exactly?'

'"Are your parents—" then a very long gap before he said, "well?" Incidentally, he sent regards to you and Max.'

'Nice of him.'

'Is that all you have to say?' Lindsey demanded impatiently.

'What do you want me to say?'

'Well, I was wondering whether to ring up and ask him what he meant.'

'*Don't*, Lindsey.'

'Why not?'

'You know damn well.'

'Look, I only want to know what he was getting at, and I never will if I don't ask him.'

'It sounds as though you've already made up your mind.'

Lindsey slammed the phone down without replying and stood breathing heavily, her hand still resting on it. All right, yes, she thought rebelliously, she *had* made up her mind. If she didn't satisfy herself on this, it would haunt her, fill her mind when she woke in the night and come between her and her sleep. It was now six o'clock – too late to phone Hugh at the office. Where was he living? she wondered. With the girl she'd seen him with, that time in Sainsbury's? Strange that in the intervening months she'd not caught so much as a glimpse of him – until today. True, his office was in Windsor Way, but that was only just off Guild Street and he must surely frequent it, for lunch if nothing else. He wouldn't drive out to the Watermill every day.

Her mind still churning, she went to prepare her meal, only then realizing that the box of groceries was still in the car. Swearing under her breath, she ran down the stairs and out on to the drive. It was almost dark, and she had to feel for the lock on the boot. As the key went in, a faint sound caught her attention, and she straightened, listening. It came from behind the bushes that screened her from the pavement, and it sounded like someone crying. Careful that the gravel shouldn't warn of her approach, Lindsey walked to the gateway and cautiously looked outside. A bicycle was propped against the wall, and astride it, both feet on the ground and head bent, was a small girl, sobbing bitterly.

'Hello,' Lindsey said softly, and the child's head shot up.

She tensed, seeming about to take off, but Lindsey went on quickly, 'My name's Lindsey; what's yours?'

'Daisy,' the child answered with a sniff. 'Daisy Yarborough.'

'From across the road? I've met your parents.' She paused, wondering if they knew she was out alone. She didn't look more than seven or eight.

Lindsey hesitated. She wasn't, she knew, very good with children, but she couldn't ignore the tears. 'What's the matter, Daisy?'

'It's Mummy,' the girl replied, rubbing a hand across her eyes. 'She fell downstairs, and when Nick and I ran to help, Daddy shouted at us to go out and play.'

Lindsey went cold. 'Is she badly hurt?'

'I don't know.'

'Has Daddy phoned for an ambulance?'

The child looked at her with frightened eyes. 'I don't know,' she repeated.

Again, Lindsey paused indecisively, reluctant to become involved. 'Where's your brother?'

Daisy's eyes went beyond her, and she turned to see the boy's slow approach on his own bike. There was no sign of tears, but in the light from the street lamp, his face was pale and tense.

Lindsey gave him what she hoped was a reassuring nod. 'You shouldn't be out in the dark,' she said, reaching a decision. 'Would you like me to take you home?'

After a minute Daisy nodded and, heart hammering, Lindsey walked with her across the road and up the drive of the house on the corner, the boy trailing behind them. She rang the bell and waited, mouth dry. Nothing happened; she rang again, and immediately the door was flung open and Philip Yarborough stood there, white-faced and hair dishevelled. He stared at them blankly, and Lindsey said quickly, 'Daisy was crying. She said there'd been an accident; is there anything I can do?'

Philip tore his eyes from her to the tear-stained face of his daughter. 'Sorry I shouted, kids,' he said flatly. 'I was worried about Mummy.'

'Is she all right?' Lindsey demanded.

'She's badly bruised and in shock, but she doesn't seem to have broken anything.'

'Have you phoned for an ambulance?'

His eyes flickered and he looked away. 'There's no need for that. She'll be all right after a rest.' He gestured to the children, and, abandoning their bikes, they squeezed past him into the house and ran up the stairs.

'Then let the Sinclairs have a look at her,' Lindsey urged. The couple at number five were a doctor and nurse.

Yarborough made a dismissive gesture. 'I'm not having the entire road involved in this,' he said sharply.

He'd not invited her in, but she'd no intention of leaving without learning more.

'What happened?' she asked.

He ran a hand through his hair. 'I don't know, she must have slipped. She'd taken up a pile of ironing and put it in the airing cupboard, and the next thing I heard was this – series of bumps.'

'She didn't cry out?'

'No. I dashed out on to the landing, and to my horror she was rolling down the stairs.'

'You were upstairs yourself?'

He swallowed dryly. 'Yes. I'd just got in from work and had gone up to change.'

There was an electric silence. Then Lindsey said doggedly, 'I know it's none of my business, but I really think you should take her to A & E. She might have internal injuries, or delayed concussion or something. If it's the children you're worried about, I'll stay with them.'

'*No!*' he said forcefully. Then, more calmly, 'If I go, we all go.' Then, reluctantly, 'But thank you for offering.'

'You will take her?'

'Yes, I'll take her.'

A sudden breeze ruffled her hair and she shivered, realizing for the first time that she had no jacket. She turned to go, then looked back at him.

'My sister met a friend of yours last week,' she said on impulse. And, as he raised his eyebrows, she added, 'Selina O'Toole.'

The lighted hall was behind him and she couldn't see his face, but the tremor that shook him was unmissable. She continued down the path, crossed the road, and had started back along the opposite pavement before he closed the door.

'Rona, it's me again.'

'You're not going to hang up on me, are you?'

'No, sorry about that. Listen – Philip Yarborough just pushed Adele down the stairs!'

'*What?*'

'He wasn't even going to take her to the hospital, but I more or less made him.'

'You – Lindsey, for Pete's sake slow down! Start at the beginning.'

Rona listened in growing incredulity to her sister's account. 'Is she badly hurt?'

'He says not, but if you ask me, it's a wonder she's not dead! He admitted he was upstairs himself at the time.'

'Admitted, or told you?'

'Whatever. What should we do?'

'There's nothing we *can* do. Are you sure he took her to the hospital?'

'Yes; at least, he took her *somewhere*. I waited at my window till I saw his car leave.' She gave a little shudder. 'When I got back, the front door was wide open, as, of course, I'd left it. Anyone could have got in.'

'In that small cul-de-sac, with you standing at the entrance to it?'

'OK, OK; I'm just a bit jumpy at the minute. I searched the flat, but all was well.' Lindsey paused. 'It looks as though Max was right, doesn't it? About Philip? Are you going to tell him?'

'I don't know. I suppose so. Linz, about Hugh—'

'Oh, and I told Philip you knew Selina,' Lindsey interrupted.

169

There was a moment's silence. Then Rona said, 'So not only do you appear on his doorstep at a decidedly inopportune moment, but you make references to a past he'd much rather forget. What was it you said, about not wanting to be murdered in your bath? You're certainly going the right way about it! God, Lindsey, for all we know, he could have killed Gemma!' She paused. 'How did he react?'

'He shivered,' Lindsey said sulkily, 'but I left before he could say anything.'

'Brilliant!'

'Oh, come on! You *said* I was in a better position to tackle him!'

'But under controlled conditions.'

Lindsey gave a snort. 'You sound like a scientist!'

'Well, he now knows we're aware of the Gemma connection.' As does Jonathan, Rona thought; had she herself been equally irresponsible? 'Just watch your back, that's all.'

She was taking a ready meal out of the freezer when, once more, she was interrupted by the phone.

Not Lindsey *again*! she thought in exasperation as she caught it up. 'Yes? What now?'

A voice said with mild amusement, 'Sounds as though you were expecting me!'

'I'm sorry,' she apologized automatically, registering that this time it had been her mobile that rang. 'I thought my sister . . .' Her voice trailed off as, belatedly, she identified her caller of that morning.

'Yes, it's me again,' he confirmed. 'I was wondering if you'd had second thoughts about our meeting? It really would be to your advantage.'

'I'm sorry. There've been so many replies, I had to take the decision to see no one personally.' It sounded a reasonable enough excuse.

'Learned anything interesting?'

'Several things, yes.' Again, not strictly accurate.

'Nothing as good as what I have, I bet.'

'Then tell me. Otherwise, I must ask you not to call again.'

He gave a low laugh that raised the hairs on the back of her neck. 'Oh, I'll be keeping in touch, I assure you. Sooner or later, curiosity will get the better of you.' And he broke the connection.

The next time the phone rang, when she was halfway through her meal, she made no move to answer it. The machine clicked on, and after her own message, Tess Chadwick's voice filled the room. 'Hi, Rona. Nothing urgent; I just wondered how things were going.'

She lifted the phone. 'Sorry, Tess; this is the fourth call I've had in about forty minutes, and the last one was a bit dodgy.'

'How so?'

'Some bloke wanting to meet me, and not taking no for an answer.'

'About Gemma?'

'Yes. He won't say what it is on the phone.'

'Then forget it,' Tess said briskly. 'I was ringing to see what kind of response you'd had. I presume you saw the letters last week?'

'Yes; Selina won't be pleased at being dragged into it.'

'Did she agree to meet you?'

'Not only that, I spent the night with her!' Rona explained what had happened. 'Thanks so much for the intro, Tess. Once she realized Gemma's daughter was involved, she was great. She's even passing on a few of Gemma's possessions that she's come across. Nothing vital,' she added, 'but it'll be interesting all the same.'

'So you owe me a meal,' Tess said.

'Which I'll be delighted to honour on my next visit.'

'Anything on emigrating families?'

'Nothing worth following up. Quite honestly, I don't think I've a cat in hell's chance of finding the father.'

'Which leaves the murderer,' Tess said caustically. 'Is that part of your brief?'

'It was suggested,' Rona answered tightly, 'but I didn't take it on.'

171

Tess gave a low laugh. 'Why don't I believe you?'

When she'd rung off, Rona tipped the remains of the cold food into the bin and switched on the kettle. *Had* Lindsey put them both in danger, by challenging Philip Yarborough? Had she, with Jonathan Hurst? This, she reflected, was what both Max and Dinah had warned her against: keep well clear of any murder hunt. And yet, even if she were successful in finding the father, she'd feel she'd accomplished only half her task if the murder remained unsolved.

What could possibly have been the motive for Gemma's death? None had ever been established. The flat had been searched, but as far as could be seen, nothing taken. Had the intruder been interrupted? Or panicked on finding someone at home? Even so, there'd been no need to *murder* her. On the other hand, had he – or she – come specifically to kill Gemma, in which case the cursory search was a red herring? But for heaven's sake, *why*?

The kettle whistled, startling Rona out of her reverie, and she made the coffee. It had been an eventful day: two calls from this unknown man; lunch with Max and James Latymer; Hugh's reported reappearance on the scene, then the business with the Yarboroughs – Adele allegedly falling downstairs, and Lindsey challenging Philip over Selina. And it was only Monday! she thought humorously.

'Come on, Gus,' she said, picking up her coffee mug, 'let's go and watch some mindless television. I've had enough of the real world.'

Twelve

The next morning when, having contacted the O'Tooles, Rona set off for Chilswood, she had still not told Max about Adele. It was cold and misty, already more than halfway through October, and her deadline for this project was November the twelfth. Why, she wondered despairingly, had she ever taken it on? At least she'd switched off her mobile before leaving home; she'd no intention of being harassed yet again by her anonymous but persistent caller.

Chilswood was known for its thriving industrial estate, rather than as a desirable place to live. The town itself had been designed in grids of parallel roads full of small semis, each with a patch of garden front and back. To Rona's jaundiced eye, they seemed to have no distinguishing features.

She pulled up outside that corresponding to the address Selina had given, walked up the path and rang the bell. It was opened by a small woman in a neat jumper and skirt, who gave her a shy smile.

'Well now, Miss Parish, isn't it?' She spoke with a lilting brogue entirely divorced from Selina's rasping tones. Had her daughter deliberately shed her accent when she made first radio and then television her career? 'Could I offer you a cup of tea, since you've driven all this way?'

Rona returned her smile. 'It's not that far, Mrs O'Toole, and I don't want to put you to any trouble.'

'Sure, it's no trouble. Isn't the kettle already boiling, since you said you'd be here at eleven?'

'Then thank you, that's very kind.'

173

Everything in the house seemed to be as small and neat as its mistress, including the elderly man who rose to his feet as Rona was shown into the front room. He was wearing an obviously home-knitted Fair Isle sweater and corduroy trousers and looked, Rona thought facetiously, like a leprechaun, with his red hair and puckish face.

'My husband,' Mrs O'Toole introduced – though he could hardly be anyone else. 'This is Selina's friend, Miss Parish, Dermot.'

He shook her hand gravely, with an old-fashioned little bow. 'A pleasure to meet you, miss.'

'Selina told us you're looking into that old murder,' Mrs O'Toole said, pouring the tea.

'For Gemma's daughter, yes,' Rona replied, feeling the need to defend herself.

'A terrible thing it was.'

Rona took her tea with a murmur of thanks. 'Did you ever meet Gemma?'

Man and wife shook their heads, and Dermot, seeming to feel an explanation was called for, offered one. 'Stokely's a long way from here, Miss Parish, and we'd no car. Selina came home every month or so, but we never visited her.' He accepted the bun his wife passed him. 'When the – tragedy happened, we were worried she might be next, and tried every which way to get her out of the flat, but she wouldn't budge. "It's my home," she said.'

'How long did she stay there after Gemma died?' Rona enquired.

'A year or so, wasn't it, Kathleen? Till she married that chap, anyway.'

Selina's first husband; Rona wondered who he was, but didn't like to ask. Had he, she wondered suddenly, been one of the tennis-club crowd? And if so, could that be important?

She said tentatively, 'I suppose Gemma must have known him?'

'For sure she would, for wasn't he her boss at the time?'

'He worked at County Radio?' At least that exonerated the group.

'That's right.'

In all conscience she could ask no more. In any case, it felt uncomfortably like checking up on Selina, which had not been her intention. Finishing her tea, she rose to her feet.

'I believe you've some things of Gemma's for me?'

'Yes, they're ready waiting on the hall stand. But will you not take another cup, before you go?'

'Thank you, no. That was very welcome, but I must be on my way.'

Out in the hall, Mrs O'Toole handed her an old shoe box. 'Not much to show for a life, is it, now?'

'Nevertheless, her daughter will be pleased to have it.'

She nodded, satisfied. 'That's as it should be.'

They stood side by side on the step, waiting to wave her off, and Rona wondered what they made of their daughter's high-profile lifestyle. She reckoned it had done little to change their own, and perhaps, as Mrs O'Toole had said, that was as it should be.

Lindsey sat nervously in the Gallery Café, watching the street below. Hugh, sounding surprised to hear from her, had not been free for lunch, as she'd suggested, but had promised to slip out for a quick cup of coffee. She wished he'd hurry; she had to be back in her own office in half an hour. Then she caught sight of him approaching from the direction of Windsor Way, watched him glance at his watch and cross the road towards her. Minutes later he appeared in the doorway and made his way over to her table, looking slightly apprehensive.

'This is a surprise,' he said as he seated himself. 'What's it all about?'

Lindsey waited till the pre-ordered coffee had been brought and poured. Then she looked up and met his eyes, trying to ignore the insistent pounding of her blood. Damn him, why did he always affect her like this?

'I want to know why you asked after my parents.'

He reddened. 'Oh God, I hoped you'd forgotten that.'

She leant forward. 'So there *was* something! I knew it!'

'Look, Lindsey, it's none of my business and I don't want to be the bearer of tales. If your parents are well, as you said, then fine. Let's leave it at that.'

'Not good enough, I'm afraid.'

He said, 'That was Jonathan Hurst you were with, wasn't it?'

Her heart missed a beat. 'You know him?'

'By sight. We've attended some of the same dinners. You two an item?'

'No,' she answered with deliberation, 'we work together.'

He smiled, and she said angrily, 'You're changing the subject! What do you mean, the bearer of tales?'

He drank his coffee without replying.

'Hugh!'

'I've missed you, Lindsey,' he said.

She caught her breath. 'There wasn't much sign of it, the last time I saw you.'

He looked puzzled. 'Yesterday?'

'No, in Sainsbury's.'

After a minute his face cleared. 'Oh, that was Sally Armitage, the wife of the chap I was staying with while I flat-hunted.' He paused, and added in partial explanation, 'I was still angry with you at the time.'

All that jealousy for nothing! Ignoring his last sentence, she said more calmly, 'Presumably you found one? A flat?'

'Yes, in Talbot Road. Quite pleasant, and handy for the office.'

Lindsey set down her cup. 'Hugh, we've fenced round this long enough, and we haven't much time. Tell me what you know about my parents.'

He sighed. 'You might regret hearing it.'

'Let me be the judge.'

'I wouldn't normally have mentioned it, but I was thrown at seeing you, and casting around for something to say.'

'I'm waiting.'

'Look, I like your father. I wouldn't—'

'What about my father?'

Hugh looked down at the table. 'All right, but don't shoot the messenger, OK? I saw him one weekend, at Penbury Court.'

'So?'

'With – someone who wasn't your mother.'

Lindsey stared at him, and something in her expression caused him to lay a hand quickly over hers. She snatched it away.

'Who was it?'

'God, I don't know! His accountant, perhaps – a long-lost cousin?'

Lindsey swallowed. 'What were they doing?'

'Walking along by the lake.' He paused, met her eyes and looked away again. 'Arm in arm.'

'Catherine Bishop,' Lindsey said under her breath.

'You *know* about her? All this twisting my arm, and you knew all along?'

'Suspected, not knew. Rona saw them once.'

'But – everything's all right at home?'

'Not so that you'd notice,' she said grimly.

'God, I am sorry.'

'Well, it wouldn't be the first broken marriage in the family.'

He said steadily, 'Nothing is broken beyond repair.'

Her eyes filled with tears. 'Stop it, Hugh.'

'I still love you.'

'*Stop* it!' She drank her coffee quickly, burning her tongue. 'I must be going,' she said hurriedly, pushing back her chair.

'Leaving me to pick up the tab as usual?'

She looked at him quickly, saw he was smiling. 'Thanks for agreeing to come.'

'Any excuse, Lindsey. You know that.'

She picked up her handbag and fled.

* * *

177

Out on the pavement, she attempted to clear her head. She hadn't time, now, to ponder the subtext of Hugh; it was her father who loomed, large and suddenly threatening, in her thoughts. How *could* he? she thought chokingly. Mum had made an effort – she really had – and all the time . . . It struck her that she'd not asked Hugh *when* he'd seen them, but thinking back, it must have been that Saturday Mum was off playing bridge. Before their shopping trip, then; perhaps her new image had made him think again?

She must get back to the office, but she'd phone Rona later, see what she thought. Still turning over possibilities, Lindsey hurried to keep her appointment.

Since she'd stopped on the way back to let Gus have a run, it was one thirty before Rona reached home. She carried the shoe box downstairs and put it on the kitchen table while she took out biscuits, cheese, and a bottle of mineral water for her lunch. Then, with a feeling of anticipation, she sat down and removed the lid.

Her first impression was that what lay inside resembled the contents of a drawer that had been tipped unceremoniously into the box. Which, quite likely, was precisely what it was. There were bottles of congealed nail polish in various colours; a couple of lipsticks, a crumpled bus ticket, an appointment card from the baby clinic. And, as Selina had told her, several airmail letters from Joyce Cowley – or Joyce Grant, as she had then been. Rona hesitated, uncomfortable about reading them, but it was possible she'd find something Selina had missed.

Her guilt was short-lived; there was nothing personal in these letters, and though they all began 'Dear Gemma' and ended 'Affectionately, Mother', little enough affection was shown in them. Indeed, they could have passed as official accounts of life in South Africa – fauna, flora, politics, climate, and a series of social engagements. Nonetheless, though according to Joyce she'd never received a reply, each one had been read over and over; the ink was smudged, and the thin paper had come apart along the creases. Rona wondered uneasily how Zara would react to this stilted, one-sided correspondence.

Only the last letter showed any maternal concern:

> It was good to speak to you the other evening, and to know you and the baby are well. I'm only sorry you didn't tell me you were expecting her. I must urge you, though, to try to contact the father. He has a duty to contribute to her upkeep. In the meantime, please let me know if there's anything you need.

Thoughtfully Rona spread cheese on a biscuit. That final letter was dated 17th December 1978; Joyce must have phoned immediately she received the Christmas card announcing Amanda's birth. She thought of the tanned, muscular woman bracing herself to meet them, and felt the first stirring of pity. Despite her new husband and opulent lifestyle, she would always be haunted by her daughter's death – and perhaps by that daughter's loss, long before she died.

It wasn't until Rona went to the fruit bowl in search of dessert that she noticed the answerphone was registering two messages. She'd been so absorbed when she came in that, unusually, she hadn't checked. She pressed the button and Lindsey's indignant voice filled the room.

'Rona, where the hell *are* you? Your mobile's switched off; I left a message on it – haven't you checked? I need to speak to you urgently – about Pops. Please ring me as soon as you get this.'

The second message, timed fifteen minutes later, at twelve twenty, was more brief. 'I can't wait any longer. I'm going to see him.'

Rona frowned and dialled Chase Mortimer. Miss Parish, she was told, was still at lunch. And, possibly in a fit of tit-for-tat, her mobile, too, was switched off.

Rona stood uneasily at the counter. What was that all about?

179

I'm going to see him. Pops, presumably. Had he been taken ill? What had happened?

Normally, she'd have gone straight round to the bank to ensure all was well; but for some time now there'd no longer been that easy relationship between them and she'd have felt awkward, as though she were checking up on him. Instead, she lifted the phone and rang through, only to learn that Mr Parish was in a meeting. Yes, she was told in answer to her diffident query, he was perfectly well.

Slightly reassured, Rona replaced the phone. No doubt she'd learn in due course what had upset Lindsey. She glanced at the box on the table. There were still the cassettes and a few cards lying at the bottom of it, but she no longer felt like going through them. Instead, she decided to go up to the study; there were some personal items to deal with – bank statements to check, an insurance policy to renew. Just for the moment, she'd had enough of Gemma Grant.

She made herself some coffee and took it up with her, put the mug on her desk, and switched on the computer to check her emails. There were a couple from friends, one from her editor with the reminder that a new biography was overdue, and—

Rona sat staring at the message on the screen, aware of spreading coldness. The sender was identified by numbers rather than a name, the addressee was shown, correctly, as Rona's own anonymous byline, and the subject, in capital letters, read GEMMA GRANT.

Mesmerized, Rona's eyes read and reread the brief message below: *Let sleeping dogs lie, or they may wake up and bite.*

Tom sat at his desk, secure in the knowledge that he wouldn't be disturbed. Mavis had been instructed to tell all callers he was unavailable – he didn't care how she did it. *Oh my God,* he kept saying to himself, *Oh my God!*

There had been the briefest of warnings: 'Your daughter

would like a word, Mr Parish,' followed immediately by Lindsey's precipitous entrance. And the door had barely closed behind her before she'd started lashing into him – there was no other way to describe it – furious, tearful, above all accusatory. 'How could you do it?' she kept crying, 'Oh Pops, how *could* you?'

It was some time before he'd calmed her enough to discover what she was talking about, but then all his worst fears consolidated. He and Catherine had been seen – by Hugh, of all people. Despite their almost paranoid discretion, their secret was now exposed, and all the people he loved most would be wounded by it. He put his head in his hands. God, if only this could have waited till after his retirement, he thought, and was immediately ashamed of his selfishness. Though a delay would have benefited him, it wouldn't have lessened the pain caused to others.

Rona! he thought suddenly. Surprisingly, Lindsey hadn't mentioned her, and in the midst of trauma he'd not thought to ask. Why hadn't she come? Had she washed her hands of him completely? As for Lindsey, she wouldn't be silenced until he suggested meeting them both in the bar of the Clarendon at six o'clock, when, he promised, they'd be given a full explanation. In the meantime, he had to go home and tell Avril.

A kind of paralysis had hold of him, slowing down both brain and body, but, mastering it with an effort, he dialled Catherine's number. It was a part of this nightmare that he reached only her answering machine.

'We were seen at Penbury,' he said flatly into it. 'I'm meeting the girls later to explain the position, and am now going home to tell Avril. I'll be in touch later.' He paused. In films, they ended phone calls by saying 'I love you', which he'd always thought inappropriate and somehow un-English.

'I love you,' he said.

He put both hands on his desk, levered himself to his feet, and made his way to the banking hall. Mavis half-rose on seeing him, and he went over to her. 'I shan't be back today,' he said. 'Would you cancel my three o'clock appointment, with apologies, and reschedule it?'

'Are you all right, Mr Parish?' Her plain, kindly face was concerned, and he wondered a little hysterically what he looked like.

'Yes, thank you. I'll see you in the morning,' he said.

Jonathan came quickly into Lindsey's office, closing the door behind him.

'For God's sake,' he burst out, 'what's the matter?'

She bit her lip. 'Nothing. Why?'

'Don't give me that. You've been crying, haven't you? Is it your ex? Does he know about me?'

Lindsey raised her head and regarded him blankly. 'It might surprise you to know,' she said slowly, 'that my entire world doesn't revolve round you. I have other interests and other concerns.'

'There's no need to take that attitude. I want to know if I'm to be on my guard, that's all.'

'*Be* on your guard, then, if it makes you feel better.'

He leant towards her, his hands on her desk. 'What's the *matter* with you? If people see you in that state, they'll start wondering.'

'And *what* they'll wonder is, why you've come hot-foot to my office.'

He stared at her.

'Jonathan, believe me, it's nothing to do with you. I've had some – rather distressing family news, that's all.'

'Oh.' His relief was evident. 'Right – well, I'm sorry. I'll call you later, then.' And he hurriedly left the room.

Back in his own office, Jonathan took out a handkerchief and wiped the sweat from his face. *Get a grip!* he told himself. Otherwise, as he'd warned Lindsey, people *would* start wondering, but about something else altogether. The truth was he'd been jittery ever since that infernal dinner with her family. Gemma Grant, for God's sake, after

182

twenty-five years! Surely it wasn't going to come out after all this time?

Lindsey, having instantly dismissed him from her mind, was on the phone to Rona, who this time had answered on the first ring.

'Lindsey! What's happened? I phoned the bank, and they said Pops is OK.'

'Oh yes,' Lindsey said dully, 'Pops is just dandy!'

'What does that mean?'

'Hugh saw him with the Bishop woman.'

There was a splintered silence. Rona said, 'When, and where?'

'At Penbury, when Mum went to the bridge tournament.'

'Linz – you didn't . . . ? Oh God, what have you done?'

'*Me*?'

'You said you were going round there. You didn't confront him with it?'

'Too right I did! We've been pussyfooting around this far too long.'

'But why didn't you wait for me? I—'

'I tried, you know I did, but you were firmly incommunicado. Anyway, the long and the short of it is he wants us both to be at the Clarendon at six this evening.'

'Does Mum know?' Rona asked after a minute.

'I think he was going straight home, to tell her.' Lindsey's voice shook, and Rona realized that her sister's sympathies lay entirely with their mother. 'Call for me at the office,' she added. 'We can wait here till six.'

'Linz . . .'

'What?'

'Don't be too hard on him. It can't be easy.'

Lindsey made a strangled sound and put down the phone.

Avril was in the back garden, pruning the roses. Thank God this wasn't one of her bridge or charity afternoons.

She turned in surprise as he came out of the back door.

'What are you doing home at this time?' Then, taking stock of him, 'Is something wrong?'

'You might say so. I've – something to tell you. Could you come inside?'

She raised her chin. 'I'd rather stay out here, thanks.'

He looked at her in anguish, all the rehearsed sentences deserting him. By some freak of chance, with her new hair-style wind-blown and a streak of soil on her face, she looked as he remembered her from years back, and his tactful, placatory words clogged in his throat.

'There's no easy way to say this,' he began miserably.

'You're leaving me.'

It was a statement rather than a question, and when he made no reply, she added, 'When, and for whom?'

He said gently, 'Are you sure you wouldn't rather come indoors?'

'Quite sure.'

'Avril, I'm so sorry. This isn't what I intended.'

'You haven't answered my questions.'

'Her name is Catherine Bishop. She's a client at the bank.'

'The woman who helped Rona?'

'Yes. As to when, I don't know. This has all blown up before we were ready.'

'How inconvenient for you. Do the girls know?'

'As of this morning. Hugh saw us together.'

'*Hugh?* Surely he and Lindsey aren't . . . ?'

'No; they apparently met by chance, at a pub.'

'So, as the cliché has it, I'm the last to know. Even Hugh had the advantage of me.'

'It wasn't what—'

'—you intended. No, so you said. Does that make it better?'

He passed a hand over his face. He wasn't sure how he'd pictured this conversation, but it hadn't been like this. He'd expected her to lash out as Lindsey had done, to be bitter, contemptuous. Instead, she was speaking in this clipped voice, entirely without expression.

'No wonder you didn't want to plan a world trip,' she said.

And then, to his horror, her eyes filled, the tears immediately spilling over to run down her cheeks. She made no move to wipe them away, simply stood, still clutching the secateurs, gazing at him like an abandoned child, and he felt a clutch of his old, protective love for her. When had he last seen her cry?

He moved convulsively forward, but she gave a small shake of her head and he stopped. 'Please let me take you inside. I can't leave you here.'

'That's something you'll have to get used to,' she said.

'We need to talk.'

'Yes, but not now. Please go.'

He said helplessly, 'But I've taken the rest of the afternoon off. I thought—'

'I don't want you here.'

'Avril . . . '

She turned her head away and, after a moment, despairingly, he went back into the house.

Rona and Lindsey sat in the office while the rest of the staff closed down their machines, tidied their papers, and, one by one, went home. Rona's mind was oscillating between the forthcoming meeting with their father, when she'd be forced to face what she'd been hiding from for months, and the ominous, inexplicable email that awaited her at home.

She glanced at her twin, tense behind her desk, and, more to distract her than for any other reason, asked suddenly, 'Do you know my email address?'

Lindsey stared at her. 'Whatever brought that up?'

'Do you?'

'No, of course I don't. When have I ever needed to send you an email?'

'Like to hazard a guess at it?'

'For heaven's sake, Rona! This isn't the time to play games!'

'It's not a game, I assure you.'

Lindsey frowned. 'All right, I'll humour you. It's probably

something like "Rona-dot-Parish at something-dot-net". Or "com". I never know the difference.' She threw Rona a challenging look. 'Well, am I close?'

'No, actually. My name doesn't come into it.'

'How clandestine! So, are you going to tell me why we're going through this pointless exercise?'

'I received an email this morning; I don't know who it's from, because the sender was identified by numbers rather than a name, but he had *my* address off pat, and I'm wondering how he got hold of it.'

'Well, from the *Gazette*, surely?'

'No, that gave my mobile number, and I never fill it in on forms, in case I get a load of spam.'

'So what was the message?'

'I thought you'd never ask,' Rona said drily. 'It was headed "Gemma Grant", and it said, "Let sleeping dogs lie, or they may wake up and bite."'

'Oh God!' Lindsey said in a whisper.

'Funnily enough, Zara's father used the same phrase, right back at the beginning.'

'Could *he* have sent it?'

Rona shook her head. 'No, I'm sure not. It's just a macabre coincidence.'

'Mightn't be a bad maxim to follow, all the same,' Lindsey commented. 'Have you no way of tracing it?'

'I don't see how; I went right through my address book, but, hardly surprisingly, it's not listed.'

'Will you reply?'

Rona shuddered. 'And say what? God, Lindsey, what with someone lurking among my emails and harassment on my mobile, I'm between a rock and a hard place. I want nothing to do with either of these creeps, but I'm not sure I can avoid them.'

'Does Max know?'

'Not about the email; it only came this morning.'

'You're having quite a day, aren't you?' Lindsey commented sympathetically.

'I am indeed. Speaking of which, it's almost six. We'd better go.'

They stood up and moved together towards the door. On reaching it, they turned spontaneously to each other – as happened sometimes – and exchanged a hug. Then, side by side, they went to meet their father.

Thirteen

Tom was waiting for them in the lounge bar, Lindsey's gin and Rona's vodka on the table in front of him. He stood as they approached, smiling uncertainly, and Rona, with a tightening of the throat, went to him quickly and kissed him, feeling his hands grip her arms.

'Hi, Pops,' she said quietly. Lindsey said nothing, merely seated herself in front of her drink.

'Thank you for coming,' he said formally.

It was a fairly large room and theirs was a corner table, with no one within earshot. Half a dozen men on bar stools were discussing football, and a couple sat holding hands at a far table. Strangely, the three disparate groups seemed to emphasize the room's essential emptiness.

As the awkward silence lengthened, Rona broke it by saying, 'Mrs Bishop said you ran her to Stokely hospital.'

Tom nodded, raised his glass to them, and they all drank.

'And I saw you with her in Barrington Road,' Rona continued. Lindsey frowned and shook her head, but Tom answered steadily, 'Yes, I thought you must have.'

Lindsey put her glass down. 'So when did this affair start?'

Tom winced. 'It's not an affair in the accepted sense. I'd like to make that clear.'

'Meaning you haven't slept with her?'

Rona moved protestingly, but Tom answered, 'Exactly.'

'Well, I'm sure that's very moralistic and all that, but it doesn't help Mum, does it?' Lindsey took a sip of her drink. 'How did she take it?'

'With dignity,' Tom replied. 'Look, I asked you both here

188

so I could tell you as simply as possible how this came about and how we intend to deal with it. It would help, Lindsey, if you could keep any further comments until I've finished.'

So he told them, those two solemn-faced daughters of his, of his growing unhappiness in his marriage – which he'd felt to be mutual. 'We loved each other very much at one time,' he said sadly, 'but somehow it got lost along the way and we finished by continually rubbing each other the wrong way.' He was being generous there, Rona thought. 'It reached the stage when I almost dreaded going home each evening, and with my retirement looming – well, frankly, I started to panic.'

'And then you met Mrs Bishop.'

'Yes, then I met Catherine, and – I don't know – it was a tonic just to be with her. Her outlook was so positive, and I found I could relax with her when I couldn't any longer with your mother. As you say, I ran her to the hospital, and that rather threw us together. Then, as a thank you, she invited me to an exhibition at the National Gallery – *Pissarro in London.*'

'It didn't occur to her to invite Mum too, I suppose?' Lindsey's voice dripped with sarcasm.

'Actually, she did; she'd bought the tickets for her son and his wife, but in the circumstances they obviously couldn't go. She offered them both to me, but God knows, your mother doesn't make any secret of her opinion of art – that looking at dried paint is no more interesting than watching it dry.' He smiled briefly. 'I always marvel at Max's restraint when she trots that one out. So, we went together, and our friendship just – went on from there. And it *was* friendship, for quite a while. When we realized how it was developing, each of us tried to draw back at different times, but—'

'It was bigger than both of you.'

'You're not making this any easier, Lindsey.'

'Why should I?' Her voice shook. 'Didn't you even *notice* Mum's efforts to make things right again? Her new clothes and make-up and hairstyle?'

'Yes, love, I noticed,' Tom said gently, 'and I know you helped her in that. But sadly it was too late.'

189

Lindsey's teeth fastened in her lip, and Rona said quickly, 'So what's going to happen?'

'Well, this has all blown up sooner than we expected. What I *had* thought was that once I'd retired, I'd take a flat somewhere till the divorce went through.'

'Why not save yourself the trouble and move in with your lady love? By that time, everyone will know about her.'

'Because I respect her, and I want to do things properly,' he said, and Lindsey was silenced.

'And now?' Rona prompted after a minute.

'It depends on your mother. We haven't discussed any details yet. If she wants me to move out at once, of course I shall. Look, twins, I really am sorry. Not for having met Catherine, but for the inevitable pain it will cause all round. When things have calmed down a little, you must meet her. I'm sure you'd find—'

'*No!*' Lindsey said violently.

'Rona?' There was pleading in his voice.

'I have met her, Pops, as you know. I – liked her very much at first.'

'And now?'

'Give me time. I – don't want to add to Mum's hurt.'

'Of course not.' Suddenly, he could take no more. This meeting had used up all his reserves, and he desperately needed to see Catherine.

'I have to go now,' he said quickly, 'but there's no need for you to; I'll order more drinks on the way out. Thank you for listening so patiently. I'll keep you up to date with developments.'

He bent and kissed each of them on the cheek. They watched in silence as he paused at the bar, indicated their table to the barman, and handed over some cash. Then, with a lifted hand, he was gone.

'I'll ring Mum,' Lindsey said, and took out her mobile. 'It's pretty obvious he's not going home. We could call round and give her a bit of support.'

But Avril, sounding calm and philosophical, didn't want company. 'It's sweet of you, darling,' she said – a rare endearment – 'but I'm not ready to talk about it yet. I'll phone you when I am.'

Having been furnished with fresh drinks, Rona and Lindsey found little to say. They, too, needed space to come to terms with what they'd heard, and they left only minutes later, separating on the pavement with a quick hug and promising to contact each other the next day.

Rona went straight to Farthings, just round the corner from the hotel. But when she let herself in to the little house, it was to find it silent and empty, and she stood in the hallway feeling suddenly desolate. It was six forty-five, and Max's class started at seven thirty. Where was he, when she really needed him – to discuss not only the sorry story of her parents' marriage, but the threatening email that still lurked at the back of her mind? A dose of her husband's common sense would have been a welcome antidote to the worries that tormented her.

Since there was no help for it, she scrawled a note and propped it on the kitchen counter before setting off through the misty darkness for home.

As it happened, though, both those topics, still exercising her when she took delivery of the take-away she'd ordered, had been superseded by the time she finished it.

Again, the news came via her mobile. She answered it with bad grace, regretting not having switched it off for the night, and a woman's voice said without preamble, 'Was it you asking about families from the Stokely area, who went to Australia?'

Instantly, lethargy vanished. 'Yes, yes it was.'

'I might be able to help you, then.' A light laugh reached her. 'It was pure chance I saw it – we don't take the *Gazette*, but it was wrapped round some vegetables I bought at the market, and when I took them out for supper, it caught my eye.'

191

Rona wasn't interested in vegetables. 'Thank you so much for phoning, Mrs . . . ?'

'Powell,' the woman supplied. 'Yes, well, as I was saying, Dr Morris and his family emigrated in the spring of '78, and they lived in Stokely.'

'Morris?' Rona interrupted sharply. 'Not Morrison?'

Her caller sounded surprised. 'No, it was Morris, all right. He was my friend's GP.'

'How old was he at the time?'

'Goodness me – let me think, now. Late forties, I suppose. He had two grown lads, at any rate.'

Rona's heart was racing. 'And the whole family went? Do you know whereabouts in Australia?'

'Can't help you on that one, dear. Anyway, though the doctor and his wife stayed on – she has family out there – the boys came home about ten years ago. They're both medics too, one's a doctor and the other a dentist. Clever family.'

'This is wonderful, Mrs Powell,' Rona said sincerely. 'Just what I was hoping for! I suppose you don't know where they are now?'

'As it happens, I do,' the woman replied with satisfaction. 'I thought you'd ask that, so I rang my friend – the one who was their father's patient – to check. She says they're both practising in Exeter. You'd find them in the telephone directory.' She paused. 'You think one of them might be that girl's father?'

'It's possible,' Rona answered guardedly. 'At least you've given me a new line to follow, and I'm very grateful.'

When she rang off, Rona sat for some minutes staring into space. Then she rummaged in her bag, extracted her diary, and looked up Selina's number.

'Well, hello there!' said the well-remembered voice, when she'd identified herself. 'Did you collect the goodies?'

Rona's eyes went to the shoe box, still on the far side of the table. 'Yes, I did, thanks, but I've not had time to go through them properly. Selina – is there the slightest chance that Gemma's lover's name was Morris, not Morrison?'

'Not the faintest,' Selina replied promptly. 'God, she spoke of him often enough.' Pause, then: 'Why?'

'A woman's just phoned with news that a family named Morris emigrated at precisely the crucial time.'

'Well, sorry to put a damper on it, but you're barking up the wrong tree.'

'Suppose they added the "son" to disguise his real name?'

'Too close for comfort, surely?'

Rona thought for a minute. 'I presume you told the police about Morrison, at the time?'

'Naturally; they were convinced I knew more, but that was all I could give them.'

And, Rona concluded reluctantly, it seemed it was all she could give her, too.

She made two more phone calls before abandoning the search for the night – to the Fairchilds, who had never heard of the Morris family, and to Joyce Cowley, who had.

'Of course I remember Dr Morris,' she said. 'He was our GP.'

'Did you know his sons?'

'Only by sight. Nice boys.'

Rona hesitated. 'Might Gemma have known them?'

'Miss Parish, I thought I'd explained how little I knew of my daughter's friends.' She paused, and her voice changed. 'Or are you wondering if one of them could be Zara's father?'

'It had crossed my mind,' Rona said drily.

'Well, at least it ties in with Australia. Please let me know of any developments.'

Like hell I will! Rona thought, replacing the phone on its charger. It promptly rang again. Max, making his regular evening call. Rona glanced at the clock, saw it was after ten.

'Sorry I wasn't here when you called,' he said at once, and some hesitancy in his voice drew her brows together.

'Where were you?'

'As it happens, I'd called round to see Adele. Why didn't

you tell me she'd been hurt? You must have known – Lindsey did.'

Rona ignored the question. 'Why did you want to see her?'

'She'd phoned to say she can't come tomorrow, and was there anything she could be preparing for next week. So I took round the notes I'll be handing out. *Why* didn't you tell me, as if I didn't know?'

'It only happened last night, for pity's sake, and there's been so much going on I never got round to it.' She forced herself to ask, 'How is she?'

'Putting a brave face on it. She seems accident-prone, wouldn't you say? I wish to God there was something we could do about it. Anyway, enough of that. You say a lot's been happening your end. What, exactly?'

'That's staggering news about Tom,' he said when she'd told him. 'I'd no idea things had gone that far. What's going to happen now?'

'God knows,' Rona said wearily.

'Poor love, no wonder you were in need of a hug. Sorry I wasn't able to oblige.' His voice sharpened. 'As to that email, is there no way of tracing the sender?'

'Not that I can see.'

'Could it be the man who keeps phoning?'

'I almost hope it is; it would halve my problems.'

'Well, you mightn't know who he is, but by the same token he doesn't know who you are, either.'

'I'm not so sure, since he has my email address.'

'But didn't you post it on the Internet in your initial search?'

Rona drew in her breath sharply. 'I did, didn't I? On the contact site! Nothing came of it, and I'd forgotten all about it.'

'So your correspondent could be anywhere in the world.'

'But to have found my address in the first place, he must have logged on to the site – perhaps after seeing the bit in the paper, which makes him local again.'

'Whatever,' Max said dispiritedly. 'Oh my love, why do you

get involved with these shady characters? It does nothing for my peace of mind.'

'Sorry,' she said.

When he'd rung off, Rona put her solitary plate and glass in the dishwasher, gave Gus his biscuits, and wearily went up to bed. It had been another long day.

And it wasn't yet over. An hour or so later, she came up slowly from the depths of sleep to hear Gus barking hysterically in the hall. Half falling out of bed, she caught up her dressing gown and ran out on to the landing. He was jumping up at the front door, still barking, his claws clicking against the heavy wood.

'Gus! Gus, quiet! What is it?' Slowly, wrapping her dressing gown about her, Rona went barefoot down the stairs, heart clattering. Something – or someone – had woken *this* sleeping dog, she thought. Then she saw it, the little shower of broken glass on the carpet, glinting in the light coming through the fanlight – the broken fanlight; its lower pane, she now saw, had been shattered and the bar twisted out of shape. *But – why?* she thought in confusion.

Careful of her bare feet, Rona approached the dog, took hold of his collar, and led him to the bottom stair, where she sat down and examined each paw in turn, talking to him softly. Finding no trace of glass, she gave him a dismissive pat, but he promptly sat down at her feet, looking at her expectantly.

Her eyes went back to the fanlight. Perhaps whoever it was had tried to break in elsewhere and, finding all ways barred, had smashed it in a fit of frustration. Fort Knox, Lindsey called the house. In the morning, she'd examine the outside for attempts to pick the lock. On the other hand, perhaps the vandal had never intended to break in, merely to issue another warning – that he knew who and where she was.

Rona shuddered. Come *on!* she told herself. She'd read only the other day that there'd been a burglary in the road. Why was she taking this personally? It happened all the time. She stood up, resolving to make herself some hot chocolate and take it back to bed, but had reached only the top of the basement stairs when she halted. She hadn't pulled down the kitchen blinds – she never did – so once she put the light on, she'd be visible to anyone standing on the pavement.

'Bed, Gus,' she said, and waited until, disappointed, he had lolloped obediently down the stairs, before going up herself.

In the morning, Rona, sweeping up the broken glass, considered phoning Max, but decided against it. He would in any case be home that evening. The glass would need replacing, but it wasn't a safety issue; not even a cat could gain access through the gap, even supposing it could reach it, and she'd been unable to detect any scratches round the lock. The breakage was probably, after all, an act of vandalism by mindless drunks on their way home.

It was with held breath that she checked her emails that morning, but there was nothing untoward. Was her unknown correspondent awaiting a reply? And who could it *be*? The man who had killed Gemma, panicking about those sleeping dogs? Or her lover? If he'd returned to this country – one of the Morris boys? – he might now be aware that she'd had his child. How was he likely to react? By coming forward to meet his daughter? Or, with a family of his own, by determining to stay firmly in the background? The latter option seemed much more likely, in which case he wouldn't draw attention to himself by making contact. Nevertheless, reluctant or not, if this elusive father was indeed one of the Morrises, she had every intention of tracking him down.

Five minutes later, via the National Health Local Service Search, she had located both Dr David and Dr Peter Morris, ascertained the addresses of their respective surgeries, and printed out the maps of how to find them. Admittedly, once in Exeter, she could look up their private addresses, but it seemed wiser to tackle them at their surgeries; they'd be unlikely to speak freely at home.

Another five minutes, and she'd booked herself into an Exeter hotel for the following night. At last, it seemed as though she was getting somewhere.

How quiet it was, Avril thought; she'd never noticed before. Once the children had gone to school and people to work, the street seemed to sink into torpor. She'd been sitting here for ten minutes, and not a car or a solitary person had gone past. Normally she'd have been vacuuming the stairs by now, but she couldn't summon up the energy. Why bother? Who would notice? For that matter, who had ever noticed?

She knew she would soon start crying again; she didn't seem to have any control over it, which was one reason why she didn't want to go out. What would people think, if she broke down in the supermarket?

The whole stupid, useless, incomprehensible point, she reflected bitterly, was that, deep down, she still loved Tom – though much good that would do her now. Impossible to remember when or why the nagging had started, but his lack of response had fuelled a growing resentment, spurring her on until she no longer took any interest in herself and evolved into the unprepossessing figure Lindsey had forced her to face. Little wonder Tom had had enough. But – another woman? Never in her wildest imaginings had she considered that possibility. Why had no warning bells sounded, that spring Sunday when Rona first mentioned Catherine Bishop?

Oddly, though, over the last twelve hours it had been the past that had occupied her mind. She thought back, for the first time in years, to her initial meeting with Tom, at the tennis-club hop. She and Kitty Little had been watching him ever since he'd arrived with a crowd of other boys, giggling over how handsome he was. She couldn't believe it when he'd actually come over and asked her to dance. The memory, buried for so long, emerged sharp and clear, undulled by the patina of time. She remembered his shy smile, the blazer he wore with the gold buttons, even the tune they were dancing to – *I don't have a wooden heart.* She'd been most impressed when he sang it in German, but he'd laughed and told her he had the Elvis record. She had been seventeen and he nineteen, and they'd married two years later. Babes in arms, she thought achingly, but they'd been so sure.

How bright the world had seemed then, how full of promise. She used to count the hours each day till they'd see each other, both of them hurrying home from work to be together. Numbly, she realized she couldn't even remember when they had last made love.

The tears were coming, she realized, feeling quickly for a handkerchief. Thank God next week she'd at least have the library to occupy her.

The train journey to Exeter passed pleasantly and, not knowing the city, Rona took a taxi to her hotel. It was mid-afternoon, and as soon as she reached her room, she phoned the number given on the website for David Morris. As she'd expected, she was greeted with a recorded message. 'The surgery is now closed. Surgery hours are weekdays from eight thirty to twelve thirty, and from five to seven in the evening. In the case of emergencies, please ring . . . '

The dental practice, however, was open, and by posing as a prospective patient, Rona elicited the information that it operated between nine and five, with late evenings on Wednesdays and Fridays. Today being Thursday, that last item was of little interest.

In which case, Rona thought, staring down into the busy street, it seemed sensible to approach Peter the dentist first, then hurry to the surgery in time to catch David – who would by then have been apprised of her coming. Also, while she'd ascertained there were only two dentists at the practice, there were likely to be several doctors at the health centre. Better to start where she had less margin for error, since she'd no idea what either of the Morrises looked like.

It was already four o'clock; not knowing how long it would take her, Rona decided to set off at once, taking in some of the sights as she went. She'd promised herself a quick visit to the cathedral, and she would also stop for a cup of tea en route. Taking a pair of flat shoes from her bag and winding a long scarf round her neck against the chilly wind, she set off on her latest quest.

She reached the dental surgery with fifteen minutes to spare. Although it was in a largely residential area, several of the front doors had brass plates alongside. The practice itself occupied a corner site, and, with time in hand, Rona went to inspect the adjacent side street. As she'd hoped, there was a small car park behind the building, with a notice reading, 'Dental staff only' to fend off trespassers. Five cars were parked there; presumably the dental nurses and the receptionist also used the facility. The back door of the building gave on to the car park, so it would be from there that her quarry would emerge.

She regained the front entrance in time to see a woman coming down the path.

'Is Dr Morris still there?' she asked quickly.

The woman smiled at her. 'Yes, he's running a bit late; his last patient's just gone in.'

'Thank you; I was afraid I'd missed him.'

The woman laughed. 'That would take a bit of doing!' she said, and set off along the pavement.

Rona looked after her, puzzled. Then, feeling conspicuous, she began slowly walking up and down the pavement, hands in pockets against the cold and hoping fervently that the last patient had only a fifteen-minute appointment.

Her wish was granted; at five-fifteen precisely the front door opened and a man came hurrying down the path and anxiously peered at the nearest parking meter. Whatever it showed, there was no notice stuck on his windscreen, and he thankfully let himself into the car and drove away. Rona rounded the corner again and positioned herself by the gateway to the car park. Almost at once, two women came out together, talking and laughing. They got into separate cars and Rona strolled on to the next gateway as they emerged on to the road. She'd just regained her position when she saw him come hurrying out – and at once knew what his patient had meant. Peter Morris was, at a guess, six foot six in height, and would indeed be hard to miss.

'Doctor Morris?' she said hesitantly, walking forward. He had reached his car, and turned impatiently, his unfastened tweed coat flapping round his legs.

'I wonder if I could have a word with you?'

'I'm sorry, surgery's over for today. If you'd like to make an appointment—'

'It's on a – personal matter.'

In the rapidly thickening dusk, she saw him frown and peer at her more closely. 'I don't know you, do I?' He had a very faint Australian accent.

'No, but I need to speak to you about someone you did know, some time ago.'

'*Need*, Miss . . . ?'

'Parish,' she supplied. 'Yes, need, Dr Morris. I—'

'Look,' he broke in, 'I've no wish to be rude, but I'm already late and I'm supposed to be meeting my brother. Couldn't—'

'Your brother?' she broke in. 'I was hoping to see him, too.'

'Then I suggest you make some mutually convenient appointment—'

'Dr Morris, I'm only here for the day. I've come specially to meet you both.'

He stared at her, his eyebrows raised in surprise. 'You've—?'

'Please, I really must speak to you. It's important.'

A cold gust of wind swept into the car park, blowing Rona's hair across her face, and she shivered.

He said brusquely, 'Well, if it's that important, and you want to see David too, you'd better come along. You can follow me; presumably your car's at the front?'

'No, I came by train. To Exeter, that is.'

He sighed resignedly and opened the passenger door. 'Get in, then.'

Rona had a brief vision of Max's reaction to her getting

into a car with a man she'd just met, who might be harbouring any number of guilty secrets. But she wouldn't get anywhere if she didn't take risks, and this tall, abrupt dentist surely posed no threat.

The car felt blessedly warm after her long wait on the street. 'I thought he didn't finish till seven,' she said, as Morris switched on the engine. His head swivelled towards her. 'My God, you *have* been doing your homework. As it happens, though, he's not on duty this evening.'

So she'd have wasted her time in going there, Rona reflected.

They didn't speak again as he drove competently down the darkening road towards the city centre. After a few minutes, he turned into the car park of a large hotel.

'We're meeting in the bar,' he said briefly, and she followed him into the warm, lighted building. Barely waiting for her, he strode through the foyer, turned into the bar, and made for the table where his brother was waiting.

'Sorry I'm late, Dave – I overran,' he said tersely. 'Then, in the car park, I came across this young lady, who tells me she's travelled from God knows where especially to meet us.'

'To meet *us*?' David Morris repeated in bewilderment, staring uncomprehendingly at Rona.

'We saved the explanations till we got here, to avoid going through them twice.' Peter paused, also glancing at Rona. 'I suppose I should introduce you, but I don't know you either. Miss Parsons, did you say?'

'Parish – Rona Parish. And I really am grateful for your time.'

His eyes flicked to her wedding ring. 'What are you drinking, Mrs Parish?'

'Vodka with Russchian if they have it. Otherwise, bitter lemon would be fine.'

He lifted an eyebrow and made his way to the bar. Rona turned to David Morris, who was staring at her appraisingly, and gave him a tentative smile. Her first impression was that both were older than she'd expected – foolish, now that she thought of it. But Mrs Powell had spoken of 'the boys', and that was how she'd continued to think of them, forgetting that they'd been boys – or young men – more than twenty years ago. The word 'rugged' applied to them both, she thought, and there was a decided family resemblance, both having thick fair hair and pale lashes over light-blue eyes. She guessed that David was the younger.

Peter reappeared, set glasses on the table, and seated himself. 'You were in luck,' he said shortly, 'they had Russchian. Now, what the hell is this all about?'

Rona took a quick sip of her vodka, aware of two pairs of eyes intent on her face.

'It's about Gemma Grant,' she said.

She looked quickly from one to the other, but if she'd been hoping for some reaction she was disappointed.

'Who?' they demanded in unison.

'Gemma Grant,' she repeated, less certainly. 'From Stokely.'

'*Stokely?*' David exclaimed. 'My God, you're going back a bit, aren't you? We left there twenty-five years ago.'

'To go to Australia. Yes, I know.'

Peter's eyes narrowed. 'You seem to know a hell of a lot about us, young lady, without volunteering any information on yourself. And who the devil is Gemma Grant?'

Oh God, Rona thought. Right – they'd asked, so she'd give them a straight answer. 'She was murdered,' she said, adding above their involuntary exclamations, 'twenty-five years ago.'

There was a pause. Then David said, 'Let me get this clear: are you trying to imply there was some link between us?'

'Surely you knew her?' Rona asked with a touch of desperation. 'At the tennis club, perhaps?'

'Our game was cricket,' Peter replied. 'You say she was murdered: how, why, and by whom?'

'I can only answer the first question: she was strangled in her bath.' Rona braced herself, and added, 'Her baby was in the next room.'

The baby's existence wasn't commented on. 'You're saying they never found who did it?'

'No; she wasn't married, and the baby's father would have been the obvious suspect, except that—'

She broke off. This was harder than she'd anticipated.

'Except?' prompted David.

She took a deep breath. 'Except that she said he'd emigrated to Australia without knowing she was pregnant.'

There was a deep, unfathomable silence, untouched by the noises of the room about them.

'She told people it was one of us?' Peter demanded incredulously.

'No, she refused to name him.'

'Well, it sure as hell wasn't us,' David said explosively. 'We've never even heard of the girl. Anyway, this is ancient history. Why start digging it up now?'

'Because her daughter – the baby who was in the flat at the time – is expecting her own baby, and wants to trace her father.'

'Fair enough, but what in the name of charity put you on to us?'

'I placed an ad in the local paper, asking about families who'd emigrated in '78, and your name came up.'

'And that's all you've got to go on? On the strength of that, you come charging down here, accusing us of God knows what—'

'I'm not accusing you of anything, Dr Morris. I just wanted to know what you remembered of Gemma, that's all.'

'And for that you came all the way from Stokely?'

'Marsborough, actually, but yes.'

'So what are you, a professional people-finder?'

'No, I'm a writer. And don't ask me why I got involved; I've been asking myself that, but it was through the offices of a mutual friend.' *Thanks again, Magda.*

There was another silence, while the brothers exchanged glances and David helplessly lifted his shoulders. Then he said, 'So tell us about this Gemma. What did she do, apart from play tennis?'

'Actually, she didn't even do that. She worked for local radio – a junior reporter. She was only twenty.'

'Just a minute,' Peter interrupted, putting a hand to his head. 'Something's beginning to come back to me.' He turned to his brother. 'Didn't we give an interview to some reporter or other who came to the house? About why we were emigrating and what we were proposing to do in Oz?'

'God, yes,' David said slowly. 'She turned out to be a patient of the old man's. Rather pretty, as I recall.'

Rona's mouth was dry. 'That sounds like Gemma.'

'Well, I'm sorry you've had a wasted journey. *If* that was her, we met her for an hour at most, and by "we" I mean the whole family. There was neither time nor opportunity, even if we'd had the inclination, for either of us to impregnate the girl.'

Another blind alley. Ridiculously, Rona felt close to tears. 'Then I'm sorry to have troubled you.' She started to rise, but Peter reached out and gently pushed her back on her chair. 'Finish your drink, then I'll run you back to where you're staying.'

'Really, there's no need; I've already taken up too much of your time.'

'No argument.' He grinned, looking suddenly younger. 'Wait till I tell Chrissie I was suspected of fathering a love child!'

Rona felt herself flush. 'I do apologize, but by this stage I'm clutching at straws.'

She hastily finished her drink, and despite her protestations Peter Morris, telling his brother he'd be back in five minutes, drove her to her hotel – as it happened, only a couple of streets away.

'I'm so sorry to have caused this upset,' she said again, as he dropped her off. 'Thanks for being so understanding.'

'Don't worry, I'll be dining off this for years!' He sobered. 'Which doesn't mean I'm not sorry about the girl; of course I am. It's a ghastly thing to have happened. Good luck in your hunt.'

*   *   *

Back in her room, Rona phoned Max, who was preparing for his class. 'It was a fiasco,' she ended flatly. 'Still, I suppose it's another possibility ticked off.'

'A long way to go for a tick!' Max responded. 'You sound tired, love. Just relax now, have a good night's sleep, and I'll see you tomorrow.'

Yes, Rona thought, kicking off her shoes, she *was* tired. She could not, she realized, be bothered to wash and change and go down to sit in solitary state in the restaurant. Instead, she'd order room service, and unwind with television.

First, though, for the record, she wrote up the interview with the Morrises while it was fresh in her mind. She hadn't dared suggest recording it.

The evening passed lazily. She enjoyed her meal, and a little later had a leisurely bath. She'd left the television on, and came back into the bedroom as the ten o'clock news was starting. She decided to watch it, and then go to bed.

Half-listening to reports from around the world, she stacked her supper things on the tray and put it, as requested, outside her door. As she closed and locked it behind her, there was a subtle change in the announcer's voice.

'The television interviewer Selina O'Toole is fighting for her life tonight after falling under a bus in Oxford Circus during the rush hour. The kerb was crowded with commuters at the time, and witnesses say she appeared to stumble and fall forward as the bus approached. There has been no official bulletin, but we understand her condition is critical.

'Selina O'Toole began her career—'

Rona heard no more. Stumbling across the room, she half fell on to the bed and stared disbelievingly at the photograph filling the screen, of a Selina vividly, vibrantly, alive. No, she thought, unconsciously shaking her head from side to side, no – there must be some mistake. She hadn't caught the name of the hospital, but it would in any case be useless to phone. For one thing it was too soon, and for another, information is never passed to outsiders.

Carefully, as though it were she herself who'd been injured,

Rona lay back against the pillows and pulled the turned-down sheet over her. She lay unmoving until the news finished, but although the incident was repeated in the closing headlines, there was no further information. Automatically, she reached first for the remote control and then for the light switch. If only, she thought as the room plunged into darkness, she could switch off her thoughts as easily.

Fourteen

It was after midnight before Rona fell asleep, and by five o'clock she was again wide awake. The early hours, she knew, were the most crucial for the seriously ill or injured, when the body's resistance was at its lowest ebb. Had Selina survived them? 'Critical', the newsreader had said, and 'fighting for her life'.

She sat up, turned her pillows over yet again and, despairing of sleep, switched on the light. The hotel room sprang out at her, austere and anonymous, her meagre possessions insufficient to personalize it. It had been, as Peter Morris said, a wasted journey; in fact, the whole enterprise, at this lowering hour of the morning, seemed doomed to failure. It was three weeks to the day since she'd embarked on it, with her visit to the Fairchilds – halfway through the six she had allotted herself. And what had she accomplished? she asked herself despairingly. Virtually nothing. She should never have given in to Zara's pleadings in the first place.

As her mind slid insidiously back to Selina, she reached for the paperback on the bedside table and determinedly opened it.

At six o'clock, having read the same page several times without making sense of it, she switched on the radio, turned low for the sake of fellow guests; but Selina was mentioned only briefly in the news summary, with no update on her condition. At six thirty, unable to remain in bed any longer, Rona made a cup of tea and carried it with her to the bathroom for a shower, gradually cooling the water and tipping her head back so the stinging stream sluiced over her face. But even that failed to revive her; she felt tired, restless and disorientated, longing above all to be home. The card on the dressing table stated that breakfast was served from seven to nine, so that needn't hold her up; however, if she caught a earlier train than she'd intended, there'd be an excess fare to pay. Grimly, she felt it would be worth it.

She had just finished dressing when the telephone shrilled, and Max's voice said, 'I take it you heard about Selina?'

'Oh, Max!' Rona sat on the edge of the bed, blinking back tears. 'It was on the ten o'clock news.'

'I didn't hear till after eleven, too late to phone. You OK?'

'Not really. I'm desperately worried about her.'

'I've been watching the box, and the latest report said she was stable.'

'Is that better than critical?'

'I'd say so. Don't worry, love; she seems a tough cookie.'

'Even a tough cookie is no match for a London bus,' Rona said, but she felt marginally better.

'What time are you due back?'

'I was thinking of catching a commuter train, but I'd have to pay excess.'

'What the hell. Get the first you can, give me a ring when you're on your way, and I'll meet you. Then we'll go somewhere for lunch.'

'Bless you,' she said.

Before leaving the hotel, she checked in her Filofax for the O'Tooles' number, but though the phone rang for a long time, nobody answered it, nor was it intercepted by an answerphone. Perhaps they didn't go in for such things. They must be at the hospital, Rona thought, and her concern deepened.

The Exeter train was crowded and she had to stand for a time, but she was able to doze on the local service, jerking awake at successive stations with a crick in her neck. Half an hour from Marsborough, she phoned Max, who confirmed he'd be there to meet her.

'Poor love,' he greeted her, as she came through the barrier. 'You look shattered.'

'I didn't sleep well,' she admitted.

'Then I suggest we go somewhere for a stiff drink, followed by lunch with a bottle of wine, and you then retire to bed for the afternoon. I'll come home early and cook something special for supper.'

Friday was the one day in the week when he had no classes and no commitments other than his own work.

'That sounds wonderful,' she said.

When she eventually reached home, she found two messages from Zara, anxious about Selina, and after the nap Max had prescribed, Rona returned her call, though she'd nothing further to contribute.

'How are you getting on?' Zara enquired tentatively, when they'd exhausted the topic of Selina.

'Slowly, I think is the word.'

'No breakthrough?'

'No; several times I thought I'd found one, but they seemed to fizzle out.'

'You're halfway through your time limit, aren't you?'

'Yes; I realized that myself. I'll stick it out as promised, but please don't get your hopes up.' She'd not told Zara of either the email or the importunate phone calls; no point in alarming her. She added impulsively, 'But be warned: if I *do* come up with something, it mightn't be what you want to hear.'

'I don't care what it is, or what he's done, as long as I know who my father is.'

Rona, thinking of Jonathan Hurst and Philip Yarborough, held her breath, but Zara added, 'And, of course, who killed my mother.'

'Is this shoe box a permanent fixture?' Max enquired as he laid the table for supper.

'Oh, sorry – I've been meaning to take it upstairs.' Rona picked it up and placed it on the bottom step.

'What is it, anyway?'

'Some things of Gemma's that – Selina found.' Her voice wavered at the name. In the later news bulletins, Selina had not been mentioned. Rona assured herself it was a positive sign, but the O'Tooles were still not answering their phone.

'Can't be anything important, surely, or the police would have taken it.'

'There are a few cassettes they didn't find, because they were mixed up with commercial ones. Selina's played them and says there's nothing significant; she suggested I pass them on to Zara, but first I want to listen to them myself.'

Max merely grunted in reply.

It was a wet weekend. Tom stood at the French windows of Catherine's sitting room, staring at the dismal autumn garden through a veil of rain. It suited his mood, he thought grimly.

The past three days had been difficult; how could they be otherwise? Avril was still refusing to discuss the future, immediately heading off any attempt he made. She addressed him only when necessary, but with punctilious politeness. Every evening they ate in the dining room in almost total silence, and every evening he thought how much easier it would be if they could revert to trays in front of the television. At least that would mask their awkwardness.

On Tuesday evening, when he'd returned from meeting the girls, it was to find the guest-room bed made up and his night things laid neatly on the quilt. The switch wasn't referred to by either of them, but was a relief to them both.

Catherine came up behind him and laid a hand on his shoulder. 'Second thoughts?' she enquired.

He turned immediately, slipping his arm round her. 'What do you think?'

She smiled. 'Actually, I meant about moving in here. You'd be very welcome, you know.'

'I know, my love, but tongues would wag, and I want to forestall that as much as possible.' He glanced at her, but she was gazing out of the window.

'In the beginning,' she said quietly, 'we didn't want to deceive Avril, go behind her back. It would somehow have – spoiled things.'

He was watching her closely, aware of her tension. 'Yes?' She took a deep breath. 'Well, she knows now. Deception wouldn't come into it.'

'Catherine . . .' His voice was choked. He could feel her trembling. God . . .

She turned towards him and with one finger gently traced round his eyebrows, nose and mouth. 'One of us has to say this,' she murmured softly, 'so it might as well be me: Tom Parish, will you please make love to me? I don't think I can wait any longer.'

The rain continued to fall on the drenched garden, but there was nobody there to watch it.

When Max had left on Monday morning, Rona went up to her study, determined to play through Gemma's tapes. There were four in all, and as she lifted them out, unsure where to start, her eyes fell on the cards lying, still undisturbed, at the bottom of the box. Idly she picked them up. The top one was a garish postcard from Majorca, and its message was brief: *Great weather, great food, great men! See you next week, worse luck! Love to all, Mandy.*

One of the tennis crowd, perhaps, or, more likely, a colleague from County Radio. The front of the next card was more subdued, an aerial view of the Corniche at Monte Carlo. Rona flipped it over and her heart leapt into her throat.

Missing you more than somewhat, she read. *Seems more like two years than two weeks! Don't you dare forget me! I'll phone the minute I get back. All love, M M.*

M M? Rona frowned. One surely stood for Morrison, but the other? She quickly scanned the last two cards, but both were innocuous, one from Selina herself on holiday, the other from someone called Sue.

Rona propped up Morrison's card and studied it carefully,

211

searching for clues as to identity. Someone who had spent a holiday in Monaco in – she peered at the faded postmark – September 1977. That should narrow it down, she thought ironically. The handwriting was well formed, though the ubiquitous ballpoint had been used, and there was a neat row of kisses under the signature, if it could be called that. He'd been in love with her then, all right. According to Selina, the affair had lasted about six months, ending in February '78, so this would have been written in the first flush of passion. If he'd only taken Gemma to Australia with him, Rona thought sadly, she wouldn't have died. But 'if onlys' were a wasted exercise.

She picked up a tape at random and slotted it into her recorder, catching her breath as a voice instantly filled the room, young, light and carefree. 'It's Friday the twelfth of January, and it's *snowing!*' it began. Rona's mouth was dry; after concentrating almost exclusively on Gemma for the last three weeks, she was actually hearing her speak. 'This is to remind myself to ask Mrs J to babysit tomorrow evening. Oh, and to tell Selina when she gets back that her library book's come in.'

There was a click as the tape was switched off and Rona's throat suddenly tightened. January, she'd said, and the baby had obviously arrived. Which would make it January 1979, the month Gemma was murdered! Was it remotely possible there might . . . ? But no; Selina had played these through and found nothing. All the same, this catalogue, if that's what it was, of Gemma's last weeks would be unbelievably poignant.

Almost fearfully, she switched on again. 'Monday the fifteenth.' In the background, the baby gave a grizzling cry. 'All right, darling, Mummy won't be a minute. Remember tomorrow to collect the—'

She broke off as the baby started to cry more lustily. There was a thud as the recorder was put down, then her voice came from further away. 'It's all right, sweet pea, Mummy's here. You're supposed to be sleepy, you know!'

Softly, barely audibly, came the sound of a lullaby, and Rona felt her eyes prick. Gemma had come suddenly, uncannily, to life; no longer someone who'd died a quarter of a century ago, but a young girl singing her baby to sleep. For the first time, Rona felt an overwhelming sadness for her, as though she were a personal friend for whom she still grieved.

'Oops!' said the voice on the tape, sotto voce but near at hand again. 'I thought I'd switched it off.' There was a click, then silence, and Rona, switching off her own machine, sat staring unseeingly at the postcard from Monte Carlo.

She was still holding it five minutes later, when the phone roused her.

'Would that be Miss Rona Parish?' asked a hesitant voice, and Rona's preoccupation fled.

'Mrs O'Toole?'

'Oh, it's yourself, dear. Thank the Lord I've reached you.'

'How's Selina?' Rona broke in.

'Well now, not too good, truth to tell, but isn't she insisting on seeing you?'

'Seeing *me*?'

'It's supposed to be family visitors only, but she's that agitated, it seems she won't settle till she's spoken to you.'

'But why? I don't understand.'

'None of us do, dear, and that's the truth. But now they're saying what they call this "anxiety complex" is slowing her recovery, and they've given permission for a short visit. Provided you don't mind, that is.'

'Of course I'll come, if you think it would help. Where exactly is she?'

'St Benedict's – do you know it? I'm not sure of the road, but I could—'

'Don't worry, I'll find it. Which ward?'

'Nightingale; she has a private room on the third floor. Could you – how soon could we be expecting you?'

'As soon as I can get a train,' Rona promised, her mind spinning.

'God bless you, dear,' said Kathleen O'Toole, and rang off.

'Selina's asking to see me,' Rona hurriedly told Max over

213

the phone. 'I'm dashing straight down there. Could you come and collect Gus at lunch time and take him for a walk?'

'I thought she was still in ICU?'

'Apparently not, but it seems she's so set on seeing me it's hindering her recovery. Frankly, I can't make head or tail of it.'

'But you'll be back tonight?'

'Of course.'

'Good luck, then.'

Rona had seen more of Marsborough station this last week than she had in months. She'd brought a paperback, but her mind was too volatile to read and she sat staring out of the window, wondering what could be so urgent that Selina was demanding to see her.

Fortunately, the taxi driver merely nodded when she gave the name of the hospital, and she sat back against the soft black cushions, anxious, now, about the state in which she'd find Selina. She'd no idea what injuries she'd suffered, but at least she must be conscious and able to make her wishes known. But then, Rona thought, smiling faintly, Selina would have to be very ill indeed to lose that facility.

'St Ben's,' said the cab driver laconically, and she climbed out and, mentally crossing her fingers, went through the large main door of the hospital.

By the time she'd given her name at the nursing station, both the O'Tooles had appeared and come to greet her, pressing her hand and effusively thanking her for coming. A nurse who had also materialized escorted her briskly to a door off the main ward, and peered through the glass pane before turning back to her.

'If Miss O'Toole becomes too agitated, we'll have to ask you to leave,' she informed Rona, clearly disapproving of her dispensation. 'And the doctors say ten minutes at most – preferably five. She's still very weak, you know.'

Before Rona could protest that it was not she who'd insisted on the meeting, the nurse had opened the door and stepped aside for her to enter, and her whole attention narrowed to the figure on the bed. She walked slowly towards it.

Selina was lying motionless with closed eyes. It was the first time Rona'd seen her without the theatrical make-up that was her hallmark, and her unaccustomed pallor emphasized her fragility. Her head was swathed in bandages, tubes from both arms led to machines on either side of the bed, and another contraption supported one leg. Rona wondered in panic if she were asleep, and whether, if so, she should wake her.

'Selina?' she said softly, and to her infinite relief the eyes flew open, and, after an instant's blankness, recognition came.

The white lips parted. 'Thank God,' said Selina O'Toole.

Rona seated herself on a chair near the bedhead. 'How are you feeling? I was told you wanted to see me.'

Cautiously Selina turned her head, until she was facing Rona. She seemed to be summoning up the strength to speak, and when she did so, her words were startlingly unexpected.

'I needed to warn you,' she said, her voice even huskier than usual, from the effort involved.

'Warn me?' Rona repeated, and a flash of the old impatience crossed Selina's face.

'I've not much stamina at the moment,' she whispered, 'and I can't waste it repeating everything. Just *listen.*' She paused, drew a painful breath. 'Rona, I didn't fall under that bus. I was pushed.'

Rona stared at her, coldness creeping up her spine.

'You *have* to believe me,' Selina went on urgently. 'There's no possible doubt: as the bus approached, I felt a distinct shove in the small of my back, and the next thing I knew, I was under the wheels.'

The blue eyes surveyed Rona with remembered cynicism. 'No,' she said in a hoarse whisper, 'I'm not delirious, nor am I suffering from delusions or persecution complex or anything else you're considering.' She moved slightly, wincing as she did so. 'And before you ask, no, I didn't see who was behind me. The traffic island was jam-packed.'

215

Rona's fingernails were digging into her palms. 'Then it could have been an accident, surely?'

'No,' Selina said succinctly, 'it could not.'

After a minute, Rona asked, 'Have you reported it?'

Selina gave a brief laugh and immediately grimaced. 'To whom? My parents? The doctors? Can you imagine the reception I'd get? And how could I prove it?' A pause, filled by laboured breathing. 'But I had to let you know, because you're also in danger.'

Rona gazed at her, her heart starting to pound. 'You – don't think it was because of Gemma?'

'Damn right it was because of Gemma!' Selina snapped, with a reassuring return to her old manner.

'But – even supposing you're right and someone did push you, you've interviewed all sorts of strange characters for your programmes. It could have been any one of them.'

Selina was shaking her head in frustration. 'For God's sake! It's taken every ounce of will power I possess to get you here. You *have* to believe me.'

Rona glanced towards the glass pane, saw the nurse's face peering sternly through.

'Look,' she began, trying to speak reasonably, 'if anyone thought you knew anything, he'd have seen to you years ago, when Gemma died. Why now?'

'In case your digging triggers a buried memory? Then there was that letter in the paper, linking me with her. That could have jogged *his* memory.'

Rona said decisively, 'All right, if you're absolutely sure about this, I'll go straight to the police.'

'*No!*'

'But—'

'You mustn't tell *anyone*! Promise me!'

'Selina!'

Selina's breathing rattled ominously. 'Promise me!' she gasped, and Rona, alarmed, did so.

'And don't – let anyone – know you've seen me – anyone at all.'

'I told Max,' Rona said.

'Then impress on him – to keep quiet. If whoever it is – finds out – you'll be in even greater danger.'

The door handle rattled, and Rona turned to see the nurse holding one finger up to the glass.

'It looks as though I have to go,' she said.

Selina gave a brief nod. The effort required to impart her warning had obviously exhausted her.

'One good thing,' she murmured, as Rona rose to her feet. 'Between us – we've rattled someone's cage. Only trouble is – it seems to be – the killer, rather than – Amanda's father.'

When Rona turned at the door, Selina's eyes were already closed.

On her journey home, Rona kept well away from the edges of pavements and railway platforms. Could Jonathan or Philip have been responsible? she wondered with a frisson. Dark glasses and a hat pulled down would have prevented Selina from recognizing them.

She had left her car at the station, and as she was getting into it, her mobile sounded in her handbag and she paused to dig it out.

'Ro – it's Pops. He's been rushed back to hospital!'

Rona put a hand on the car to steady herself. 'When? Is he all right?'

'I don't know any details; the bank contacted Mum, who phoned me. Where are you? I tried you at home first.'

'At the station; I've just—' She broke off, remembering Selina's warning, but Lindsey wasn't listening.

'I'll see you there,' she said, and broke the connection.

Did Max know? Rona wondered, as she switched on the ignition. She'd ring him from the hospital. It seemed as if her whole life was disintegrating; threats on all sides, Selina attacked, her parents' marriage breaking down, and now, to crown it all, Pops back in hospital.

Ten minutes later, for the second time that day, she found

herself in a hospital corridor, and moments later joined her mother and sister at her father's bedside. To her profound relief he was propped up on pillows, looking much as normal. He reached out a hand and she hurried to him, bending to kiss his hot cheek.

'No need to panic, sweetie,' he said. 'All this fuss!'

'What happened?' Rona glanced from one member of her family to another, and it was Avril who answered.

'He was in severe pain, and with his previous history, the bank wasn't taking any chances.'

Rona thought back to his heart attack earlier in the year, and how frantic her mother had been then. Now – though admittedly it didn't seem nearly as serious – she was calm and composed, even if pale. Didn't she *care* what happened to him? Rona asked herself savagely.

As though bearing out the thought, Avril retrieved her handbag from the floor and stood up. 'Well, since the panic seems to be over and you're both here, I might as well go.' She glanced impassively at her husband. 'I'll phone this evening to check when they're sending you home.'

And, ignoring her daughters' stunned gaze, she nodded at them all and walked out of the room.

Tom said quickly, 'Don't blame her; she was worried enough when she first came in.' He paused, then added, 'She started a new job today – at Belmont Library.'

'Mum's gone back to work?' Lindsey asked incredulously. 'After all these years?'

'Best thing for her, in the circumstances.'

'Are you really all right, Pops?' Rona asked him.

'Really. They think it was a false alarm; talked about stress, and so on.' He smiled crookedly. 'They could be right; life hasn't exactly been plain sailing of late.'

The sisters left twenty minutes later, when Tom's check-up was due, and were standing talking by Rona's car when a blue Peugeot skidded to a halt beside them and Catherine Bishop half fell out of it.

'Rona – how's your father? I had an appointment at the

bank, and he wasn't there. At first, they wouldn't say what had happened, but I insisted. . .'

Lindsey had turned abruptly away, but Rona answered steadily, 'He seems all right. They think it was a false alarm.'

'Oh, thank God!' Her voice shook. She glanced towards the hospital, then, tentatively, back at Rona. 'Is – your mother with him?'

Lindsey said harshly, 'No, you're quite safe.'

'She's just left,' Rona replied. 'He's being checked at the moment, but it shouldn't take long.'

Catherine hesitated, glanced at Lindsey's averted face, then said quietly, 'Thank you. I'll go in and wait.'

'What a nerve!' Lindsey broke out, when she was barely out of earshot. 'How *dare* she come waltzing along as though she's every right to be here?'

'She loves him, Linz. That's pretty obvious. And it's also pretty obvious that Mum doesn't any more. Try to accept it.'

There were angry tears in Lindsey's eyes and Rona felt the wrench she always experienced when her twin was unhappy. 'Look,' she said, 'I've been – out all morning and missed lunch. How about trying out that new teashop in Market Street?'

Lindsey hesitated. 'I'm supposed to be at work.'

'Compassionate leave,' Rona said, and Lindsey grudgingly smiled.

'All right, but I mustn't be long. Is your car OK here?'

Rona nodded. 'Not knowing the score, I clocked in for two hours. I presume you walked?'

Lindsey's office was barely five minutes away.

'Ran, more like.'

They walked together along Alban Road and turned into Market Street. The new café was, in fact, almost opposite the bank, and they both glanced across at it.

'Pops has been there for as long as I can remember,' Lindsey commented. 'It's odd to think he soon won't be. Because of his retirement, I mean,' she added hastily.

They went inside and were shown to a table. The café was doing a good trade in afternoon tea. There were blue and white checked cloths on the tables, and the crockery bore the willow pattern from which it had taken its name. Rona ordered a toasted bacon sandwich. She'd still not phoned Max, but since there was now no urgency, this evening would do.

She glanced across at her twin. 'Anything more on Hugh?'

'No,' Lindsey said, adding after a minute, 'Thank God.'

'And Jonathan? Still dancing attendance?'

'Uh-huh.'

'When did this start between you?' Rona asked curiously. 'I thought at first he was new to the firm, but at dinner he said he'd been there yonks. If you'd known each other for years, why the sudden spark?'

Lindsey shrugged. 'At first I was married to Hugh and not looking elsewhere, though I always thought he was dishy. Also . . .'

'Yes?'

'There was talk he was seeing someone in accounts.'

'Quite the philanderer.'

Lindsey bit her lip. 'Then, of course, I met Rob.'

There was a brief silence, while they both reflected on that disastrous episode.

'And as soon as that ended,' she continued, 'Hugh started his weekend visits, so to some extent I was involved with him again. It was really only after our latest bust-up that Jonathan . . . hove to, as it were. Said I was looking miserable, and would a drink cheer me up, and we went on from there.' She paused. 'Weird it should turn out he knew that girl whose death you're working on.'

'Indeed it is,' Rona agreed.

Catherine sat gripping Tom's hand, her eyes continually searching his face. 'But it's my *fault*!' she insisted for the second time. 'God, Tom, if anything serious had happened as a result of my suggesting—'

He smiled and squeezed her hand. 'My darling, that's the best *release* of tension known to man! If it hadn't been for that episode, I might really have kicked the bucket.'

'Don't talk like that!'

'Well, it's true.' He paused, looking at her anxious face. 'But if you really feel responsible, let me scotch it once and for all. As it happens I did have a word with the doctor; asked if it could have had any ill effects, and he said no.' His mouth twitched. 'Though he advised me not to overdo it for a while!'

Catherine flushed, laughing in spite of herself.

'So you don't have to hie yourself to a nunnery, all right?'

'That's a relief!' She bent forward and gently kissed his mouth. 'I do love you,' she said.

Fifteen

When Rona returned to her study the following morning, it was to find Gemma's tapes still on her desk, as she'd left them when Mrs O'Toole telephoned. Fortunately, her call to Max the previous evening had been taken up with the drama over her father, and it was only at the end that he'd thought to enquire about Selina. Rona reported that she was still seriously ill but making progress, and no more was said. He seemed to have forgotten the urgency of the summons to her bedside, which was just as well; she'd no intention of telling him Selina thought she was in danger.

Rona sat down and stared for a couple of minutes at the postcard from Monte Carlo, reaching out absentmindedly for the phone when it started to ring.

'Hello?'

'Well now,' said the remembered voice, 'not doing too well, are we? And now that woman mentioned in the paper is in hospital. Coincidence, would you say? Don't you think it's time you agreed to see me, before anything else unpleasant takes place?'

Instinctively, Rona slammed down the phone – and immediately regretted it. Without hope, she dialled one-four-seven-one, to be told, as she'd known she would be, that the caller had withheld the number. Pushing him from her mind, she switched on the recorder, backtracking slightly to remind herself of Gemma's last words. *I thought I'd switched it off*, she said.

For the next twenty minutes or so she sat listening as Gemma reminded herself of dental appointments, trips to the clinic, cinema bookings and a dozen other things that had made up her life. Selina was right, Rona concluded regretfully; there was nothing of interest here. However, the tape had barely two more minutes to run; she'd hear it through to the end, then turn her attention to something else. In fact, it would be a relief when it finished; it was becoming increasingly difficult to sit listening to the dates Gemma gave at the beginning of each memo, knowing they were moving steadily and inexorably towards the day of her death. Which had been—

'January the twenty-fifth,' supplied Gemma on cue, and this time her voice sounded clogged, as though she'd a cold or had been crying. 'Selina will be late home, so remember to record the serial – *if* I can get the video to work.' There was a pause, while she blew her nose. 'Clinic appointment, but must be back by five, for Jonathan. Check there's enough beer; he—'

There was a final click as the tape ran out. Rona scarcely heard it. She sat staring at the machine for some minutes, then briefly rewound it. No, she hadn't misheard: January the twenty-fifth, Gemma had said. Which was the date she was killed. And Jonathan had been expected at five o'clock. Either Selina hadn't played this tape, or had got bored and switched off halfway through, as she almost had herself. And the police, though they'd taken the recorder, would have found only a new, blank tape in it; Gemma must have tossed this one on the shelf with the others, until she could be bothered to clear it.

God! she thought. What should she *do*? Would the police be remotely interested in such flimsy evidence? After all, there was no saying whether Hurst had actually *gone* to the flat, or even if he was the Jonathan she'd been talking about. Yet surely, as her unknown caller had hinted, it was too much of a coincidence? And was it the expectation of seeing him that had upset Gemma?

Rona thought back to his manner at their dinner table, when she'd questioned him about her – the spilt wine, the hunted look in his eyes. He'd carried it off well, she had to admit, but he'd certainly given the impression that once Gemma had dropped out of the crowd, he'd never seen her again. Let alone on the day of her death.

Suppose she did go to the police? Even if they decided to look into it, it could be days, weeks, even months before they took any action, during which time he would presumably be at large. And with Lindsey. What he'd done once . . .

Rona gave herself a little shake. Suppose she told Max, then – asked his advice? But she already knew what it would be. Drop it – get out while you can – it's not your problem; the girl's been dead over twenty years, and the world's kept turning.

It seemed, then, that she had two options: one was to put the whole thing out of her mind and forget she'd ever heard the tape, the downside being she'd continue to worry about Lindsey. The second was to tackle him herself. Her skin prickled at the thought, but she'd no intention of being foolhardy. She would take someone with her, meet him in a public place, and let him know she'd told a number of people her suspicions – even if this last was untrue.

Her mouth was dry and she plugged in the kettle to make coffee. So – where could they meet, and who should be her escort? Dave Lampeter was the obvious choice; an ex-student of Max's who'd still not found long-term employment, he'd acted as her bodyguard before. She wondered if he was still available and, while she drank her coffee, looked up his number.

'Dave? It's Rona.'

'Hi there. How are things?'

'A little fraught; hence the call.'

'Uh-oh!'

'How are you fixed at the moment?'

'Literally at the moment?'

'More or less.'

'Well, at this precise minute I'm on my way back from delivering an order.'

'You're not still stacking shelves, then?'

'No, I've been elevated to deliveries,' he said drily. 'We're on the Internet now, and doing a roaring trade. They needed more drivers, I have a clean licence, so I applied. Gets me out and about, at least.'

'Any free time?'

He said cautiously, 'You're not on the track of another murderer, are you?'

'You could say that.'

'God, Rona, where do you dig them up? And I suppose Max is in blissful ignorance, as usual?'

'More or less. Look, this isn't a long-term thing.' She thought rapidly. 'Could you make yourself available around lunch time?'

'Today? Shouldn't be a problem.'

'I'm not sure if I can swing this, but I'm hoping to meet someone, and I'd like you to be there.'

'To do what?'

'Have lunch while keeping an eye on us, and afterwards see me safely back home.'

'And that's all?'

'I'm hoping so. First, though, I'll have to see if I can ensnare my quarry. I'll ring you back as soon as I know.'

'I can hardly wait,' he said.

Rona finished her coffee, her mind turning over possibilities. Where could she meet Jonathan that would ensure there'd be plenty of people around, but still afford them a little privacy? For various reasons she discarded the Gallery, the Clarendon and Dino's – which left the wine bar where she and Lindsey had once met for lunch. It had waist-high partitions between the tables, giving at least the illusion of privacy.

What, she wondered, did Jonathan do at lunch times, apart from make love to her sister? A casual phone call to Lindsey should, with luck, reveal his plans. She rang Chase Mortimer, only to be told that Miss Parish wasn't in today.

'She's working from home? It's her sister speaking.'

'Oh, hello, Miss Parish. No, unfortunately she has one of her migraines. She hopes to be back tomorrow.'

Rona thanked her and rang off. A quick call to Lindsey

established that she was, in fact, confined to bed and feeling sorry for herself.

'It's a full-blown one this time,' she reported, 'flashing lights and the lot. I can't even lift my head off the pillow. Mum's coming round later, to minister to me.'

'I'll pop over myself this evening,' Rona promised.

She'd have to think of something else, then. Jonathan was unlikely to agree to meet her without a plausible reason, but . . .

An idea was forming in her mind; it was duplicitous, but it should prove effective. He and Lindsey must have the same lunch hour, since they often spent it together. Crossing her fingers, she again phoned Chase Mortimer, this time disguising her voice.

'Mr Jonathan Hurst, please.'

'May I ask who's calling?'

'It's a personal call.'

'One moment, please.'

Then: 'Jonathan Hurst.'

'Jonathan, it's me.' Rona waited breathlessly, but even Max couldn't distinguish her voice from Lindsey's on the phone.

'Hello, angel. Feeling under the weather, I hear?'

'Actually, it's easing off a little and some fresh air wouldn't go amiss.'

'Oh?'

'Especially if it took in a bit of lunch.'

'Oh honey, when I heard you weren't in, I arranged to meet Frank.'

'You can change it, can't you? I really need to see you.'

'Well, I don't know what he'll think—'

'Please, Jonathan.'

'All right. Where do you want to go?'

A potential trap here. Had they, or had they not, visited the Bacchus together? 'How about the Bacchus? I'm still a bit sensitive to light, and it's nice and dim there. Don't mention you're meeting me though, or they'll think I'm playing hooky.'

He gave a low laugh. 'It's a date. One o'clock?'

'One o'clock,' she said aridly. It had been almost too easy. 'One o'clock at the Bacchus,' she confirmed to Dave, minutes later. 'At least, you'd better make it ten to. Can you manage that?'

'No problem. Are you likely to want me to leap to your defence, because those partitions could do me a mischief.'

She smiled. 'No leaping should be required, and your lunch is, of course, on me. Thanks, Dave.'

Rona arrived at the wine bar at twelve forty-five, with Gus as added protection. The head waiter looked doubtful, until she assured him he always accompanied her to restaurants and lay quietly under the table. At her request, she was shown to a booth at the back, and seated herself so she could watch the entrance. She ordered a bottle of Muscadet and smoked salmon sandwiches for two, doubting that either of them would have much appetite.

Five minutes later, Dave came in, saw her, and took a table in the centre of the room, not close enough to overhear conversation, but within easy reach should the need arise. The scene was set, and all they were lacking was the principal player.

He arrived at five past one. As soon as she saw him in the doorway, Rona put a hand to her head, screening her face. She heard him approach and slide into the seat opposite.

'Still suffering?' he asked sympathetically.

She raised her head and looked at him, saw the shock in his eyes, followed by dawning anger.

'Rona?' he asked uncertainly. Then, with more vigour, 'What the hell's going on?'

The waiter's arrival saved her replying, and Jonathan watched in growing bewilderment as he was shown the bottle of wine and invited to taste it. He hesitated, glanced at Rona, and after a minute did so, nodded briefly, and sat in silence as it was poured into two glasses. The man had barely moved away when a smiling girl brought the sandwiches, appetisingly garnished with parsley and lemon.

'Enjoy your meal,' she said.

227

Jonathan met Rona's eyes. 'Is there any reason why I shouldn't get up and walk out of here?'

'Quite a pressing one, actually.'

'Which is?'

She took the recorder out of her bag and, putting it on the table between them, pressed the switch. Immediately, Gemma's tear-clogged voice started speaking, as clearly as if she were sitting next to them. Jonathan hurled himself back in his chair, his eyes riveted on the machine and the colour draining from his face.

. . . must be back by five, for Jonathan. Check there's enough beer; he—

A click, then silence.

'Oh God!' he exclaimed convulsively. 'Oh, my God!'

He dragged his eyes from the machine to Rona's intent face, moistening his lips. 'Where the *hell* did you get that?'

'Selina found it among her things.'

'God!' he said again, shakily. He reached for his glass and drained it, seemingly wishing it were something stronger.

'She gave the date earlier,' Rona said, above the thundering of her heart. 'It was the day she was killed.'

'I know that, damn it. God, how well I know it!'

Rona reached for her own wine glass, her hand as unsteady as his. 'So?'

He wiped a hand across his face, and she saw beads of perspiration on his forehead.

'Did you tell the police you'd just seen her?'

He gave the travesty of a laugh. 'You know damn well I didn't.' He looked up suddenly, frowning. 'Is Lindsey in on this? Was her migraine a blind?'

'No, it's genuine all right; she's at home in bed. She doesn't know what I'm doing.'

There was a taut silence. Absentmindedly, Jonathan reached for a sandwich and began to eat it. 'You were suspicious of me from the first, weren't you? As soon as you met Selina, and found out I'd known them? I could tell, at your house that evening.'

'I did wonder why you'd not told Lindsey, when she'd mentioned Gemma earlier.'

'I thought I'd explained why.'

'And I was prepared to believe you. Until I played the tape.'

He nodded, accepting this. He finished the sandwich and started another, and Rona, hoping to fill the emptiness inside her, did the same, though she scarcely tasted it.

'The question is, will you believe me now, if I tell you what actually happened?'

'Try me.'

He gave a deep sigh. 'I suppose I've nothing to lose.' A pause. Then: 'To be frank, I'd always carried a torch for Gemma, even after we stopped going out together. But then she dropped out of the crowd altogether, and eventually I met someone else – Carol, in fact, who later became my wife.'

Someone laughed loudly at an adjacent table. Two waiters collided at the door to the kitchens, and an empty tray fell to the floor, clattering on the tiles.

'Then one day,' Jonathan continued slowly, '*that* day –' he nodded at the tape – 'I bumped into her in town and we went for a coffee. To be honest, I was worried about her; she'd obviously been crying, but she wouldn't say what was wrong. I asked after Selina, and Gemma said she was going to a leaving do that evening and would be late home. "Just when I could do with some company!" she said.'

He refilled both their glasses. 'Well, to be honest, I wondered if I was in with a chance. I still hankered after her, and her bloke was no longer in the picture. So I suggested dropping in after work, to cheer her up.'

There was a long silence.

'And you went?' Rona asked at last.

'Oh yes, I went. We drank beer and played some music, and I was hoping to stay at least until Selina got back, but at half past six Gemma said it was time for the baby's bath, and though I'd have been happy to watch, or help her or something, it was clear she expected me to go. So – I went.'

'And that was it?' Rona demanded, when he didn't go on.

229

'Yes. The next day the whole place was buzzing with the news Selina'd found her dead when she got back. I just couldn't believe it. I was numb, horrified. And when it dawned on me I must have been the last person to see her alive, I just – flipped, went into complete panic mode. Fortunately I'd not told anyone I was seeing her – I didn't want it to get back to Carol. I convinced myself there was no way anyone could find out, and that if I kept my head down, it would be all right. I was questioned, of course, along with everyone else who knew her, but the gods were with me and nothing came out.'

'So to save your skin with your girlfriend, you withheld evidence in a murder enquiry?'

Jonathan gave her a twisted smile. 'I'm well aware of your opinion of me, Rona. However, I hope I've enough decency to have come forward if it could have done any good.'

'It would at least have narrowed the time of death to between six thirty and eight. According to newspaper reports, she'd not been seen since leaving the clinic at four fifteen.'

He shrugged. 'The post-mortem cleared that up. Basically, I knew no more than anyone else; no one had phoned or called while I was there, and I'd heard enough about miscarriages of justice to be terrified of being wrongly accused. They could have made out a case for jealousy or rejection that sounded plausible enough, and how could I have disproved it?'

He met her eyes challengingly. 'Well? Do you believe me?'

Reluctantly, she found that she did. Once again, a promising lead had drawn a blank, and despite the disclosures on the tape, she was no further forward.

'Yes,' she said quietly, 'I think I do.'

'So what are you going to do about it?'

'Nothing; but if you're expecting an apology, I have to disappoint you. You've not emerged exactly smelling of roses.'

'And Lindsey? Will you tell her?'

'I think I'll have to.' She eyed him steadily. 'And I'd be grateful if you didn't pre-empt me. I'm going to see her later, and I'd rather explain myself, face to face. She'll probably be furious with me.'

'And me.'

Rona shrugged. 'I shouldn't think it will make much difference.'

Surprisingly, the two plates in front of them were empty. Jonathan poured the last of the wine into their glasses, and drained his in one draught.

'I doubt if we've anything further to say to each other, so I'll leave you in peace.' He felt for his wallet, but Rona shook her head.

'The least I can do is stand you lunch.'

He hesitated, enough of the man-about-town to be uncomfortable with a woman paying for his meal, even in these circumstances. Then he nodded acknowledgment. Rona watched him as he strode across the room and disappeared through the door without a backward glance. Dave was looking enquiringly at her, and she beckoned him to join her. He stood up and came over, carrying a half-eaten plate of scampi and chips and a glass of white wine.

'Well, that was a damp squib!' he commented. 'I was expecting some shouting, at the very least. Did you unmask him?'

'Unfortunately, he's not the killer,' Rona said, sipping at her wine.

'You're sure?'

'Quite sure.'

'So the real one is still on the loose? Will you need protecting from him?'

She smiled. 'I might, if I'd the faintest idea who he was.' Briefly, she thought of Philip Yarborough. He was still a possibility, but she was now so disheartened she felt like abandoning the whole enterprise.

Dave finished his meal and wiped his mouth on his napkin. 'That was good. I must try this place again.'

'Thanks for stepping into the breach, Dave. Now, let me settle up with you.'

'You already have. You're paying for the lunch, and all I've actually done is eat it.'

'Much to your disappointment, apparently!'

'I suppose there's a touch of the knight errant in me. You never said what you're working on this time?'

She shook her head. 'It's a long story, but don't worry, I'll let you know if danger looms.'

'Still want me to walk you home?'

'No, it's not necessary. I have Gus, anyway.'

'Supplanted by a dog!' Dave complained humorously.

They parted on the pavement outside, and Rona dejectedly walked home.

Lindsey was up but not dressed when she called at the flat, later that afternoon. Her face was pale, her hair bedraggled, and she sat huddled in her dressing gown.

'Will you be fit for work tomorrow?' Rona asked.

'Probably. If I get a good night's sleep, I should be OK.'

'Did Mum come over?'

'Yes, straight from the library.'

'How was she?'

'Seemed OK. She told me all about her job, but nothing personal; says she's not decided what to do, and doesn't want to discuss it till she has.' Lindsey smiled. 'She insisted on steaming some fish for my lunch. Remember how she always gave us that when we were ill?'

Rona said carefully, 'Talking of lunch, I have a confession to make.'

'Oh?'

'I played a dirty trick on your boyfriend. Come to think of it, it was quite Shakespearean, twins being mistaken for each other, and all that.'

Lindsey was staring at her. 'What on earth are you talking about?'

'Promise not to hit the roof till I've finished?'

'I'm not promising anything.'

'Right, then I might as well jump in: I phoned Jonathan pretending to be you, and arranged to meet him for lunch.'

'You *what*? Why? Whatever for?'

Briefly, ignoring her sister's indignant interruptions, Rona told her about the tape, Jonathan's reaction to it, and his subsequent confession.

'You really have a nerve,' Lindsey said, when she'd finished. Then: 'Actually, it was quite brave of you.'

'Well, I did have Gus at my feet and Dave Lampeter across the room.'

'You didn't tell *him* you suspected Jonathan of murder?'

'Actually, I told him very little.'

Lindsey thought for a minute. 'You say there are more of these tapes?'

'Yes. I considered skipping the rest of them, especially since Selina'd said there's nothing of interest. But if she missed the bit about Jonathan, there might be something else even more important.'

The phone interrupted them, and Lindsey answered it. 'Oh, hello.' She glanced at Rona. 'Yes, she's here now . . . So I hear . . . Of course I want to see you, you dope!' Another glance at Rona, accompanied by a smile. 'I think she's just leaving. Yes, fifteen minutes would be fine. See you.'

'Was that my marching orders?'

'You don't mind, do you? Poor lamb, he sounded quite worried.'

'So he should. All right, I know when I'm not wanted.'

Lindsey stood with her and gave her a hug. 'Next time you decide to impersonate me, make sure you have my prior permission in writing. You're dealing with a solicitor, don't forget.'

As Rona drove home, she reflected that the day's happenings hadn't improved her opinion of Jonathan Hurst. It seemed he'd always been a two-timer, ready to ditch his new girl-friend for the chance to get back with Gemma. Serve him right that it rebounded on him. But who had gone to the flat after he left, and found her relaxing in the bath? Perhaps they'd never know.

The phone was ringing as she opened the front door.

'Rona?' said Dinah's voice, bright and reassuringly normal. 'I know it's short notice, but are you free for supper this evening?'

Rona's spirits suddenly soared. 'Oh, Dinah, yes I am! I'd love to come. I've been meaning to invite you all here, but haven't got round to it.'

'You seem a bit fraught, lovey. How goes the perilous quest?'

'You make me sound like Hercules! As it happens, it's thoroughly bogged down. I'm scarcely a jot further on than when I last saw you.'

'Well, you can tell us all with a glass in your hand. Seven thirty?'

'I'll be there. Thank you.'

The evening with the Trents was exactly what Rona needed after the emotional roller-coaster of the day. The informal atmosphere, the delicious meal that Dinah produced so effortlessly and stories of the children's latest achievements, all helped her to unwind, to pause and take stock.

She heard about Mitch's recent visit and snippets of his life in the Middle East; of Barnie's latest problems with the printers; of a new recipe Dinah was anxious to try out. Looking fondly from Barnie's familiar figure to Dinah, with her wiry dark hair and bright eyes, and Melissa, every inch the proud mother, she reflected, as she often did, that she was more comfortable with this family than with her own. Especially now, she thought with a sigh.

Throughout the meal, no mention had been made of Rona's project, for which she was grateful. Now, though, relaxed in comfortable chairs by the fire, with Gus and the cats amicably sharing the rug, Dinah finally broached the subject that had obviously been worrying her.

'You say you're not making progress on the father hunt?'

'Virtually none.'

'How long are you going to give it?'

'Six weeks in all – three more to go.'

'And the mother's killer?' Dinah asked quietly, handing round chocolate mints.

'Likewise. Not an inkling.'

'Then all I can say is, thank God.'

Barnie stirred. 'Hey, you're writing off a possible series!'

'But you wouldn't commission it,' Rona reminded him.

He regarded her from under beetle brows. 'No; I admit I had qualms. Still have. Not received any threats this time, I hope?'

Rona hesitated. 'None you need worry about.'

'Which means yes,' Dinah said, regarding her anxiously.

'Just a crank making nuisance calls.' And the email, which unaccountably worried her more. Thank God they didn't know of her connection with Selina, whose attack had been widely broadcast.

Sensing her unwillingness to elaborate, they reluctantly let the subject drop, and more general topics occupied the next half hour. Eventually Rona put down her coffee cup. 'If I don't make a move, I'll fall asleep here!' she said.

It was disconcerting, though, when Barnie opened the front door, to find a thick mist had descended, rimming the outside lights with misty haloes and completely obscuring the gate. Dinah immediately suggested she stay the night, but Rona, anxious to get home, declined.

'It's probably only out here, where there are open fields,' Barnie said reassuringly. 'As you get nearer town, it's sure to lift. Drive carefully, though, and give us a quick call to confirm you're safely home.'

Rona set off cautiously, following the limited beam of her headlights down the lane and along the main road. Once or twice other lights loomed up on the far side of the road, but thankfully there was little traffic and she reached home without incident. As Barnie had anticipated, visibility was a little better here, but she still didn't fancy garaging the car and having to walk home, and was relieved to find a parking space opposite the house next door.

She made two brief calls, one, as promised, to the Trents, the other to Max, who had rung earlier. Then, having given Gus his ration of biscuits, she went wearily to bed.

Sixteen

By morning, the mist had thickened into almost impene-trable fog. Rona stood at her bedroom window, staring out at the suffocating whiteness that effectively shut her off from the world. Fortunately she'd nothing planned for today, and she decided to put her incarceration to good use by ploughing her way through the three remaining tapes; and Max would be home this evening.

After breakfast she took a cup of coffee upstairs with her, put it and the tapes on the little table by the chintz chair, and settled down to listen to them in comfort. The first one she selected began on July the 19th 1977, and was a hotchpotch of interviews and commentaries on local events such as school prize-givings and golden-wedding celebrations. Even then, Gemma was making use of the tapes as a personal aide-memoire, inserting reminders to collect the dry-cleaning or to buy stamps. It did not make for riveting listening, and Rona found her attention wandering.

The next, dated December '78 – almost eighteen months later – was one of the recycled tapes, and must have imme-diately preceded the one she'd originally played. No mention this time of Jonathan, but again her luck held; following a note of the baby's weight, Gemma, seemingly thinking aloud, said suddenly, 'Selina's nagging me to phone Morrison Morrison; but how can I, after all this time?'

Instantly Rona stopped the tape and rewound the last couple of minutes. No, she hadn't missed a lead-up to this statement, nor did anything relevant follow. The next entry was dated a week later, a note to book Mrs Jones as babysitter for a

Christmas lunch, and the tape continued with similar unimportant notations until it clicked to an end.

Rona sat back in her chair, frowning. Morrison *Morrison*? she repeated to herself. Why the repetition? Gemma had spoken clearly – no question of its being simply hesitation. And the postcard, she remembered with rising excitement, had been signed with two Ms. She'd guessed one stood for 'Morrison'; did the other, as well? And if so, why?

Her interest reawakened, she slotted in the last tape, which proved to be another of the early ones.

'It's Saturday, 29th July,' announced the young voice, five minutes into the tape, 'and I'm at Gramercy Park for the flower show, which is to be opened this year by Mr James Latymer, MP, who is here with me now. Good afternoon, Mr Latymer.'

So Gemma had met James. Not surprising, considering her job, but a coincidence from Rona's perspective. His voice, recognizable though noticeably younger, responded, expressing delight at being invited, an interest in horticulture and a fondness for the town, which he had lived in as a boy. The interview lasted barely three minutes, but Gemma had gone on to record James's speech as he opened the show, which was greeted with enthusiastic applause. She then interviewed several of the exhibitors and attempted to describe their displays, frequently having to ask the names of the plants, and the entry ended with James presenting the prizes and briefly congratulating the winners.

And that, it seemed, was that. Rona stood up and stretched, glancing out of the window. Fog still shrouded garden and boundaries, hiding the familiar view and giving a sense of dissociation. Lunch time was approaching, and she wondered if the Pizza Pronto man would be able to find his way to her; she fancied something hot and spicy to lift her mood, and breathed a sigh of a relief when her phoned order elicited no reservations regarding the weather. Twenty minutes later she opened the door to the delivery man.

As she slipped the pizza into the oven, Gus looked up reproachfully from his basket. He'd had a lonely morning,

Rona thought guiltily, and there'd be no walk today.

'Just for two minutes,' she promised, as she guided him to the French windows and gently pushed him outside.

She laid the table with a glass of bottled water, the fruit bowl, and a knife and fork for the pizza. *Morrison Morrison*, she thought again – and somewhere in the far reaches of her memory an echo stirred.

There was a scratching at the glass door and she readmitted Gus, who promptly shook himself all over her. Tit-for-tat, she thought ruefully, rubbing down her skirt. She switched on the lunchtime news, only half-listening as she ate her pizza. No mention of Selina; if she phoned the hospital, would they let her speak to Mrs O'Toole?

Why, she thought with exasperation, had she allowed herself to become embroiled in this? A series of snapshots flicked through her mind: Zara and her plump, solicitous husband; the Fairchilds, troubled about the parent search; Joyce Cowley, the Morris brothers. And there were those to whom she could not put a face but who were also connected to the case – the mysterious caller and the sender of the email. Were they one and the same? She doubted it; they had different styles.

She put her glass and plate in the dishwasher, replaced the fruit bowl. Morrison Morrison. Why was the repetition somehow familiar?

She glanced at the clock: one fifteen. Max would be preparing for his afternoon classes. Would Adele turn up this week, she wondered? On impulse, she lifted the phone and pressed the Farthings button.

'Max Allerdyce,' said her husband's voice.

'Max, it's me.'

'Hello, Me. Filthy day, isn't it?'

'Yes; I haven't set foot outside.'

'Very wise. I had a plethora of apologies for the first class, so I've cancelled the second.'

'Good; you'll be home early, then?'

'Yes, but at the moment I'm in the middle of assembling the still life; did you want something in particular?'

'Sorry, yes. I know this sounds mad, but does the name Morrison Morrison ring any bells?'

He sounded amused. 'As in "Weatherby George Dupree"?' *'What?'*

'Christopher Robin, isn't it? "James James Morrison Morrison Weatherby George Dupree, took great care of his mother, though he was only three." There's the doorbell – I must go, love. See you later.' The phone went dead.

Rona continued to hold it, staring unseeingly ahead of her. *James James* Morrison Morrison. And like an echo came Hester Latymer's voice: *'A penchant for quoting A. A. Milne.'*

Was it possible *James Latymer* was Zara's father and Gemma's secret lover? But – Australia?

Rona drew a deep breath, trying to adjust to this staggering supposition. Say they'd first met at the flower show that July. Had an affair started soon afterwards? He must have been thirty-two or three at the time, Gemma only nineteen. The Morrison Morrison soubriquet – shortened, for convenience, to a single word – would be, as she'd told Selina, a private joke, effectively disguising his identity. And if, as was accepted, the affair ended before Gemma knew she was pregnant, it was possible James had remained unaware that he had a daughter. Until, perhaps, he learned of the current search.

Rona checked herself. All this, she reminded herself, was pure speculation. Dare she put it to the test, as she had with Jonathan?

First, though, she needed to list all known facts and see if the hypothesis would hold water. She ran up the basement stairs en route for the study, but as she reached the hall the doorbell rang. Gus, who always assumed she was deaf on such occasions, came bounding up behind her, barking loudly, and, holding his collar to restrain his enthusiasm, she opened the front door.

On the step, seeming to have materialized out of the shifting whiteness, stood James Latymer – for all the world, thought Rona in confusion, as though she'd telepathically summoned him. For a split second time hung suspended and she was aware, with penetrating clarity, of the acrid smell of fog, of its coldness seeping towards her and of beads of moisture on the coat of the man in front of her.

'I hope I'm not disturbing you?' he said.

Sanity came flooding back and she hastened to redeem herself. 'I'm so sorry – no, not at all.' There was positively no option but to invite him in, and this she did, stepping aside with a silent gesture.

'I realize I should have phoned in advance,' he apologized as he came into the hall, but offered no reason for the omission. 'May I take my coat off? It's rather wet, I'm afraid.'

'Of course.' She took it from him, hung it on one of the pegs, and showed him into the sitting room. The radiator wasn't on, and she lit the gas fire to dispel the chill. Gus, having confirmed his recognition of James and received a pat in return, settled contentedly in front of it.

'Can I get you some coffee?' Rona asked as they seated themselves, but he shook his head.

'No, thank you; I've just had some.'

He didn't look well, she thought. His face, which on the two previous occasions she'd seen him had been florid, was pale, and there were pouches under his eyes.

To break the lengthening silence, she asked facetiously, 'Is a by-election looming?'

A brief smile touched his mouth. 'Quite possibly,' he said. Then, 'Sorry; of course you want to know why I'm here. I'm just wondering where to start.'

She waited tensely, hands clasped in her lap.

'This – assignment you're working on,' he began, and came to a halt.

'Yes?'

'How's it going?'

She met his eyes. 'Things are beginning to slot into place,' she said carefully.

'Ah; I thought they might.' A pause, then: 'Do you mind telling me why you undertook it?'

241

'I've been asking myself the same thing.'

'I understand it was the girl herself who approached you?'

'Yes.' Rona braced herself: time to put her theory to the test. 'You're her father, aren't you?'

For a long moment he held her gaze. Then he gave a deep sigh. 'Yes,' he said quietly, 'I am.'

That, at least, had been easy. 'You met Gemma at the flower show?'

His eyes widened. 'Good God! Have you got a crystal ball?'

'Something of the kind.'

He bent forward, hands clasped between his knees. 'It's at times like this I wish I still smoked.'

'Is that what you came to tell me? That you're the missing father?'

'I had to get it off my chest, and there's certainly no one else I could tell. So here goes: as you guessed – God knows how – we met at the flower show, and I – well, she completely bowled me over. Basically she was shy, but being a reporter she tried hard not to show it, and the result was – endearing, somehow. Also, let's face it, she was extremely pretty. Anyway, she was on my mind all afternoon, and when I'd handed out the prizes, I invited her for a drink. Before I knew it, I was totally infatuated with her. I think the clandestine element added to the attraction.'

'Morrison Morrison,' Rona supplied.

He stared at her incredulously. 'God, I'd forgotten that bit. You really are a witch, aren't you?'

'You were married at the time?'

'Yes,' he acknowledged heavily, 'I was married, and, as a rising young politician, I knew I was playing with fire. I kept telling myself it was madness, but I hadn't the will power to end it. Until Hester became pregnant.'

'And you didn't know Gemma was?'

He sat back, looking reflectively into the gas fire. 'You know, the ironic thing is, I don't think she was. Not when I told her, I mean. I don't know what I'd expected, but she took it extremely badly – became quite hysterical, in fact. She'd

242

thought I was going to get a divorce and marry her, though I'm sure I never said so, and when I mentioned Hester's pregnancy, she went ballistic. It hadn't occurred to her that I was still sleeping with my wife.'

No, Rona thought achingly; in her innocence and naïvety, it wouldn't have.

'But if she wasn't pregnant—'

'Lord knows, I hadn't meant it to happen; but she kept clinging to me, sobbing that she knew I really loved her, and I told myself one last time wouldn't make any difference. My God, if I'd only known!'

'She never contacted you, when she found out about the baby?'

He shook his head. 'In the end, mainly to stop the hysterics, I'd had to be pretty brutal, insisting she never got in touch again. But if I'd known—'

'It would have made no difference,' Rona said.

He flashed her an angry glance, then his eyes dropped. 'You're probably right.'

'Her murder must have come as a shock.'

'An enormous one, made all the worse because I had to hide my feelings.'

'The baby was mentioned in all the reports. Didn't it cross your mind it must have been yours?'

He shook his head. 'Not at that stage; I convinced myself it was impossible – that she must have gone with someone else on the rebound. By then, of course, our son Rupert had been born.' He paused, adding reflectively, 'There can be only a few months between them.'

'So,' Rona pursued, 'life went on. Until what?'

He ran a hand through his hair. 'Deep down, I must have come to accept I was the father, but it didn't hit me till Hester saw that paragraph in the *Gazette*. "Why do people do it?" she said. "Do they really think their parents will welcome it all being dragged up again?"'

'A lot of parents do,' Rona said from a dry mouth.

'Not this one.' He gave a bark of laughter. 'Dear Hester –

she never knew what a shock she'd given me.' He glanced at
Rona. 'When we had lunch that day, at Max's studio, I'd no
idea you were working on it. It was only when I got home
and mentioned seeing you, that she told me it was you who'd
instigated the search.'

'So,' Rona said, as the fact leapt out at her, 'you sent me
an email, warning me off.'

He flushed. 'I'm not proud of that. I'm not into issuing
threats.'

'How did you know my email address?'

He wasn't meeting her eyes. 'It was on the letterhead, when
you wrote to thank Hester for the lunch.'

After all her ponderings, such a simple explanation. 'And
the phone calls?'

He looked blank.

'Did you also phone anonymously, wanting to meet me?'

'Certainly not. Why do you ask?'

'Because someone did.'

He frowned. 'Probably just a malicious call. People cash in
on news items, you know. It happens all the time.'

No doubt he was right. 'So another reason for coming here
was to ask me to stop the search?'

Slowly he shook his head, and she felt the first prickle of
unease. She thought back over what he'd told her, about the
end of the affair and his reaction to Gemma's death – and
went suddenly, icily, cold before she understood why. Then,
as though a button had been pressed, a sentence obediently
repeated itself in her head.

*The prime suspect would normally have been the father, but
he'd emigrated to Australia.*

Only he hadn't, had he?

God, she thought in sudden panic, *that* was why he'd come;
he was sure she was on his trail – and she was alone in the
house with him! If she could only get outside, the fog would
hide her – but she'd no chance of even leaving the room
without his catching her. And Gus, beloved Gus, sleeping
peacefully on the hearth: he'd met this man before, heard her

244

invite him in, talk to him. How could he be expected to understand he was now the enemy?

Though she dreaded looking at James, she couldn't prevent herself and, as their eyes met, he saw that she knew. 'Oh Rona,' he said softly, 'I so hoped it wouldn't come to this.'

Above the suffocating beat of her heart, defiance unexpectedly came to her aid; she was damned if she'd die not knowing the end of the story! Aloud, she said, 'So what really happened?'

There was a long silence. He was staring into the fire again, seeing God knew what. Eventually he began to speak.

'It was true, that I didn't know about the baby. Not until after it was born, when, completely out of the blue, she phoned me. I was – poleaxed. I'd managed to put the whole thing behind me, and when I heard about the baby, I panicked.' He paused. 'It was January '79, remember, just months before Margaret Thatcher came to power. And I'd been told I'd a chance of being in her cabinet – one of the youngest members on record. The last thing I needed was an illegitimate child crawling out of the woodwork.'

Did he realize how brutal that sounded? Rona wondered dully. Probably not.

'What did she want?' she asked. Although part of her brain was concentrating on his story, intent on finally learning the truth, another part still worked on her escape. Could she say she needed the loo? Offer coffee again? Anything to free herself from her dangerous proximity to this man, this – murderer. She no longer had any doubts.

'Maintenance,' he answered her. 'She said her friends were insisting I take some responsibility – which gave me the hell of a jolt, I can tell you; I thought she'd told them who I was. But she said not, that to stop them pestering her, she'd said her boyfriend had gone to Australia. Apparently she'd interviewed a family who were emigrating, which gave her the idea.'

The Morrises. So there *had* been a connection, albeit a nebulous one.

'You refused to help?'

'I'd no option; if I'd done so, I'd have been admitting paternity. But she became more and more upset; said she wouldn't have asked for herself, but she wanted the best for the baby and she'd virtually no money. I advised her to contact her mother, but I couldn't shake her.'

He stood up abruptly and Rona stiffened, poised for flight, but he moved to the fireplace and leaned an arm on the mantle. Surreptitiously, she measured the distance to the door: escape was still out of reach.

When he began speaking again, his voice was harsher, flatter. 'She told me her friend would be late home that evening, so it would be safe to call round. We could talk things over face to face, come to some arrangement.'

'And couldn't you have done?' Rona asked.

He shook his head violently. 'Once you start on that kind of thing, you're on a slippery slope; there's no saying where it will end. I just couldn't risk it. And when I still refused, she – threatened to contact Hester.'

Oh, Gemma! A fatal mistake. 'So you decided to go after all.'

'Only later, after she'd rung off. The more I thought about it, the more I panicked. I'd so much to lose – my career, perhaps my marriage. Then I remembered she'd be alone that evening; and it struck me that a chance like that might not come again.'

'A chance to kill her,' Rona said in a whisper.

He didn't seem to have heard. 'I was going to ring the bell, but I tried the handle and the door opened, so I went in. There was no sign of her in the kitchen or living room, then I heard sounds coming from the bathroom.' He paused, his breath becoming laboured. 'And that door wasn't locked, either.'

There was a long silence. Rona was having difficulty breathing, each intake a sharp pain in her chest. God, the tragedy of it – the waste. What was it he'd said to her, the first time she'd met him and handed him his teenage

manifesto? *Oh dear, is my past catching up with me?* Well, it
had certainly caught up with him now.

James cleared his throat. 'Afterwards – I had a quick look
round to check there was nothing that might lead back to me.
I couldn't see anything, so I – let myself out and – went home.'

'And duly became a cabinet minister in Mrs Thatcher's
government.'

'As you say.'

'And never spared a thought for your little daughter?'

He passed a hand over his face. 'I did see her – while I was
searching the flat. She was awake, and looked up at me with
Gemma's eyes. It – freaked me, I can tell you.'

For a long time, neither of them spoke. Then Rona said,
'Even if I'd worked out you were Gemma's lover – and you
couldn't know I had – it didn't follow that I'd think you killed
her.'

'I was pretty sure you would.'

'Because the lover's the most likely suspect?'

'That's one reason.'

'And the other?'

'I had a sitting with Max yesterday. Did he tell you?'

'No. Why is that relevant?'

He turned then to face her, and she didn't care for the look
in his eyes. 'Because,' he said slowly, 'it came out that you'd
met Selina O'Toole.'

Rona's hands went slowly to her mouth as she gazed at him
in dawning horror. *'You tried to kill her, too?'*

He flinched. 'I'd never met the woman, but Gemma often
spoke about her and she'd always worried me. Once, a few
years ago, she tried to interview me for some programme or
other, but I backed down; I couldn't get it out of my head that
she knew more than she'd said. But time went on and nothing
happened, and I gradually relaxed. Until this bloody search
began. It was like opening Pandora's box; first the article, then
a letter connecting Selina with Gemma. I was afraid you'd
contact her.'

'I already had,' Rona said hoarsely.

'I didn't know that. I reasoned that if you met, she'd start remembering things she'd not thought important at the time. So – it seemed best to prevent that meeting. Yes,' he added heavily, 'I don't blame you for looking at me like that. I can't even face myself. God!' he said explosively, making Rona jump. 'I've spent my life trying to deny what happened with Gemma, only to discover, when another crisis threatened, that I reacted in precisely the same way.'

He gave a twisted smile. 'A prime example of the ruthless politician, intent only on furthering his career.'

'They usually stop short of murder,' Rona said through dry lips.

'Yes; well, at least it turned out not to be murder this time. No thanks to me, she survived.'

'And Max told you I'd visited her in hospital?'

James nodded. 'When I asked how your assignment was going. And that was what clinched it for me.'

Oh God! she thought. *Oh God!*

'Which brings me to my third reason for coming here.' She watched, incapable of movement, as he reached into his pocket. What was he going to produce? A gun? A knife? A syringe? What actually appeared was an innocuous-looking envelope, though she stared at it as though it, too, might be lethal.

'I felt you deserved to know the whole story. Well, now you have it. In return, I want you to do one last thing for me. Before I left home just now, I wrote three letters; one I sent to my solicitor, one I left for my wife, and this is the third. I'd like you to give it to my daughter.'

She stared at him as the sick fear began to recede, not daring to believe that she wasn't, after all, in mortal danger.

'I'm not going to ask you about her – her current name, what she looks like, anything. It's better for me not to know. Just tell her – that I'm sorry.'

Rona's voice came as a whisper. 'What are you going to do?'

'Crash my car,' he said simply. 'Into a brick wall, for preference, though in this fog it might be difficult to find one.'

'But—'

'I told you I can't live with myself any more; why should anyone else be expected to live with me?'

He held out the envelope, but when she made no move to take it, he laid it on the coffee table.

'I'll let myself out,' he said.

She didn't argue; reaction had set in, and she was incapable of standing. As he crossed to the door, Gus opened one eye and thudded his tail sleepily on the rug. Out in the hall, James took down his coat, shrugged into it, and let himself out of the front door.

Rona was still sitting there when, twenty minutes later, Max's key sounded in the lock.